Setting Sail for Golden Harbor

A Humorous Memoir About
the Final Years of Life

John Vance

ISBN: 978-1-61296-997-8
PUBLISHED BY BLACK ROSE WRITING
www.blackrosewriting.com

Printed in the United States of America
Suggested Retail Price (SRP) $17.95

Setting Sail for Golden Harbor is printed in Minion Pro

Special thanks to all the staff at Black Rose Writing; to my children Hope and Jimmy for their love and support; to my wife Susan for her enthusiasm and keen editorial eye; and to my mother for all she gave me.

Setting Sail for Golden Harbor

"If we couldn't laugh, we would all go insane"

Robert Frost

Preamble

"The human race has only one really effective weapon and that is laughter."
Mark Twain

As the Victorian author Samuel Butler observed, "If Life must not be taken too seriously—then so neither must death." I think he was absolutely right—and so did my mother—a remarkably strong and especially talented and loving woman named Nan. Indeed, why should there be any shame or hesitation in recalling the humorous moments provided by aging parents during the final miles of life's journey, especially when the humor in no way diminishes the affection and respect felt for a loved one? My mother Nan provided so much of that humor—in many ways both familiar and unique. Because the journey toward the end of a parent's life is fraught with challenge and poignancy, laughter often becomes a wonderful antidote to depressing reality and allows one's memory of the experience to escape the clutches of regret and sadness. As Langston Hughes noted, "Like a welcome summer rain, humor may suddenly cleanse and cool the earth, the air, and you." We recall the welcome laughter at a funeral or memorial service, not simply because it breaks tension and somber reflection but also because it reminds us that the deceased has lived, has amused, has warmed our hearts, and will remain alive through the memories of words said and actions taken during the final period of life.

This book shares the moments, events, and remarks that made Nan simply unforgettable to those who knew her. But Nan was also a remarkable woman owing to the challenges she faced throughout her life, including working as a "Rosie the Riveter" during World War Two, holding down a series of jobs while most of her contemporaries stayed at home, beginning her own successful business, suffering two abusive husbands before finding Mr. Right—all while setting an admirable example to her only child (me), who shared with her the difficulties of a frustrating and at times dangerous home life. Hers is a story worth sharing, one that can inspire as well as delight the reader.

The individual chapters, which cover topics rather than mere chronology, address facets of Nan's life and concentrate on the humorous to hilarious stories and comments she made relating to each subject. Whereas some moments are serious and not always pleasant, I follow Nan's credo that reflection on one's life must be filtered through the lens of humor. At one point during the final year of her life, I teasingly threatened to write a book about her. She put down her martini, thought a moment about the prospect, and then pronounced, "If you do tell my story, just be sure to make it funny." In the following pages, I have tried to do just that.

Chapter 1

"I'm Fine, Doctor"

"Always laugh when you can; it is cheap medicine"
Lord Byron

"And how are you today, Nan?"

"I'm fine, doctor."

Nan swung her legs back and forth on the examining room table as if she were waiting for the school bus to take her home. As she did so, she also swayed her head contentedly back and forth while her doctor took the stethoscope and inserted the headset into his ears. With an impish smile, Nan grabbed the chest piece and brought it to her mouth. "How come I can't listen to your heart, doctor?" He smiled patiently and attempted to take the chest piece back, but Nan resisted just enough to force from him the kind of benign sigh pediatricians characteristically expel whenever a child plays rather than cooperates during an examination. The only problem was that Nan wasn't a rebellious six-year-old but rather a somewhat feeble woman of ninety-two.

That was my mom—the incomparable Nan to everyone else.

Accompanying my mother in her later years to her various doctor's appointments (cardiologist, pulmonologist, ophthalmologist, internist, audiologist, and surgeon) provided us considerable and memorable moments of delight and hilarity—in spite of the unfortunate conditions that prompted and required these appointments. Through it all, Nan demonstrated resolve and playfulness and offered a bushel-full of post-visit "observations." At the beginning of the visit, when asked how she was feeling, she typically replied with "I'm fine, doctor" or "I feel great." The responses became so habitual that I assured her that one of those phrases would be her last words on the day she died, a prediction she never contradicted.

Nan grew up in Baldwin, Long Island—a healthy girl of hardy Italian stock—always well fed, even during the Depression years of the 1930s. Normal medical issues were often dealt with at home, with heaping bowls of *minestrone* as a general palliative and the application of unusual remedies and Italian poultices (*cataplasma*) for other ailments. Honey and whiskey down the throat and fried onions placed on the chest for colds, beet juice into the ear for earaches, a slug of whiskey for toothaches and canker sores, and digested fried eggs for diarrhea were prescribed in many Italian homes, hers included. A combination of bread, milk, and soap was a favorite poultice for various infirmities. Back problems would be treated by a coin wrapped in a cloth soaked in olive oil. A flame would be applied to the cloth, which would then be pressed on the back—once the flame went out, that is. Italian children like my mother wore gold earrings to ward off eye problems, and fevers could be checked by carrying an onion in one's pocket or eating dry figs on the first of May.

But eventually the family grudgingly conceded to modern medicine—all in the mustachioed form of Dr. Lagorio, the handsome family physician, who made house calls for just about anything—from a deep splinter to the chicken pox. Later, I discovered that "Lagorio" meant "green lizard" in Italian, and I momentarily wondered if the good doctor didn't actually *give* his patients chicken pox rather than treat them for the ailment. It was here that Nan developed a reverence for physicians, who always made her talk like a skittish seven year-old whenever she saw one—"Yes, Doctor. Whatever you say, Doctor," even if some of them were forty or fifty years her junior. Of course, the unavailability of affordable health care prevented most consultations, tests, x-rays, and minor procedures. The generosity of men like Dr. Lagorio and just old-fashioned luck was often the only preventive care within the family's price range.

Yet not all medical needs were met—one in particular for reasons of habit and tradition of the worst kind. It was expected that during a lifetime one would keep just the teeth which managed to escape the ravages of decay. Teeth that failed to escape were evicted by force or remained as foul tenants throughout one's life. Full dentures were the choice of those who could afford them—and such was the case with my grandmother and later Nan as well. I still shudder at the unpleasant—no, ghastly—memory of seeing my grandmother talking to me without her teeth in. As for seeing my mother similarly untoothed, I witnessed that only twice—in the hospital near the end of her life and on the night she died. She was always careful never to be seen by anyone without her dentures. For that, I thank you, mom.

As the American humorist Erma Bombeck remarked, "There is a thin line that separates laughter and pain, comedy and tragedy, humor and hurt." One might add that without experiencing the hurt one can never fully appreciate the humor. And such it was in Nan's life. Her first serious medical issue was likely the result of my biological father's nasty habit. After a "few" drinks, he seems to have had no compunction in being physically abusive. Nan informed me years later that on her wedding day she wished her leg would break so she wouldn't have to walk down the aisle. Her instincts were certainly proved correct, but at the time she couldn't insult her parents and besmirch the family name by backing out of the ceremony.

As many know, following the death of an elderly parent, families frequently discover papers, diaries, letters, and photos that reveal incidents, peculiarities, and reflections about which the family has been unaware. Often these revelations fill in gaps, solidify existing assumptions, and provide delightful surprise and amusement. But they can also shock and sadden. Among Nan's papers, we discovered a copy of a deposition given when she was attempting to seek a divorce from my father. The record revealed that while particularly inebriated he pushed his way into my grandparents' home and attempted to take me (then an infant) for a car ride. When my grandfather told him to leave the house, my father threatened to kill him and had to be subdued by my mother's older brother. This event understandably led to a separation from her husband, which did not fully alleviate Nan's bouts of anxiety and depression. A divorce was finally granted, although Nan's mental state wasn't helped by the knowledge that she was the first in either her father's or mother's family to get a divorce.

Yet even such dreadful memories could also trigger humor. Around the age of ninety, Nan shared with me one of her Dr. Lagorio stories from that period of her life. As was the case with most family doctors of the time, Dr. Lagorio was an internist, gynecologist, obstetrician, pediatrician, dermatologist, and psychiatrist rolled into one. Needing to talk to someone about her mental stress, she made an appointment and told him she was having considerable difficulties with her marriage, which affected everything from performing her duties as telephone operator (think Lily Tomlin's Ernestine character "One ringy dingy") to getting enough sleep. Yet she couldn't admit that she was living in fear of violence, let alone that she was being psychologically abused as well. During the talk with Dr. Lagorio, Nan did offer an admission that she was feeling inferior in several areas. She believed she couldn't measure up to what she, her parents, and her acquaintances expected of her—an understandable and unfortunate by-product of her psychological state. Registering very low on the sympathy scale, Dr. Lagorio was a practical physician who preferred dispensing a remedy over lending an ear. "Nan, the next time you think of yourself as inferior to someone, just imagine that person sitting on the toilet taking a crap and then wiping his or her ass." Nan shared that lovely tidbit with me when I was an insecure teenager.

As helpful as that graphic advice could be, Nan's spirits and psychological health hardly improved after she married her second husband a few years after her divorce was finalized. Depressed by her "status" as a divorced Roman Catholic from a traditional Italian family and by the fact that I (now five years old) had no father to teach me how to play baseball or lift me above the crowd at the circus or during the 4th of July parade (my real father never took advantage of his visitation rights), Nan dated and soon married a man who seemed gregarious, caring of me, and appreciative of my mother's very attractive looks. Besides that, her status was again "elevated" to that of a married woman. Years later she confessed to me that she didn't love him, but married him anyway because she feared she'd never get another chance—she had just passed thirty at this time—and, after all, he seemed good to me. But reality struck hard on the wedding night, when this husband launched himself into a jealous tirade over the fact that men were staring at my beautiful mother.

Looking back, I have judged this man as an overgrown petulant child—boorish and slovenly at home, both passively and actively aggressive, at times cruel and brutish, and generally miserable over his small place in the world. But what was Nan to do? Admitting to the family that she had made another mistake in her choice of mates and wanted a second divorce was to her thinking utterly impossible. And this husband had the gift (it may have been his only one) of fooling everyone but my mother and me with his fun-loving public persona. He was one of those "lampshade-on-the-head" types, quick with a joke (often crude) and deft with a compliment. My grandmother (Nan's mom) thought he was a swell guy, and he was invariably attentive to her. As for me, I soon grew tall enough to see over crowds and I learned how to play baseball on my own. Unfortunately, he legally adopted me, getting my real father off the hook financially and leading to my initial name change when I was in the first grade. But for some apparent legal reason his last name (admittedly an unattractive eastern European one) had to be changed when I was in the fourth grade, and once again I stood in front of the class and announced that I was now a boy named John Vance instead of that other name, let alone the name I had at birth. Nan teased me in later years by saying that I was one of the few males with three names *not* wanted by the F.B.I.

For thirteen years, Nan endured the relationship with husband number two (or H2), which also featured the habitual complaints about food choices for dinner. If it was a hamburger, he'd complain that he didn't have steak. If it was steak, he'd moan that my mother was spending too much on food. The string of such immature and insulting actions and remarks was long indeed, and he wasn't shy about injecting doses of humiliation when his fancy desired. Whether it was the particular curve of Nan's nose or her choice of clothing, he had a full arsenal of insulting and abusive reactions at his disposal. That he was no prize in the looks department (Neo-Neanderthal might be an apt description) made no difference. But I shouldn't leave the impression that Nan took all of his insults, immaturity, and cruelties without fighting back. I heard far more than my share of arguments between them, but such efforts took their toll on her spirits and health. What was also sad was that she didn't have a confidant with whom to share her frustrations and fears, primarily because she felt trapped by the need to keep this unhappy marriage a secret, especially from her family.

But all came to a head when I returned home, at age seventeen, to hear H2 cursing Nan. She appeared stunned as I caught sight of her, and in a second I found out why, as H2 grabbed her by the shoulders and for a second time (as I learned) slammed her into the full length heater that was on the hallway walls of many South Florida homes at the time. As my mother crumpled to the floor, he turned and berated me for not cutting the lawn as he had expected me to. (As a cheery side note, he once made me cut the grass with a pair of scissors for failing to do it on the day he had deemed I should.) As he pushed me into the living room, that little red button lit up in the brain that says "push in case of an emergency" or "push when you've just had enough." I told him to leave my mother alone and then dropped him to the floor with a judo chop across the throat. I lit out the front door daring him to chase me, but he was too heavy and out of shape to give much pursuit. (That he made his way to the street wearing nothing but a pair of boxer drawers added a nice touch of humor to the episode, I will admit.) Instead, he took off in the car—likely headed to his favorite watering hole. As soon as he left, I returned inside the house to tend to Nan. I told her we no longer had a choice—we had to call her sister and mother and tell them what had happened not only on this night but for the past thirteen years.

We never again saw H2, but for a full year, every time we heard a car pull into the driveway, we both tensed and looked at each other as if to say, "He's come back just like we knew he would." Happily, H2 never attempted to contact Nan after the divorce was settled and she entered a much happier period when she fell in love with Tom, a handsome, funny, and simply terrific guy, who loved her romantically and fully. His death from lung cancer at just age sixty-one was for her, as it would be for anyone, a deeply depressing and personal tragic loss, but at least she had eighteen years with him—even if the last six months were a nightmare. The one positive result of his death was that Nan quit smoking—cold turkey. They had both smoked fairly heavily—two packs a day on the average—and Nan hadn't been without a cigarette in her mouth since she was sixteen, when she used to sneak out to smoke. Fortunately, she constantly discouraged me from taking up the habit, but she could have saved her breath. I hated the smell of cigarette smoke even since I can remember—but even more so an ashtray full of cigarette butts and even a pack of open matches, which I used to cover whenever I was seated near one. By the time of the Surgeon General's warning in the mid-1960s, it was too late for Nan to regret having smoked throughout her pregnancy or exposing her son to second-hand smoke. Yet for as strong a grip as cigarettes had on her from the age of sixteen to right after she turned sixty-two, she quit the day her husband learned he had lung cancer (and coincidentally the very same day our second child, her grandson, was born, named for her husband).

Other than the normal rounds of arthritic pains, stomach ailments, and assorted fever and colds, Nan's health remained pretty good—until the effects of her long habit caught up with her around the age of seventy. A chest x-ray caught cancer low on one of her lungs, and she immediately scheduled surgery to have it removed. She hated being in a hospital for a week—"the food stinks"; "I feel fine now, so why can't I go home?"; and "I can't figure out how to change the channel on this damned thing" were her constant refrains. I reminded her that the prognosis was more than we hoped for. The surgery got the cancer—so there would be no need for follow-up radiation or chemo. She agreed but not without, "So I have half a lung left. What does that mean for my breathing?" I reminded her that she actually had *one and* a half lungs left and that the surgeon said whatever she did physically, she could keep doing it without too much difficulty. To that she grunted and said, "I miss Dr. Lagorio," who unfortunately had been dead for some thirty years by this time.

She recovered nicely from the surgery, even though she was hounded at the hospital by her self-appointed bosom buddy Martha, who never met a moment of silence she couldn't fill by dispensing unwanted advice, indulging in character assassination, or reminiscing about some personal adventure about which no one seemed to care. Now in her early seventies, Nan returned to her workouts—the type of which always seemed to change, depending on what she had just snipped out of a cheap woman's magazine or taken from a television infomercial. Once a devoted disciple of the remarkable Jack LaLane, she had by this time lost his booklet and the "Glamour Stretcher" she used to swear by. A little running in place, lifting of three to five-pound weights, and squatting gave her a toned appearance to go along with her age-defying looks. If I had a dollar for every time I heard someone say to her, "Nan, you can't be _____" (fill in the age), I could buy a political candidate (local level, that is).

At age eighty-four, Nan encountered another medical snag: she needed immediate surgery to address an aneurism in her abdominal region. Once more she came through it like a champ and recovered quickly. But three years later, shortly before we were to leave for Orlando for our daughter's wedding, Nan complained of cramp-like pain, and her surgeon found that in the intervening time, the scar tissue/adhesions had led to small bowel obstruction, requiring follow-up surgery. A laparoscopy was performed and the adhesions were cut and released. Here too, she handled the procedure well, and she was expected to be discharged from the hospital in a day or two, but her post-op tests revealed that she wasn't breathing effectively. She was given oxygen and was required to blow into the device that registers breath power. "What the hell is this?" she complained. "I breathe in as hard as I can and the black thing won't go up the tube. The damn thing is broken." And boy, did she "love" that oxygen mask. "Can you ask them to give me something that doesn't smother me? I came in here to get better not to die of suffocation. I look like the damned Man in the Iron Mask." But what most troubled her was that they didn't let her go home, and the day we were to leave for the wedding was coming fast upon us. After a week and on the afternoon before we were to travel to Disney World, the hospital relented and released her. Nan's "thank God—finally" was soon replaced by another phrase that also had "God" in it when they informed her she would have to travel with a large oxygen tank to keep her breathing regulated. We were supplied with several extra tanks, and the following morning we drove nine hours to Orlando from Athens, Georgia, where we lived. For understandable reasons, Nan wasn't her chipper self, and when we arrived at the Grand Floridian Hotel, she just wanted to go to her room and sleep. The next day, she rested and had room service, while the rest of us did the Disney thing. Showing that she was a good patient, she used her oxygen—which nevertheless we had to insist on.

The day of the wedding she felt much better. She had a marvelous time at the ceremony and the reception—without her oxygen, needless to say. "I can't embarrass my granddaughter by looking like an alien." The next and last day, she was back on the high saddle, enjoying her meal and lounge time—and even garnering a "proposal" from my new son-in-law's brother, who treated her the way she expected to be treated—like a queen. Another medical incident safely navigated—or so we thought.

But the trouble with Nan's lungs eventually returned, prompting another hospital stay. She had been suffering from stamina loss and breathing difficulties for some time—and the ways she determined something was wrong were unconventional at best. Her ability to weed her small garden was affected, she complained—even though she was approaching ninety and dealing with the at times brutally hot Georgia summer sun. "I feel out of breath coming back from the curb when I drag my trash roll cart and carry the recycling bins down to the street," as she did every Monday. But most peculiar and amusing was her admission one afternoon: "I can't believe it."

"What's that, mom?"

"I tried jumping rope this morning, and I couldn't do it."

"Well, mom, you're ninety now."

"I still can't believe I couldn't do it."

And I couldn't believe that she actually thought she could. I imagined racing over to her place and finding her on the floor trying to escape Houdini-like from the tangled jumble of arms, legs, and jump rope.

That failed attempt at "street sports"—I was grateful she didn't try hopscotch—reminded us of when she returned to the roller rink some eight years earlier. She was adamant about reconnecting to her past—to those glorious high school years when she would, as she recalled, "sail across the rink like Sonja Henie on rollers rather than on blades." (To update the reference, substitute Tara Lapinski, Gracie Gold, or Michelle Kwan for Henie.) Sadly, her attempt at age eighty-two was more like Sonja Henie on rolling pins. I spent my rink time keeping Nan afloat, and when we went down I at least broke her fall with my body—with blade-like pain shooting from my hips and ankles. When we were unlacing our skates, I suggested that if she wished to recapture some of the glory of Old Baldwin High, she should take a math test.

One morning, my wife and I received a call asking us to stop by because she had something important to talk to us about. Since she lived within five miles, we were there right away.

"I'm feeling anxious. I'm afraid I'm going to stop breathing." Suddenly the inability to jump rope didn't seem so devastating. We checked her into the emergency room, and the staff was stunned to discover that her blood oxygen level reading had fallen to 65. That number had no meaning for me, until the ER nurse noted that a "normal" reading is between 95 and 100. 90 to 95 is considered low but not reflective of any significant problem. A 65, however? Picture an outdoor thermometer and a reading of twenty below Fahrenheit. At this point our medical vocabulary was expanded with such rollicking fun terms as "hypoxemia," "spirometry," "lung diffusion capacity," and "plethysmography." Nan's reaction to these terms? "When can I get this damned plastic tube out of my nose?"

The six-day hospital stay got her breathing regulated, and she felt rested and ready to go home. One of the physicians came in and explained the situation to her. She had COPD (chronic obstructive pulmonary disease) and congestive heart failure. All those years of smoking finally caught up with Nan—as well as her having lost part of one lung to cancer. The doctor patiently explained the need for Nan to be constantly on oxygen from this point forward and talked of options when she had to leave the house for appointments, dinners, and other activities. Nan nodded throughout the session, punctuating sections of his talk with "Yes, doctor" and "I understand, doctor"—and of course several exclamations of "I feel fine" and "I feel great."

When the doctor left, she looked at my wife and said, "What the hell was he talking about? Did you get all that? So when am I getting out of this place? I want some real food."At ninety, she could be excused for not absorbing every detail, but in this case her mind was impenetrable--as solid and confident as a medieval fortress as enemy cannon balls bounced harmlessly off its walls. But the biggest reaction was saved for the announcement that they'd be delivering to her house an oxygen machine and fifty-feet of "nose-hose" as well as several portable bottles of oxygen. "What the hell do I need that for? I'm breathing fine." That her breath was being supplemented at that moment by hospital oxygen seemed to be lost on her.

Yet, part of her inability to comprehend all (any) of what the doctor told her was the result of her poor hearing. Not surprisingly, her hearing began to fade in her later seventies, but after she moved up to Georgia in her early eighties, the fade rate increased to the point that she lost much of what the priest delivered in his sermons. Spanish and Irish accents bedeviled her—to the point that she yearned for the voices she heard at St. Leo's, her church in Florida—that is, the sound of the priests who were there in the 1960s. When I reminded her that the priests were Father Donnan with his thick Irish accent and Father Lacrima with his incomprehensible Bulgarian one, she dismissed my reminder with her familiar "You don't know what you're talking about." When she joined a church discussion group, Nan could only hear the women sitting on her immediate right and left. If someone else posed a discussion question and asked her what she thought, she'd simply offer a "I'll have to think more about that before offering an opinion" or "I can add nothing, really, to what Betty just said." I just hoped that Betty said something more profound than absurd.

Conversation in a lively (noisy) establishment is a challenge regardless of how strong are one's audio capabilities, but with Nan it was a challenge worthy of Everest or the Amazon. At times she simply resorted to the smile-and-nod technique—adding laughter whenever we happened to chuckle. When we asked her a question in such a setting, we tried to increase the volume to aid in comprehension, but there were times when her answers left us groping for what it was she thought she heard.

"How do you like my full beard, Mom?"

Then why did you grow it now? It's only spring.

"You want to take that home?"

No. If I had tried to cook it, mine wouldn't taste half as flavorful considering what I have in my pantry. We need to go to the store soon.

"Would you like more olive oil?"

I love you too, baby.

As time went on, we noticed that her chair in the TV room had been pulled out several inches from the wall against which it was placed. I pushed it back, but the next time it was pulled out again. Why, mom?

"I can hear the television better."

"Well, just turn up the volume a little." Mistake on my part—a great big mistake. It came to pass that whenever we'd go to see her, the television was on so loud our own thoughts were drowned out by the screaming match between two characters on *Days of Our Lives.* But they were just talking normally, not screaming—as we found out when we turned the volume down to something approaching normal levels. The CD player also made communication impossible. Try asking if she's had a good day with Sinatra bellowing "Fly Me to the Moon" at a volume that literally could be heard up there. Nan's poor hearing also made car conversations a struggle, seeing that she preferred to sit in the back seat when my wife and I took her out. "Are you two talking to me?" every time I made an observation about the traffic. "Are you both whispering?" whenever I commented on recent events. And of course dead silence when I offered a "What are you hungry for, Mom?" or "Did you watch *Dancing with the Stars* last night?"

As one might expect, Nan often had troubles answering the phone. Mishearing the caller, she tended to dig herself into a number of holes. When she received a "come-on" call about "winning" a cruise or being eligible for a "loan," she remained on the line trying to convince the caller that she had already paid for her recent cruise and wondered if she were mistakenly being charged for her niece and husband (who took her on her latest cruise) as well. "I told that person to call Trudy [her niece] and take it up with her," she told me. As for the bank "loan" call, she panicked believing she was in arrears with her equity loan payment. "I'm sure I paid it. I'll have to get my check book." Most often, the caller gave out first—surely a rarity in these annoying telemarketer times—and hung up. "John," she'd tell me, "call the bank and straighten this out. Damn it, I pay my bills, and I resent getting calls saying I haven't." Suffice it to say that I convinced her to tell them to contact me if she didn't understand what the call was about.

Yet, there was the occasional slip-up. When I took over her bills in the last year and a half of her life, I discovered that she had two insurance companies covering her house. She had received a call asking her about her homeowner's coverage from a representative of a well-known name in the industry. Somehow she ended up purchasing a new policy. "I thought it was the same as when your mortgage company tells you they just sold your mortgage to another company and you have to start paying them now." On another occasion she called an 800 number after seeing a television commercial for big-band CDs. She saw the one she wanted (the featured disc at a discounted price) and called to order it. She apparently didn't hear the part of the commercial or the phone conversation that reminded her that she'd be sent more CDs every several weeks or so. When the second came in the mail, she called me. "They sent me something I didn't order. Can you phone them?" When I explained what she'd done, she fumed at those "crooks" who mislead the public.

Following a year-long campaign, we convinced her to try hearing enhancements. Now ninety, she grumbled about not needing any, but our arguments won out—somehow. "How would you describe your hearing, Nan?" the audiologist asked at the initial visit.

"It's fine."

"No it isn't," my wife and I chimed in perfect unison. The testing proved us right, and Nan reluctantly conceded to the auditory truth. She was in such an accommodating mood that she okayed the purchase of six thousand dollar's-worth of enhancements. When she put them in and the adjustments were made, her face exploded in surprise at what she could now hear. The ride back from the audiologist's introduced a whole new vocabulary."You don't have to raise your voice; I can hear you fine" and "Be careful what you say; I can now hear everything." I couldn't wait to see her reaction when she turned on her television, which was still set at mega-volume. She reached for her ears and howled at the nuclear explosion of sound. Now my wife and I could communicate with her more effectively and we believed we'd never have to have our eardrums shredded by those screaming *Days of Our Lives* characters or the moon-shots delivered by a crooning Sinatra at full volume. But as they say, all good things . . .

Because she accepted that she'd have to be on oxygen when she was in her home (she was supposed to be on it 24/7, but vanity wouldn't permit her to be seen in public with a plastic tube inserted into both nostrils), Nan found that hooking the tube around her ears made wearing the hearing aids more difficult. When she took the tube off for various reasons (going to the bathroom, for example), she'd pop off the hearing aids and end up needing our help to find them. And so, for the last fourteen months of her life, she returned to the shouting soap characters and roaring Sinatra songs. Six grand right down the old ear canal as it were.

Would that Nan's hearing was all that bedeviled her daily life. But her sight went as well. After she moved to Georgia, she began having difficulty reading restaurant menus. Admittedly and depending on the lighting, many of us have to hold the menu at bizarre angles to catch the light that bleeds from the kitchen or bar. Pulling out iPhones to illuminate the menu is also common, but Nan's difficulties seemed beyond all that. Matters came to a head when at eighty-seven she went to a strip-mall optometrist about getting a new pair of reading glasses. He gave her an examination and noted that cataracts had likely formed in both eyes. At least we now had an explanation for her vision problems. A local ophthalmologist was recommended and the cataract removal surgery was scheduled. All went well, according to the post-op report and follow-up. Yet, Nan's sight seemed to be getting worse as the weeks went by. A further check led to a referral, which led to another referral to a specialist in vitreo-retinal diseases and surgery. The diagnosis wasn't cheery: macular degeneration. Nan went to another ophthalmologist for a second opinion, and in this case the second was identical to the first.

Still, Nan dismissed the diagnosis of both specialists. "They're just covering up for the botched cataract surgery. That man [the original surgeon] took away my sight." Her logic was just as firm as it was flawed. "All I know is that I saw fine before I had the surgery, and now I can't see much at all." In truth, she hadn't seen "fine" before the surgery, but without question her vision was now worse and getting more so. Until she went to Golden Harbor Assisted Living, she frequently echoed the same refrain—"All I know is that before the surgery . . ." Occasionally, her ire rose to the level of asking me to see about getting an attorney so she could sue the "bastard" who "blinded" her. A day later she'd tell me to forget it because the other ophthalmologists would only lie for one of their own—even on the witness stand under oath.

But her complaints were fired off quickly and then she put her weapon away. Otherwise, she never whined about her poor sight and made whatever adjustments she could to make do with what she had left. "Who's that who just talked to me?" and "Is that you, John?" as I was walking down her hallway without her having heard me come into the house. I found it remarkable that I never once startled her. Maybe a mother can smell her son coming from yards away—I don't know. Soon her writing became illegible and her signature could wind up anywhere on the 6 by 3 inch checks she wrote. I would fill in her checks and then point the pen where she needed to sign, but even that was too difficult; therefore, I had the bank put my name on the account so I could sign all the checks. "I'm having you audited, John, just in case you want to take off with the money," she'd tease. Although she didn't often use them, Nan had more magnifying glasses lying around than did Sherlock Holmes.

The seemingly simple and daily chore of taking pills was also made quite formidable owing to Nan's poor eyesight. The plastic weekly pill thingamajig would make the task easier, we foolishly thought. Just take one pill from each compartment and *voila!* But Nan would lose track of the day and occasionally open the Thursday compartment when it was only Tuesday, and two days later, when she had the calendar straight, she believed she had taken the pills earlier in the day when she hadn't. And then there were the occasions she tried to place the plastic pill holder near the edge of the bathroom vanity but missed, leaving the pills scattered on the bathroom floor like chicken feed. "John, can you guys come over?"

Moving from the bathroom to the kitchen—refusing to have all her meals out or brought in, Nan insisted that she could still cook. Each time we went over, we'd remind her not to touch the top of the stove. But challenges remained, such as seeing what the temperature was set on, finding something behind something else in the refrigerator, and figuring out measurements. Her greatly limited eyesight also missed smudges, stains, and drippings, which remained until we or the housekeeper we hired cleaned them off. Pepper became salt and vice versa. Glassware was set down on the very edge of the table or counter—with a few going the way of all flesh, so that we ended up with several matched sets of one. And in the kitchen was a wall monitor placed there by the security service she contracted with. When we left the house she'd set the alarm, and when we returned we'd have to disarm it within so many seconds to prevent the damned thing from waking the dead. At times she'd set it and forget that she had. A walk out the back door to the patio, a trip to the mailbox, or a desire to water the bushes could result in the alarm being triggered. And when it was, we'd get a call at our place to inform us of that fact. We came; the police came; the police left shaking their heads; and Nan cursed technology. When her sight problems increased, she had trouble punching the right buttons, resulting in . . . you guessed it. We finally arrived at a sensible solution. Disarm the blasted thing—permanently. But Nan insisted on paying the bill month after month, because she didn't want the security company angry at or disappointed in her for canceling the service.

As mentioned, she had moved her favorite chair closer to the T.V. in order to hear better, but eventually it was a mere twenty inches away when most of her sight left her. It was a miracle she could squeeze in between the cushion and the front of the big-screen TV. Sometimes I'd see her like that and I couldn't help thinking of the scene in the first *Poltergeist* film. I expected Nan to put both her palms on the screen and whisper, "They're heeeeere."

By the time she turned ninety-one, we were taking her to a full complement of doctor appointments—namely, to her pulmonologist, cardiologist, family physician/internist, ophthalmologist, audiologist, dermatologist, and vascular surgeon. Her left knee had by this time given over to arthritis, so each time she sat in or got out of the car, she endured additional discomfort. In addition to her regularly scheduled appointments, we took her to whatever test she needed—at the hospital, doctor's office, or medical annex. Nan's attitude toward her many appointments ranged from "Maybe she can make me better" to "He doesn't do anything to help me get better." In addition, whereas she never disagreed with doctors' recommendations or orders while she was listening to them—her go-to response was a cooperative nodding of the head—she saved her displeasure for the ride back home from her appointment. The first reaction was a simple question to me and my wife. "What the hell was Dr. So-and-So talking about in there? I couldn't follow a thing he/she was saying." When we explained what Doc So-and-So suggested or ordered, Nan would pull out from her bag of complaints such reactions as "Why the hell do I have to do that? I can breathe just fine"—or, "Now how is that going to help? I think they just want me to do these things because it's more money for them." Yet, speaking of these medical costs would always bring out her altruistic and patriotic side. We would say, "Mom, Medicare will take care of that," and she'd invariably reply, "This is stealing from the government. I feel guilty about that, so I'm not going to spend its money on that treatment." Sometimes when she'd get frustrated with what she had to do or go through, she'd moan, "Can't I just go to Dr. Such-and-Such and forget about Doctor So-and-So?" We had to remind her that these doctors had different specialties. "Your lungs and heart are different areas, mom."

"Well that wasn't that way it was when Dr. Lagorio took care of me. It's just a money grab."

At one point, she was convinced she had breathing and stamina difficulties primarily because she was out of shape. "I just sit around here and watch television all day." Fair enough, but her remedy was to get back on the home treadmill she hadn't been on for several years. We pleaded with her not to get on until she first cleared it with her general physician. When she asked him if she could climb aboard the treadmill, his face expanded to three times its normal width. "Nan, no. You can't afford to risk falling off." We reminded her that years earlier my wife's mother fell on the treadmill and broke her clavicle, elbow, wrist—and hip. Nan kept silent and just nodded when her doctor asked if she understood what he had said. As soon as we got to the car, she launched. "I love that man, but he made me mad today." Why? "He won't let me get on the treadmill. He's trying to make an old lady out of me." She was right. How dare he? She was only about to turn ninety-two.

Because Nan usually had several questions about her health issues, we encouraged her to be sure she brought them up at her appointments. She would always reply, "Oh, I will—don't worry about that." But she didn't because it would bruise the beauty of the phrase, "I feel just fine, doctor." We determined that we had better go in with her and make sure the issues were raised. When asked a specific question, she'd habitually turn to my wife (who was super-organized and had all the details written down) and say, "Tell the doctor." On one occasion, my wife provided the physician the latest issues plaguing my mother, after which Nan said in all seriousness, "I don't even know why I come. You might as well go in there for me so I can stay home." At another time, she called us over and complained of an upper respiratory problem, causing her to expectorate more than her fair share of phlegm. We made a doctor's appointment for two days hence, but when we met with the physician, she forgot what it was that ailed her. Therefore my wife explained about the expectorating of two days previous. My wife received no thanks for revealing that fact; rather she was met in the car with a "I'm mad." Why, my wife inquired. "I don't appreciate your making up things that never happened." I guess we only dreamed about the expectorations—sigh.

Of course she had to be checked out personally by stethoscope, blood pressure cup, et al. But the one instrument she hated most was the scale on which she had to stand at the beginning of each appointment. It wasn't her weight that bothered her, because she was down to 115-120 on the average, which seemed good enough. It was rather the additional reading of her height that set her off. In her prime, Nan was five-six. By this time of her life, however, she struggled to make five-three. Whenever a nurse announced that reading, Nan would unfailingly counter with "I'm not five-three; I'm five-six." We tried to explain that bones have a way of settling after ninety years or so, but she wouldn't hear it. My wife is five-two and change, so they were now almost identical in height, but Nan would force my wife to stand back to back with her and then say, "Look at the two of us. I *tower* over her." I told my wife not to fret; they're making towers a bit smaller these days.

Problems with her oxygen levels continued and soon her desire to do without it in public couldn't be realized. When we took her shopping, she could make it down all the aisles without too much difficulty, but soon she limited the number of aisles she could traverse until the day she gave out in the cereal aisle of Publix and had difficulty catching enough breath to leave the store. Church was a little easier for her to negotiate. She'd use the portable oxygen tank on the way to mass and make it in all right. When we picked her up she was sitting on an outside bench, and some kindly man or woman would help her to the car. As expected, some days were less worse than others, so she could walk into a physician's appointment with the portable tank on Monday and then barely make it through the door on Wednesday. As the weeks went by, her protestations of "I don't need the oxygen; I can breathe fine" became faint echoes of the past. How she hated walking anywhere with that pull-tank and plastic hose up her nose. She jumped on any excuse to pull the hose out. If you asked her a question, she pulled it out. If *she* wanted to ask a question, she pulled it out. If a fly flew near, she'd pull it out. If nothing happened, she'd pull it out.

Living on her own (*her* demand—so please don't accuse her son of insensitivity) led to an increase in phone calls to our house. If she didn't wish to explain on the phone, she'd just say "Come over." Seven to ten minutes later, we opened her door not knowing what to expect. "I can't get any air out of the machine." She couldn't see that she had inadvertently pulled out the plastic tube from the oxygen machine. "Can you take this thing out of my room? It's giving off too much heat." We countered that she merely needed to move it out of the bedroom (she had a fifty-foot tube, remember). "I've been thinking of doing that while I couldn't sleep. Can you put it in the garage [on the complete opposite end of the house from her bedroom] and then drill a hole into the living room for the hose, and then drill one through the guest room, and then another into the TV room, and then across the hall through the wall into my bedroom?" Fortunately, she settled on a compromise of having the machine in the TV room with the tubing running under her bedroom door, which she always kept closed anyway.

Nan also belonged to a service she could reach by pressing a button on a necklace she sometimes wore and at other times couldn't find. The problem with such devices is that they occasionally get pressed accidentally, especially if they get sat or rolled over on. Understandably, Nan was always highly embarrassed when the service called her and she was forced to tell them she didn't mean to press the button and that everything was fine. But on one very early morning—5:30 early—our phone rang. It was the emergency service calling to inform us, "Your mother says she needs you to come over right away." Leaping out of the bed and into our clothes, my wife and I pulled out of the garage in record time. When we arrived, we rushed into her bedroom. I'm sure both our faces were wide-eyed with concern as we stood at the foot of her bed. "Mom, are you all right? What's wrong? What do you need?"

"Well, I could use a cup of coffee. Make me a pot, baby."

What? No "Make me some coffee before I go to my final reward"? Or at least "Make me some coffee before you take to the hospital"? No, just "I could use a cup of coffee." My wife and I stumbled to the kitchen and made the coffee, looking at each other as if we'd entered the Twilight Zone. In a moment, Nan made her way to the kitchen and thanked us for brewing a pot. I might have waited a full thirty seconds before I asked, "Mom, you had them call us to come over and make you a cup of coffee?" The benign look on her face suggested that she was about to gaze at the cup and remark, "It's the best part of waking up" and then after she took her last swallow, "Ahhh, good to the last drop." Instead, she blithely explained that she had rolled over on the necklace and accidentally called the service. When they called her back, she was too embarrassed this time to say she hadn't meant to call, so "I told them to call you and say I needed you to come over. I didn't know they'd call you right away and wake you up." You're right, Mom. They should have waited until I was showered and dressed before calling. How thoughtless of them.

For Nan, the fifty-foot plastic oxygen tubing was like living with a reticulated python. One description of a reticulated python reads, "Some reticulated pythons are sweet-tempered and trustworthy; however, many have nervous and irritable dispositions and simply do not make satisfactory captives" (or houseguests). This oxygen tubing was of the latter variety—

nervous, irritable, and dangerously cuddly. We'd enter Nan's TV room and find her sitting in her chair incarcerated by tubing, which was wrapped around her legs, or waist, or neck—and even once inside her underwear, on a line from between her bottom cheeks, then up between her breasts, down over one shoulder and around her waist and then looped around one knee.

Nan's walking through her house, especially with her bad sight, rivaled the astonishing feats of southwestern Asia, such as sleeping on a bed of nails and flute-charming a speckled cobra. At times she would be jerked backwards as she walked to the kitchen when the tubing was wrapped under a chair leg or bed post. Occasionally the tubing would elevate and drag to the floor a full glass of wine or a fragile knick-knack. Nan tried to avert such mini-disasters by grabbing and looping the fifty-foot hose like a ninety-two-year-old Annie Oakley, releasing a little more the further she walked in the house, but the serpent seemed to have a mind of its own and would drop around her ankles, causing her to get caught up in it more with each step she took. That strategy was quickly abandoned. She also had a difficult time remembering to remove the tubing from her nose and ears before dressing, and as a result she secured the tubing under her shirts. She would take the tubing out when she ate, and at times it would slip under her shirt where she couldn't see it. Then the search began—her hands reaching under her blouse or through the top of her shirt as though she were Houdini trying to escape his shackles. A perfect summation of Nan's feelings for the oxygen tubing came near the end of her life, when she blurted out, "I wish Hitler was still alive."

"Why do you say that, mom?"

"Because I'd like to bequeath him this damn oxygen tube."

After four hospital trips within ten months—all because of breathing difficulties and frighteningly low oxygen levels, her doctor told her that she couldn't any longer live by herself.

"I do fine, doctor."

He spoke of how she was in that "gravy" time of life, and asked her to think about going to an assisted living community.

"I will," she promised. At this time, she had started on a Coumadin regimen (blood thinning), ordered by the hospital doctor during her most recent stay, but there was a problem in getting the right dosage for the level she was supposed to attain, causing her considerable frustration. Her personal doctor told her to forget about the Coumadin, which raised her (and our) spirits considerably, arguing again that she was in the "gravy" period and that not every possible medical problem needed to be directly treated. "I'll be fine at home now," she assured us. So had she thought about assisted living as she promised? Perhaps for a fleeting moment. "I don't see why I need to go there. I do fine at home."

Nan had a wonderful philosophy when it came to relying on others: "I refuse to lose my independence." She watched her mother live alone from the time her husband died when she was sixty to her death at eighty-seven. "I'll never ask to live with you," Nan told us—and she never did. But what finally got Nan out of the house and into Golden Harbor Assisted Living was an accident quite common among the elderly. A broken hip. We received a call on a late afternoon in May asking us to come over.

"What's wrong, mom?"

"Nothing. I'm fine, but I need to talk to you."

We drove over assuming it was a further problem with the oxygen unit. When we arrived she was sitting in her chair in front of the TV. I noticed a spilled glass of wine and an upended plate of crackers and cheese on the floor.

"What is it, mom?"

"I fell." She had just gotten up from her chair and apparently lost her balance, sending her straight down on her knees. Later, she would insist that she merely slid forward on the chair to her knees, but her chair had a soft cushion that tended to swallow up the sitter and required a two-arm push up just to get out of it. If a naked body was coated with motor oil, one still couldn't slide off that cushion. Like most of us, Nan hoped to minimize the damage by altering the details a tad. As we know, "I took an awkward step on the staircase and somehow broke my leg" really means "I tried to go down to the basement after my fourth margarita and fell down the stairs."

We immediately looked to her head for any bleeding or bruising. We saw none. A year earlier, Nan had tripped and fallen in her bedroom, when she stumbled getting out of bed, but she had insisted that even I could fall like that (she was right) and that it wasn't a sign of anything worse than clumsiness. But this time she knew something was wrong, because the pain in her hip was excruciating. "We need to get you to the hospital. I can call an ambulance if you can't move."

"I can get to the car." Making it there was of course very difficult and painful for Nan. I asked if she wanted me to carry her, but she insisted she'd get to the garage by herself, which she did by using a light chair and pushing it along the floor before sitting in it when the pain was too much and then pushing it some more, and so on. I had to lift her to get her across the door stoop and down into the garage, causing her to howl and then laugh. "So now it's you carrying me." We made it to the emergency room and awaited the verdict: a bad bruise, since the x-ray showed nothing. So back home we went, but not before picking up a transport chair (light wheelchair) at the medical supply store. That Sunday was Mother's Day and we were able to dine at a nice eatery, which turned out to be our last restaurant meal together.

But the pain continued without cease, so we scheduled an appointment with her doctor. He immediately recommended seeing an orthopedic surgeon. But he also insisted on something else. "You're going to have to give up living at home, Nan." This time she didn't quarrel. She had just spent a few days at Golden Harbor Assisted Living when my wife and I were away for an academic conference. She liked the staff there, and told us she was just fine with going back. I knew something wasn't quite right about her cooperative attitude, but our attention was directed at the report from the orthopedic surgeon: a broken hip which needed surgery, followed by several weeks of rehab. Nan was all for it, owing to the pain she was enduring. But one problem the surgeon's assistant shared with us. Given Nan's difficulties with her lungs, it would be too risky giving her a general anesthetic. "We'll get her to the hospital and have the anesthesiologist see if she can have a spinal." Wonderful.

The next morning we arrived at the hospital and after completing the paperwork, we sat in a room waiting for the anesthesiologist. Nan was immediately put at ease by his personality and sense of humor, and she did her standard "This is my son and he's done such-and-such" routine, much to my usual embarrassment. One would think I was well used to it by now and I'd let it roll off like water on a duck's back, but no, I never did. It was more like hot tar seeping in rather than cool water rolling off.

Fortunately, the anesthesiologist was able to give her a spinal and the operation was a success, according to the post-op report. Later we visited Nan in her room and besides the effects of her drugs, she seemed fine and most happily out of pain, albeit the result of her medication. The next day would tell more, however. To our further delight, she was her usual self. Yes, there was discomfort from the surgery, but she knew it would subside and was looking forward to "getting out of this damn place" and on to her therapy. We couldn't blame her for feeling impatient to leave, since this was her fifth hospital visit in the space of fourteen months. She ate at least part of her meal, although we had difficulty identifying what lay on the lunch plate. It's never good when you have to preface your description with "I think this is . . ." But for her just having undergone hip replacement surgery, my wife and I were thrilled that Nan came through it so well. Or so we thought.

The next day we were stunned to see the change in her appearance and breathing. Apparently during the night her renal (kidneys) system began to shut down. She was disoriented and unaware she even had surgery. The next several days were most difficult ones, with discussions about hospice care and the pros and cons of dialysis at this late stage, which we decided against (being true to Nan's living will), much to the doctor's relief. I went over the next afternoon and looked in on her, and I truly thought she was gone. This was the first time I ever saw her without her dentures and the sight was, forgive me, utterly ghastly. This couldn't be my stylish mother—but it was, and we assumed she'd pass away during the night. We discussed options with the Palliative Care nurse, who counseled us wisely. She believed that Nan would be best off going to assisted living for her final days as long as she was under hospice care.

The staff at Golden Harbor was perfectly fine with having Nan spend her last days there, but it was the recommendation they gave regarding the hospice component that we most appreciated. The hospice organization they suggested was named Compassionate Care, and I will never fail to appreciate and admire the professionalism, compassion, friendliness, and skill they demonstrated in their care of my mother. They, and others like them, are the true angels on this earth.

Nan recovered her sensibilities well enough to understand that she'd be going to Golden Harbor, but her physical state was dire at best. When the head hospice nurse examined her, she told us, "I'm sorry to say this, but your mother may not live through the night." But then she didn't know Nan, who had quite a surprise waiting for all of us.

Chapter 2
Bird Hands & Gold Lamé

"With mirth and laughter let old wrinkles come."
William Shakespeare

To the very end, Nan maintained fierce pride in how she looked and carried herself. She not only nodded toward vanity but bowed to it constantly. A large part of the magic of her spirit was her concern for her appearance and utter refusal to act and look her age by allowing her hair to display its true gray or to cut it in a length commonly worn by septua-, octo-, and nonagenarians—and by her damning rejection of bedecking herself exclusively in "age appropriate" outfits. There was something quite charming and exhilarating seeing her in "Brooklyn Dodgers," "I Love New York," "Love Me—I'm Italian," and "Austin 3:16" tee shirts (the last being a gift from her grandson). She also liked patriotic wear—stars, stripes, flags, etc.— and Miami Dolphins garb. And these shirts would often be accompanied by a pair of jeans, which she would also complement with colorful and attractive blouses and, in the winter, with her black leather jacket. Black on black was one of her favorite combinations until the end of her life. In short, she never got anywhere near flower-print dresses, powder-blue sweaters, shawls, side-snap pants, and flat sturdy shoes—the usual wear of women her age and even twenty to thirty years younger. In spite of her youthful tee shirts and jeans, Nan's "serious" clothing was elegant and impressive. Her closet reminded one more of Dior, Harrods, Gucci, Armani, and Versace far more than it did Penney's, Stein Mart, Khol's, Target, or Walmart. Her shoe collection didn't quite rival that of Imelda Marcus's, but it included stylish pumps, sandals, and boots.

As expected, when she entered her eighties her high heels began to present a few problems. Walking further than ten feet was one. We soon got into the "sidewalk dance" routine with her. Ten feet—stop. Eight feet—stop. Ten feet—hold her up. Eight feet—look for the police, who might misconstrue Nan's difficulties with her heels as proof of her affection for martinis. A compromise was reached: I'd drop her and my wife off as near to the door of the restaurant as possible and hope for the best. The high heels were eventually retired in favor of the medium to short heel, which still didn't alleviate all her difficulties. For one thing, sidewalks didn't cooperate by being completely smooth and level. My wife and I became pretty proficient at preventing Nan from tipping over and commiserating with her as she cursed the shoddy sidewalk construction: "When I was growing up, cement layers used to take pride in their work." On one occasion, she stepped up from the parking lot to the walkway at Olive Garden, but her heels slipped on the edge of the step up and she fell straight back on the asphalt next to the car. As I helped her to her feet, she refused to cast aspersions at her heels and blamed the fall on the fact that the step-up wasn't painted orange to warn the hapless victim to lift her feet. And even though the higher heels were eventually put out to pasture, Nan had no intention of parting ways with them. They remained in her closet: "I may need to wear this pair because they're the only shoes that go with my gold and black ensemble." When we emptied her closets after Nan passed away, my wife and I estimated the height of all Nan's heels placed end to end as approaching a three-story building.

But the true star of her closet was her waist length gold lamé jacket, which she last wore on her 91st birthday outing. Elvis in his famous gold lamé suit had nothing on Nan, believe me. Her belts were always more stylish than utilitarian; her jewelry more dramatic than authentic or valuable. Although the stones and gems in her rings, necklaces, bracelets, and pins were illegitimate, they never looked it. And these trinkets were bought in shops in New York, Las Vegas, Palm Beach, London, Rome, and Madrid, which gave them an extra hint of value. After Nan died, we took her collection to a local jeweler who found only three items top-end enough to buy from us, but she recommended another shop where the owner took costume jewelry. The reaction from the second woman was "Wow. I've never seen so many lovely and impressive pieces in one collection like this." Nan would have been proud.

My mother didn't begin her life as a fashion diva of course. There wasn't any additional money for any of the stylish infant and little-girl monogrammed outfits one sees today. By the time her father began to make his money—moving from tailor to bar owner after Prohibition was repealed—Nan was in her teens facing the pressure of measuring her wardrobe against others her age. Fortunately (or not) she attended Catholic school until high school and wore what all the other girls wore. But at good old public Baldwin High in the later 1930s, she did what she could to dress up what she possessed and could afford to purchase. (Rather tough when she gave the family two-thirds of everything she earned in after-school and summer jobs.) Nan experienced her full share of embarrassment over what she wore in comparison to the outfits donned by other high school girls—and she endured considerable teasing by those better off. Even though her father was by now doing quite well with his tavern, handing out clothing allowances for his two daughters wasn't exactly a high priority. My mother told me it was then that she vowed someday to dress as stylishly as she could.

She was eighteen and a high school graduate when the calendar turned to 1940 and with it came the decade of Rita Hayworth, Lana Turner, Vivian Leigh, Veronica Lake, Hedy Lamarr, and Ava Gardner—all stars that significantly influenced women's styles, Nan's being no exception. Photos from the period show her in finer clothing, though certainly not overly expensive, wearing hair styles that marked the period. Nan's looks in her late teens and early to mid twenties reveal that she could have passed easily for someone in Metro's stable. But one feature of hers stopped her from agreeing with what I just wrote. She inherited from her Italian pedigree a larger-than-one-might-want nose.It wasn't ghastly or even unsightly—it was just too large for her, and it affected how she saw the rest of herself. That others made fun of her for that feature was true, and as we all know a humiliation felt at twelve can resonate just as strongly a decade or more later. There was one period right before and right after I was born—when Nan was twenty-five through twenty-seven—when she took scissors to her photos and removed her head as deftly as those severed by the guillotine in 1789 France. There was one shot of her holding the infant me, looking like the wife of the headless horseman of Ichabod Crane fame. Since she wasn't working for the CIA, the photographic decapitations could only have been prompted by a misplaced

John Vance

sense of inferiority.

After passing through the trauma of my abusive father and the onus of being the first in the family ever to be divorced, Nan regained her interest in contemporary style—if one can define the clothing of the early 1950s as stylish. In spite of her own estimation of her face (her nose particularly), she certainly turned her share of heads, as I learned from her brothers, mother, and friends of hers. And at this time she inspired the devotion of a gentleman who was quite well-fit financially. He met Nan in my grandfather and grandmother's now bar/restaurant on Long Island. Not surprisingly, he found the food and beverages very much to his liking and was a several-times-a-week customer. The man was ten years older than Nan—previously married but not any longer. He promised to care and respect my mother and make her life easier than she had experienced since her disastrous marriage to my father. It sounded simply ideal—financial security with extra money to purchase nicer clothes and a larger screen television (twenty-one inches), to name but two of the benefits. Yes, all ideal—except for one tiny matter. The gentleman just wasn't keen on taking Nan with that five-year-old son of hers hanging around. He wanted to travel and show her the world—or selected big cities in the U.S. A rambunctious tow-head would tend to put a damper on the life he wanted to lead with Nan. The boy could live with his grandparents or his uncles and aunt, couldn't he? Nan thought about it for quite some time—one or two seconds—before rejecting the life the man wished to give her. Not quite Sophie's choice, but one I was happy she made. Nan never reminded me in any moment of frustration or anger that she sacrificed a life of relative leisure for her son. I didn't learn of this incident until she told me about it when she was in her eighties. Then she felt free enough to teasingly taunt about having given up a life of leisure just for me.

It wasn't long afterward that she caught the eye of another personable and attentive man, who would soon be transformed into the selfish and abusive character who became husband number two (H2). As I mentioned, he thought so much of Nan's looks and style that he saw green (jealousy's favorite hue) whenever a man gave her a long look or if she gave a man an innocent short one. "Do you have to wear that?" "Change your clothes." "What are trying to do—get other men's attention?" These were the familiar (and edited) refrains of the day.

Our move to South Florida when Nan was thirty-three changed nothing as far our less-than-ideal home life, but it did open up another avenue as far as her fashion sense was concerned. It was at this time she began wearing "pedal pushers" (forerunner of modern Capri pants), a style she would never abandon. Her physical appearance just seemed to get better and better, and it was during the later 1950s that she had her nose worked on—at a time when middle class women rarely had a rhinoplasty. (My guess is my grandparents helped her financially.) But it was the early 60s that brought Nan to her peak in beauty and style. And her inspiration was the number one name in fashion at the time: Jacqueline Kennedy. A number of my mother's outfits were reminiscent of Jackie's more expensive ones (including pill box hats), and her dark(ened) hair was of course styled a la Jackie. Soon, Nan was being called "Jackie" by friends and relatives. Nan was without question quite a beautiful woman—now having reached forty—some eight years older than Mrs. Kennedy. Nan made up her mind to reject the style choices made by many women who were sensitive to the fact that they were "now forty" and therefore should start dressing "accordingly." Nan would have none of that for the rest of her life.

But with her enhanced physical appearance came the continuation of complaints and accusations from H2, who wanted to enjoy the fact (delusion) that his wife was a beauty who reflected favorably on him—on his physical appeal, which again wasn't exactly notable—far more Ernest Borgnine than Clark Cable. Yet at the same time he wished to avoid anything that would titillate his insecurity—such as actually seeing a man appreciating Nan's looks or hearing another man compliment her while he was in the room. Having been married to H2 for close to ten years and far stronger psychologically than she was at the end of her first marriage, Nan developed a kind of stoic yet defiant attitude toward her miserable home life. She wouldn't "dress down" or "tone down" the makeup, which, I should add, was never garish. No hideous pencil drawn eyebrows; no bulbous bright red lipstick; and no Gothic rouge in her cheeks. My mother never liked circus clowns and she damn sure wasn't about to look like one.

It was during the early 60s that she developed a peculiar walking habit. She dropped her arms straight down and then flexed her hands at the wrist with fingers extended, which I dubbed "bird hands." In addition, she took a "coquettish stride" when she walked. It wasn't so overt that one's face would clench, but it was distinctive and not at all bizarre for a woman as beautiful as she was. Of course when the bird hands and walk continued when she passed fifty—and sixty—and seventy—and eighty—*and* ninety, it did begin to seem a little unusual, I had to admit.

Nan and I occasionally got out of the house without the oppressive male presence to see a movie or spent some time downtown window shopping or sitting at the lunch counters at Woolworth's, where I relished eating grilled cheese sandwiches and French fries. But the most memorable escape occurred when I was about to turn sixteen and Nan was forty-one. We decided to take a summer trip down to Key West for a few days, while H2 was away for some work-related event (or so he claimed). Just getting 240 miles from home was quite a rush. Without question, distance gave us a sense of security and a nice taste of freedom. We indulged our appetites at one of the old- fashioned drive-ins—usually off limits owing to my adopted father's antipathy for wasting money on food my mother could cook herself. Nan and I delighted in the peaceful ride past Miami and then on the series of bridges linking the Keys. When we started our sightseeing around Key West, I noticed men checking out my mother. Although she never encouraged any of their attempts to interact, I know I wouldn't have blamed her if she smiled at them or engaged in small talk. But the highlight came when we were on the White Street Pier looking south toward Cuba (less than a year after the Cuban Missile Crisis, mind you). I had gone off to another part of the pier, leaving Nan to her coffee. After a time, I looked back and saw a man approach her and begin a conversation. I headed back to make sure she wasn't being bothered, and when I got to within shouting distance—I said something along the lines of "Hey, mom. You should come over and look at the water." The "Hey, mom" spoken by a teenage boy completely unnerved the male visitor, who scurried off in another direction. Nan and I laughed at that then and throughout the rest of that day—and for fifty years after. During the night, someone mistakenly knocked on our motel room door, and I was quick to say, "I bet it's your boyfriend from the pier," which got us chortling again.

When we drove back north, we spent the night on Miami Beach and took in the blockbuster of the year—Elizabeth Taylor's epic and costly *Cleopatra.*

Here again I saw further evidence of the looks my beautiful mother could draw from men, with or without a spouse in tow. Yes, it was a fun trip, but alas, we had to return to the less-than-pleasurable reality of our home life. But 1964 was a watershed year in that Nan was reaching a point that she felt good enough about herself to fight back more vigorously against H2's abusive childishness. Later in life, she told me that during that year two men she had met when she worked in real estate had a thing for her and weren't hesitant about admitting it. One was divorced and the other was having marital problems himself. She confessed she was tempted to allow them to continue expressing their interest, but she couldn't bring herself to have an affair with either of them—and so the men disappeared from her life. Again, she had physically hit her peak when she was in her early forties—still being called "Jackie," even after JFK's assassination.

By the fall of 1964—when I began my senior year in high school—we had become friends with one of my grandmother's tenants (she had an apartment and two efficiencies attached to her house that she rented.) Around my mother's age, Tom was as handsome a man as Nan was beautiful. If one can imagine a combination of Dean Martin and Cary Grant, then one would have described his looks accurately. I liked him from the start, and he and his then wife were favorites of my grandmother, who often invited them to dinner whenever we were there. He played golf with H2 and invited me to play with them. My adopted father never made the invitation, mind you. I hadn't started playing at the time and I declined the invitation—the less time with the father presence the better, as I saw it. I could tell that my grandmother's tenant and his wife weren't exactly a loving couple—so I'm sure, especially since I liked him, I gave some thought to what an attractive and happy duo he and Nan would make. I had absolutely no idea that the both of them were thinking the same thing.

Half way through my senior year in high school, I came to the realization that they were in love and were finding it impossible—especially after a few drinks—to contain their affections for each other. Not that I minded, but I was concerned how this would play out—with two existing spouses still in the picture. At our place the matter came to a head when H2 shoved my mother and I judo chopped him in the throat. (Ah yes, the bucolic memories of my youth.) As for Tom and his wife, their confrontations was more verbally violent, even though by this point the wife knew the truth. My grandmother also knew—after she witnessed her daughter and her tenant's physical attraction to each other. Shortly after Nan's and Tom's individual divorce proceedings began, the four of us went out to dinner, and after three martinis each, Nan and Tom were what we used to call "making out hot and heavy" in the back seat, while I, driving Tom's car, tried to keep my eyes on the road and not on the rear-view mirror, while my grandmother pulled out her rosary beads and started praying.

When we returned to my grandmother's, Tom asked me to take a walk just with him—during which he told me to punch him in the face for getting carried away in the back seat. I did react physically—by hugging him and telling him I was very happy that he and Nan were apparently in love. Tom and I did far more together than I ever had done with H2. Golf, movies, neat eateries, sporting events, and the occasional tavern (I was underage, so I had coke) were the new activities I delighted in. Tom was voracious reader and a big Ian Fleming fan—so he took me to see the first four Sean Connery Bond films. He taught me a number of things I have kept with me to this day. He was truly a great guy and I loved him very much.

He worked at Pratt and Whitney Aircraft in Florida, and after I graduated from high school he got me a job there (just another gesture to express his love for Nan)—since I hadn't planned on going to college. But because of the Vietnam call-up, I ended up enlisting in the U.S. Army right before I turned nineteen. Tom was around that age when he jumped into Germany near the end of 1944, and Nan, like so many parents of the day, viewed the latest war through the lens of WWII. "I don't know what I would have done if you didn't love your country enough to fight for it." (Later, she would drastically alter her view of the Vietnam War.) While I was awaiting an October induction, Nan's and Tom's divorces finally made their way through the court, and soon they were on their way to Valdosta, Georgia to get married. Nan had finally found her Mr. Right.

During their years together, Nan continued building her wardrobe and maintained her good looks throughout her later forties and fifties. Tom aged gracefully—as Cary Grant did—and they continued turning heads as a most attractive couple. The clothing fads from the late 1960s through the 1970s had some effect on Nan—but she didn't (thank goodness) stroll into restaurants or appear at parties in a mini-skirt, a pair of hot pants, platform shoes, go-go boots, pinstripe suits, gangster hats, mannish jackets, or any other kind of androgynous wear. She subscribed to a number of glamour magazines and enjoyed seeing the latest from Givenchy, Dior, Saint Laurent, Halston, Bill Blass, Armani—and of course whatever Jackie K (later O) was wearing. In this period Nan embraced elegantly styled hairdos, paler lipstick and nail polish, pant suits, long shawls, ponchos, capes, and fashionable denim. Her jewelry and earrings became more elaborate and fashionable as well.

But in 1983, Tom's health began to deteriorate, and on the very day my son was born he received the dreadful news that he had an advanced case of lung cancer. Tom's condition worsened rapidly, and for his last six months the disease and the by-now useless chemotherapy ravaged him inside and out. This incredibly handsome and virile man was reduced to a frail and deathlike figure until he mercifully died. He and Nan had a great eighteen years—but it was only eighteen years. They both deserved so many more as man and wife.

Immediately after the funeral, Nan moved to the condo where some of her friends and my wife's parents lived, and as the months went by, her love of fashion returned. She began to travel, and what she wore was an important aspect of her European and North American tours and cruises. She was now in her mid-sixties and wished to show herself at her best to her contemporaries, many of whom were widows or divorcees themselves. Further purchases of items such as soft and poofy pants, long dangling earrings, all-black outfits salted with rhinestones, and all white outfits peppered with gold and black trim and accessories enhanced her overall wardrobe. Throughout her seventies, she maintained that look and added to it, and of course no one saw a gray hair on her head. With one exception, to the end of her life she was a brunette—a shift from her natural black.

Regarding that color exception, around age seventy-five Nan decided she'd follow the example of Norma Jean Baker and have some fun time as Marilyn by dyeing her hair blonde. Actually, it was more goldish than blondish, but the overall dish was fairly unpalatable. For one, the color really didn't do much for all white and gold outfits, because there was an overload of gold in the overall look. Fortunately, she returned to her roots (or rather what her roots were forty years earlier) and re-launched as a brunette after about three months of channeling Marilyn. Nan colored her own hair for the most part, with application of the spray-on brown or mascara for touch-ups between colorings. When she reached ninety we encouraged her to have her hair colored at a nice salon where my wife had her nails and hair done. Nan agreed, and when I picked her up after her appointment, she walked out of the salon's door and immediately began picking at her hair. When I asked what was wrong, she replied that they didn't style it the way she liked, so she was trying to reshape it into the more familiar look. I'll have to say that she looked like her hair was infested with termites the way she was pulling, tugging, and twisting. By the time she was done, she resembled a midwestern woman who got into the tornado shelter thirty seconds too late. But all future beauty sessions at the salon were cancelled after one visit to get a manicure and pedicure. Because the stylists and manicurists had different levels of training and experience, the price would be adjusted accordingly. My wife, who had her own nail appointment at the same time, scheduled Nan with the most experienced manicurist, owing to my mother's advanced age and the shape her nails were in. When they were both done and were paying separately, Nan learned that her work cost more than my wife's. Well, when Nan sunk her teeth into principle, there was no letting go. It was unfair that she had to pay more, she howled. The analogy that I (as a professor) would be paid more than a young high school teacher—owing to my experience and advanced degree—was met with ridicule. "If you were both teaching the same book, you should both be paid the same, John." I only hope she meant that the young high school teacher would get my pay and not vice versa. The amount of the difference in her and my wife's bill wasn't that much, really— but that didn't matter when Nan's principles were involved. Thus began a boycott, which held firm until Nan was situated at Golden Harbor Assisted Living.

When she reached her eighties and her eyesight weakened, she began to have problems with her cosmetics—and I just don't mean that her base was roughly applied or her eyeliner was drawn a bit crooked. For some reason, she went with a darker base than she normally used. As an Italian-American, Nan had a nice olive tint to her skin that helped enhance her dark brown eyes. But one summer afternoon we picked her up for lunch and thought initially she had been out in the backyard for too long. Either that or she spent several minutes with her face in the microwave. Her base had a strong orange hue, making me wonder who would ordinarily wear that color. Was it part of a Halloween make-up kit? A failed attempt to mix creamy beige with mango or pumpkin?

It is a given that telling an elderly woman her makeup, hair, or clothing isn't quite cutting it isn't something one looks forward to with any pleasure—and initially we took the prudent way out and said nothing, hoping Nan would make an adjustment and apply a foundation that was more appealing. Unfortunately, our grown children joined us for dinner out, and after dropping Nan back home following the meal, her grandchildren summarized the look about as well as anyone could. "She looks like an Oompa-Loompa!" I had to admit that there was a resemblance—facially—to the orange skinned characters depicted in the 1971 film *Willie Wonka & The Chocolate Factory*. That did it. My wife and I decided we had to risk angering or hurting Nan by sharing our views about the makeup. The next time we picked her up, my wife noted that Nan's base was a little rough around her chin. While my wife smoothed Nan's face, she softly said, "Mom, I think your foundation may be a little too dark for your coloring. You need to go back to what you were wearing before." While my wife gently spoke, I had one foot out the front door, ready to take the coward's walk down the block until the storm subsided. Nan did explode but not in the way we feared.

"It's too damn dim down the cosmetic aisle at the store. They need to put in higher-watt bulbs so people can see what they're buying." Now that didn't explain how she could apply it and not detect the orange glow in the bathroom mirror, but Nan had that covered as well. "John, put some brighter bulbs in the bathroom. I can barely see myself in the damned mirror." And then the clincher. "John, you let me be seen in public wearing this makeup? Why didn't you say something?" I replied honestly that I didn't want to hurt her feelings. So what was her response to her kind and thoughtful son? "But you let me go out looking like a fool, didn't you?" If there's a lesson in this tale, I hope someone learns it.

Part of Nan's "comfy" inside-the-house wear was a faux leopard-spotted and short nighty. Such a garment falls under the classification of "don't-let-anyone-see-you-in-this" wear. But in her late eighties, Nan had entered that stage where one occasionally loses track of how one looks at any given time. All dressed to head out to lunch with four curlers still in her hair and bedecked in an orange shirt with yellow pants were just two examples of what I mean. But one afternoon, when Nan was ninety, our daughter brought Nan's fifteen-month old great-granddaughter over for a visit—one planned but forgotten by my mother. My daughter rang the bell and knocked loudly so Nan could hear her at the door. Whenever Nan heard such knocking— about one-fourth of the time—she took a peak through one of the glass panels running the length of the door on either side. Seeing that it was her granddaughter and great-granddaughter, Nan opened the door with an extra-large smile on her face. But it was the item on her body that was far more memorable. There she stood in that faux leopard-spotted and short nighty. My daughter was aghast at her grandmother's slinky appearance, and all that was needed to complete the moment was a ninety-five-year-old man emerging from the bedroom in a bathrobe with a martini clutched in his hand. But it could have been worse. At least it wasn't her grandson at the door.

When we were packing her clothes after Nan recovered from her surgery and began her stay at Golden Harbor, we were amazed at the amount of clothing she had accumulated—in spite of a bi-monthly contribution of items to Goodwill and church-related charities. Even though she had long stopped wearing dresses, she had a number of attractive to gaudy items of that kind. Blouses I'm sure she hadn't worn in ten to twenty years. Pants that could no longer fit—since she had lost weight as well as height in her last years. Gorgeous coats she brought up with her from south Florida, where there might be one night in four years cold enough to wear one of them. And shoes, and more shoes—from four-inch heeled pumps to Nike running wear. I know that in her last few years she rarely wore anything other than three or four "go-to" pairs of footwear; therefore, the retaining of all her shoe collection was rather unnecessary. Certainly, we all collect and keep a host of items for sentimental or other reasons—photos, baseball cards, dolls, video tapes, receipts, as well as clothing—but shoes that no longer fit or are impractical to wear? My wife and I made some "executive decisions" on which ones to bring to Golden Harbor, but we still brought many more pair than would be worn. We thought we'd give Nan the choice in which few pair she would keep. But when we went through the shoes, she decided to keep every pair and wanted to know where the rest of her shoes were. In the seven months at Golden Harbor she wore a grand total of two pair (excluding her soft "scuff-arounds").

Removing her clothing from her apartment after her death was therefore both a sad and amusing experience, topped off by my wife and daughter donning Nan's politically incorrect full-length faux fur coat and doing an abbreviated runway bit. Where and when my mother purchased this item, I cannot remember. From my youth, I recalled her wearing one of those fox stoles that had four separate pelts sewn together—each with a fox's head, tail, and claws attached. I fully expected the whole thing to suddenly come alive and go for Nan's throat in some version of the Four Foxes of the Apocalypse. I guessed that Nan might have felt the same way, because the apparel disappeared from her closet in the 1960s. Perhaps she felt Jackie K wouldn't be seen with heads and claws around her neck. The faux full-length number, whenever it was purchased, remained in Nan's closet. Other than the year-round south Florida heat, she just never went to any appropriate place where the coat would make sense wearing. When I teased her about wearing it during winters in northeast Georgia, she shook her head. "I don't need to be attacked by those animal rights people from *FETA*." FETA? I wanted to reply that she'd be more likely to be attacked from that group because of her love for provolone than for wearing a fake fur coat.

Yet memories of her outfits and how they emboldened her remained vivid. In her middle eighties, she would be all gussied up in black pants and a black and gold sweater—with accompanying gold jewelry and bird hands working their magic—and flirt with much younger men--telling my son-in-law that it was lucky she wasn't forty years younger, because then my daughter wouldn't have stood a chance. Nan, who was an excellent dancer in her day, liked to cut the carpet with my friend Randy, dubbing him Fred and herself Ginger (Astaire and Rodgers, that is). She sauntered up to another married friend of mine and told him he would make an excellent Mr. Darcy (from Austen's *Pride and Prejudice*). On several occasions she'd cavort with my male friends and then come to me and ask who it was she was flirting with. With the right amount of vodka and vermouth in her system, she extended her flirtations to hand holding and light pecks on the cheek. In her last years, when her sight was very bad, she'd take the embraces of one of my demonstrative male friends and banter with him for minutes at a time and then ask me who it was. Sad to say, it was someone she had known for a number of years, but she just couldn't make out his features.

Still, my favorite memory of Nan out on the town was on New Year's Eve when she was eighty-nine. My wife and I took her to a local show and afterward headed down the sidewalk to the restaurant where we had our dinner reservation. Nan was in her sartorial best—black pants, black and gold blouse, and that killer gold lamé jacket. We set a good walking pace to accommodate her age, and since the show was good, Nan was in a vivacious mood. She linked her arm in mine and my wife did the same. I'm sure our conversation was stimulating and witty, and we laughed and chuckled about whatever it was we were talking about. Up ahead, I saw two young boys—about ten and seven, I estimated. They were staring right at us—at me in particular. Our trio shifted to the right a bit to give the lads a chance to pass on our left. As soon as they reached us, the younger boy said to the older one, "Look at that man. He's a playa." Indeed I was—with my wife on one arm and my saucy mother on the other. I turned my head after they passed, and the older boy pointed his index finger at me as if to say, "You got it, brother."

We brought the outfit she wore that night—as well as many, many others—to Golden Harbor to allow Nan to sift through and choose a few she'd like to hang on to. What we failed to understand at the time was that Nan believed she would be getting better and would therefore need her outfits when she resumed her activities—shows, restaurants, and trips. However the truth was that she would not be making any further improvements after her rally from her near-death state after her hip-replacement surgery (see Chapter 9). But we were not strong (inhumane) enough to tell her differently. So Nan went through the bags and boxes of clothing throwing very little into the "get-rid-of" pile. Instead we heard phrases like "I'll need this sweater when I go out in the winter" and "I always wear this outfit on cruises—so I'll keep this." Oh, there were a few items she tossed (literally tossing them toward me so that I could stuff them in a plastic garbage bag for Goodwill)—a pair of shorts here and a long-sleeve blouse there. But since I was getting so little thrown my way, I started looking out the window and admiring a June rain shower. That is, until I got smacked in the face by an article of clothing Nan decided she didn't want any more. Remember that this is my own mother we're talking about—so it came as a bit of a shock when that sexy black bustier made contact with the left side of my head. I swear I did everything I could NOT to imagine Nan wearing that piece—"Think baseball; think baseball!" my inner-self screamed. Yet I couldn't help giving some thought to when she might have worn it last and for what reason. Tom had been gone for thirty years, after all. Surely it was purchased when they were first married—eighteen years before that. The alternative to that time-line was too unfathomable to contemplate.

Nan's unique and often impressive taste in fashion had its downside as far as the rest of the family was concerned. Namely, she wanted to dress us according to her own tastes. Birthdays and Christmas brought shivers whenever we opened her gifts, with the accompanying "If the size isn't right, you can exchange it" disclaimer. I'm sure she dressed me decently enough when I was a baby and a young boy—at least the existing photographic evidence suggests as much. But when I reached (and throughout) my teens I can remember the disappointment of receiving clothes as birthday and Christmas gifts instead of what I really wanted—money to buy the latest singles and albums of my favorite groups. There'd be a Florida-themed buttoned-down shirt instead of the latest Paul Revere and the Raiders disc or a pair of shiny beltless pants instead of the recent Stones album. I'd get ties I never wore and vertically striped shirts that only looked good on the Beach Boys.

Into my twenties my mother's practice of clothes-giving continued. I could see Nan was delighted whenever she'd present me with the latest in male fashion—of another era or planet. But on one occasion she was right in step with the times. Unfortunately that step was for all times to come a major male fashion stumble: the leisure suit. I'd been ridiculing the look ever since I first saw it, and it didn't matter to me that Johnny Carson wore them on the *Tonight Show*. At least Carson probably never wore the color Nan picked out for mine: lime green. I do know for certain, though, that *I* never wore that leisure suit or any other regardless of the color. Well, I did have to put it on that Christmas Eve and watch Nan's face light up with pride and delight. I stood there helpless, like poor Ralphie in the pink bunny suit in *A Christmas Story*. But there was another suit that comes to mind—one Nan bought me several years later, after I had received my doctorate. I was one of the fortunate ones; I had a faculty position in hand when I got the degree. Realizing that fact, Nan, who came up to Florida State to attend the ceremony, decided that if her boy was going to be standing that fall in front of a classroom at the University of Georgia with a "Dr." in front of his name, he better look the part. Try as I might, I couldn't convince her that faculty members don't have to teach class dressed as though they were being inaugurated president of the United States. So I ended up the proud owner of a new and expensive suit, with five costly ties, and a set of sparking cuff-links thrown in for good measure. Sorry to say, I never wore the suit except in the store that afternoon. Of course I always said I did wear it whenever Nan asked—the kind of fib one might classify as universal if not forgivable.

As the years went by, the choices she made became more peculiar, daring, inexplicable, and even horrifying. For Christmas and my birthday, I received V-necked sweaters, which I didn't like; beltless dress pants in colors I felt uncomfortable wearing; and several pairs of loafers, which I gave up wearing twenty years ago. Nan announced before one gift that she was sick of seeing me in Ralph Lauren Polo shirts "with that silly little man riding a horse" over my left breast. So I opened my big Christmas present and pulled out two very expensive shirts "made in Italy."

They were indeed of excellent construction and looked every penny of what they likely cost. But nothing is less me than a silk shirt with muted designs all over the front, a front pocket, and the first button some seven and a half inches down from the base of my neck. "This way you can show off your chest, John," Nan proudly announced. I have—maybe—seven dark hairs on my chest that can be seen with the naked eye—not the Italian masculine look the shirt makers likely had in mind. She would have been far better off finding me shirts designed by Chinese or Native American designers, I think.

But I also had a wife and later a daughter and son for Nan to dress as well as her own boy. As for my son, Nan did fine with sports-team tee shirts until he reached his teens. Then came the attempts to style him up a few notches. On one occasion, after my son asked for one or two Polo shirts, we convinced her that she wouldn't have to buy him the helmet and horse to go with the shirt. However, she discovered that a polo shirt (small p) was a style of casual wear. But my son hoped for the Polo shirt (with the capital P), which he didn't receive. Later Nan would often note of her grandson (as she did with me), "Why is he always wearing that kind of Polo shirt? He's dating now, so he needs to dress up a bit more." A bit more? With Polo shirts then at $70.00 to $75.00 a pop? Did she mean a tuxedo shirt? My son was always very sweet about receiving a short-sleeved dress shirt with dual pockets. He would thank his grandmother and wait until we were in the car going home. "Here, dad. Can you drop this at the Goodwill the next time you go by."

Our daughter suffered even more—because after all she was female. Her misery began when she was about eight, when Nan bought her what we think was supposed to be a sweater. It was a pink furry sweater/shirt that seemed to be in the high Cro-Magnon style. I might have seen something like this on a *Flinstones* episode from the early 1960s. I shudder to add that Nan bought a matching blue one for our son—who at least was only three and didn't suffer as much mortification as did our daughter. And speaking of things Cro-Magnon, Nan gave her a large sleep shirt, fringed at the bottom and on the sleeves, with a caveman and cavewoman cartoon on the front, complete with "your cave or mine" printed in big letters across the chest. Perhaps Nan forgot that her granddaughter was only ten at the time—not quite ready for cave hopping.

When our daughter reached the age of serious fashion consciousness, she would literally dread opening her grandmother's presents on Christmas Eve. And Nan never failed to justify that dread. Shirts, pants, matching outfits, shoes, and belts were invariably of the "dress up" variety—as if her thirteen or fifteen or seventeen-year-old granddaughter was going night clubbing at Studio 54. And for the first Christmas with my daughter's new husband, Nan presented her with a faux denim jacket with copious rhinestones and matching faux denim elastic-waisted pants, as well as matching faux denim and rhinestone covered shoes. How proud Nan was to give this gift. She had spoken to us about it for several weeks before Christmas. Needless to say, this was an outfit Nan herself would have worn—as was the cropped faux fur vest that my daughter opened up on another Christmas Eve when she was twenty-five. At least this item was worn—and worn publicly in front of some 150 persons. My actress daughter wore it on stage when she was playing the part of a gum-chewing prostitute named Ray-lo.

When our daughter reached her twenties, she thought it would be wise to ask specifically for items of clothing she wanted, cutting out photos, which my wife and I would show Nan. My mother wasn't pleased, even though we reminded her that she would still be buying her granddaughter clothes—the only gift she wished to give. Nan looked at the photos and lamented that her granddaughter "used to have such great taste in clothing." When both our daughter and son suggested to her that gift cards would be welcome gifts, Nan nearly had an apoplectic fit. "Wrap a gift card? What kind of Christmas present is that?"

When she realized that her granddaughter had damaged that part of her brain that identified all that was stylish, Nan decided to double up on my wife's clothing gifts. Yet long before, right before my wedding, she bought my wife a "First Night" ensemble. We had just made it to the hotel after the reception and my wife excused herself for a few moments. When she emerged from the bathroom, she was bedecked in a flowing white peignoir that one of Dracula's daughters would have donned on a windy moonlit midnight out on the moors. The outfit was "enhanced" by a pair of puffy mules (shoes, that is) with kitten heels that might have been worn by Jayne Mansfield in the 1950s. I suppose Nan thought the eroticism of the outfit would stimulate the proper reaction from her son. A reaction was stimulated—but it was raucous laughter on the part of the newlyweds. Later Nan informed me that she picked out the ensemble because it was something she would have liked to wear on the first night. Wonderful linkage—her desires to *my* wedding night. I then placed a call to Vienna: "Is Dr. Freud taking any new patients?"

This is not to say that every gift she gave my wife was a clunker, for there were shirts and sweaters that were pulled off the hanger or out of the drawer from time to time—but they were the "preliminary" presents to the "big" gift. If one could poll my wife about the kinds of clothing she would never wear or want to be seen dead in, Nan's presents would be well represented. Maxi skirts, four-inch wide vinyl belts, leopard-spotted silk blouses, gaucho pants, plaid shirts, shirts with billowing sleeves, turtle-neck sweaters, and thick-heeled shoes. But without doubt, the mother of all such unappreciated outfits consisted of a solid *white* vinyl trench coat *with* a pair of *black* shiny faux leather boots with *four-inch* stiletto heels. Needless to say, my wife had to marshal every ounce of her good and kind nature even to eke out a "This is definitely something I don't have. Thank you, mom."Nan beamed with pride and added with a wink, "I bought this with you in mind, John." Now that certainly begged a massively huge question. I never remember claiming to love odd black and white combinations, whether faux leather nor not. I was finding it hard imagining a woman wearing at the same time the mini white trench coat and the high black dominatrix boots with half a dozen straps with buckles on each boot. Would there be a checkerboard hat to go with it? Was Dalmatian the latest inspiration for *haute couture*? Then I tried to imagine my wife wearing this get-up. I couldn't do it. I didn't want to do it. I was afraid to do it. Yet what did Nan mean when she said she had *me* in mind when she bought it? No. Impossible. She couldn't have meant the mistress boots, could she have? Did she think my wife and I were into S & M scenarios? What had we done to suggest that, I wondered? I know I most assuredly would have suffered if my wife walked around in that outfit and she made it clear to me that she would suffer as well if she ever put it on. So an M & M scenario? My darling wife is the kind of soft-hearted woman who keeps unwanted gifts at least for a month or two before making the decision to give or throw them away. In this case, however, the trench coat and boots were placed in a large paper bag for give away on the day after Christmas. As I drove to the Goodwill, I realized I could never hand the bag to someone working there and have that person look in the bag and then stare at me with either a stunned or bemused look on his or her face. Therefore, I drove behind a strip mall and found a clothing bin sponsored by another charitable organization. I looked around several times to be sure no one saw me before I tossed in the bag and speedily drove off, as if I had just deposited a body for the local *caporegime*. As luck would have it—and luck was sure good to us— Nan never asked my wife to wear the outfit to dinner or to a show.

But there was one fashion item that Nan wished me to have was quite special: her mother's—my beloved grandmother's—diamond ring. After my grandfather made his money following the repeal of Prohibition, he replaced the original engagement ring he gave my grandmother with one far more impressive—1.4 carats. When my grandmother died at age eighty-seven, the ring went to Nan and her older sister, who passed away the following year. My mother then kept the ring secured for some twenty years, until she showed it to me on my birthday. "I want you to have this, John. We'll reset the stone into a man's ring." I was naturally touched by her generous offer, but I had to tell her I didn't wear any other ring except my wedding band, and that I didn't feel comfortable even wearing a watch. (I've always believed I was hanged in an earlier life.) What I couldn't say is that even if I wanted to wear another ring, this chunk of ice would be a bit pretentious (for me) to display on one of my fingers. Luckily, Nan seemed to understand my desire to wear nothing but the wedding band and closed the box which held the ring and put it aside. That was in August. On Christmas Eve, I noticed under her tree a small present about the size of a ring box. I was sure Nan couldn't have forgotten what transpired only four months earlier—so I assumed that she was giving the ring to my wife—whose diamond on her engagement ring had very little monetary but plenty of sentimental value. I was concerned how my wife would respond to Nan's saying something along the lines of "You've spent too many years wearing that cheap chip of diamond my son gave you. You deserve a serious upgrade, and here it is."

But the gift was for me. So she *did* forget what transpired on my birthday. No, she didn't. I opened the box and there was the 1.4 carat diamond—this time set in a tie tack. First, I wear a tie maybe three or four times a year at best. Second, if I thought wearing the ring was pretentious, the tie tack would be pretentiously ostentatious. And third, tie tacks pop off—at least for me they always do. So wearing it was simply out of the question. But I didn't tell Nan that. I was honored to have my grandmother's diamond—even as a tie tack—and I made sure it was tucked away safely at the house so that I would always be able to show it to Nan if she ever asked to see it again. The story does end on a happy note, however, and the diamond in a more appropriate place. Three months after Nan died, my son asked his girlfriend to marry him. The occasion was made even more special because the ring he gave her had my grandmother's diamond set in the band. We decided that Nan would have been so pleased, especially since she really loved my son's girlfriend and vigorously interrogated the both of them right before her death about when they were getting married.

Again, if I had a dollar for every time someone expressed shock at my mother's age—given her more youthful appearance—I could easily buy another 1.4 carat diamond ring. "She is not eighty. No way," "My grandmother is sixty-seven and looks twenty years older than you're eighty-five-year-old mother, John," and "When they brought your mother in and I saw on her chart that she was ninety-two, I was sure I was in the wrong room" were just three of the comments made about Nan's more youthful appearance—and general attitude. "I love young people," she would often say. "I don't feel my age, and I'll be damned if I'm going to look it, either" is probably my favorite of her assessments about aging.

Given her good looks and spunky manner, one might guess that she eventually dated again after the death of Tom in 1984. As I mentioned, she had offers years earlier, after she divorced my father and when she was married to H2. Beginning in the fall of 1985, when she had completed her year of mourning, I imagined she would start taking in a movie or having dinner with a man roughly her age. By this time, she had moved into a condo overlooking the Intracoastal Waterway in Lake Park, Florida—a little north of West Palm Beach. The residents there were for the most part a social bunch, with scheduled dinners, parties, and meetings. The problem was that the overwhelming majority of residents were the single-woman or married-couple variety. Nan became active on the condo board of directors, and there are plenty of photos of her blowing party horns and wearing straw hats during looser (booze-served) gatherings. She would join groups going to theatre productions, but never alone with a man. Part of the problem, it seemed to me, was her hooking up with another single (divorced, not widowed) woman who had one of those "truck-crashing-into-storefront" kinds of personalities. Sheila was the authority on whatever topic that came along. Overly made-up cosmetically with a snort-and-bellow voice, she wanted to take Nan under her wing, when Nan was the kind who literally worked *on* airplane wings during the Second World War. Rather than "Nan under the wing," it was more "Sheila under the skin," making Nan's enjoying travel impossible. Nan preferred to stay around the hotel if Sheila decided to see the town—and vice versa. Therefore, this wasn't the proper climate for attracting the attention of men.

Nan did much better when she went on cruises—without Sheila of course—and especially when she traveled with my cousin and her husband. Nan would tell me after she returned that she met "so many nice people," but other than commenting on how handsome the Captain looked, she offered little on any kind of communications she had with the opposite sex. That is, until she came back and unloaded on a man who appeared to be stalking her (she was in her mid-eighties at the time). It appeared he waited for her to be alone on deck before he'd come over and strike up a conversation. He'd try to flatter her by being flabbergasted that she was older than he thought—and he may well have been—but Nan took it purely as a come-on line. When she'd tell him she was with my cousin, he'd ask if she could break away for a few hours. When she tried fending him off with "My husband died not too long ago," he made the same claim about his "wife." He'd watch her from a distance and wink and wave when he was closer. "I know he was trying to get me into bed," Nan remarked to me—without irony.

I let that slide, of course, but from that point on she often spoke to me about dating. "I'm not sure I could do that to Tom" (then deceased for twenty-five years). I told her he would understand if she wanted to have dinner and see a show with someone, but she'd always say, "That would be nice, but I know what they would want eventually."

I couldn't say, "Mom you're ninety-one. I don't necessarily think they would want that." I could have added, but didn't, that they couldn't do it even if they did want it. Nan did occasionally admit, "I'm not sure there's any man who's my age or older who's not in a wheelchair," but she wouldn't let go of the notion that she'd be expected to have sex if she dated a man. As an example, a man at her church usually sat right behind her every Sunday. He'd talk with her and walk her to the car when she was still driving and then out to meet us when we took and picked her up. Nan thought he was a very nice and wanted me to meet him, which I did. He looked somewhere in his forties—some forty plus years younger than Nan. On one occasion a woman—who had promised to drive Nan home from church when my wife and I had a lunch engagement with another couple—didn't show up at church and left Nan without a way to get home. The nice male offered to take her home, but she told him that I wanted her to call if something like this happened. She had the church call my wife's cell phone and we ended up leaving our lunch date prematurely to fetch her. The following week, the nice man offered to pick up Nan and take her home after mass *every* Sunday. Nan turned him down. I was happy she did because I have a suspicious nature about another person's motives in situations like this. But that wasn't why she turned down Mr. Nice Guy. "I'd be afraid he'd want sex if I depended on him for taking me to church and then home again."

That was my mom. She was a knock-out in her prime and a very attractive woman at every age. Add that to her stylish clothing and flirtatious bird hands, and it's no surprise she feared the desires of the man she attracted—regardless of the age difference between her and the man. Finally, her sexual concerns came to a head when she asked me at age ninety-two, "John, I would so love to go out with a man for dinner and some nice conversation about things that interest me. You do a lot of theatre. Do you know any older gay men who might like to take me out?"

Chapter 3
"I Need a Project"

"We are all here for a spell. Get all the good laughs you can."
Will Rogers

Nan's taste in clothing had its soulmate in her sense of style in home furnishings. Decorating, re-arranging, and painting were the holy trinity, the *mirepoix* of her household existence. Especially as she got older, she had an incessant need to change things up in her home. In fact, she moved from a lovely townhouse in Athens to a ranch-style home because she had "run out of things to do" at the former residence. That move occurred when she was eighty-six. All she lacked as far as a sign of her devotion to redecorating was a ladder and paint brush tattooed on each arm. She painted (walls and furniture, not sunsets and daisies), wallpapered, dragged around heavy furniture, hammered, and nailed until she was ninety-two and forced to move into Golden Harbor after breaking her hip. All warnings against mounting ladders and pleas for caution fell on deaf ears, even after she grudgingly agreed to hearing enhancement.

Nan was influenced in this area by her mother, who after my grandfather began making good money, secured attractive furniture, vases, rugs, and draperies—not to mention assorted and interesting knick-knacks. Nan's first ten years of failed marriages showed little evidence of her furnishing style, primarily because the money brought in was rather meager. Just the basics sufficed in the home—beds, sofa, living-room chair, small kitchen table (no dining room), and eventually a black and white television—then offering reception of only three channels in stunning black and white.

Matters changed for Nan at age thirty-seven when H2 was promoted at work and a new house was secured. Now she was able to decorate a full living and dining room—as well as a patio. The furniture was stylish for the time—matching light green sofa and chairs in the Danish Modern mode, dark wood dining table and chairs, coffee table, and a nicer stand on which to put the black and white television—now receiving four channels instead of three. Eventually, some art work—much of it admittedly the product of S&H green-stamp redemptions—adorned the walls. After a few years the Danish Modern furniture was transferred to a new area off the dining room, the result of having the patio fully enclosed—completely Nan's idea. The living room now had plusher chairs and a sleeper sofa, which weighed three tons—or so it seemed whenever I had to help move it.

The builder responsible for enclosing the patio was just one of several men who became enamored of Nan and was willing to risk the wrath of a jealous husband. It was clear Nan liked him very much, as I'd get back from school and discover them in a friendly tête-à-tête at the dining room table. But it went no further owing to a number of factors, including her fears, upbringing, and concern for me. But this builder did seduce her into pushing for a swimming pool to embellish the back yard. H2 went along with the plan, primarily because it gave him the status of having the only pool in the immediate neighborhood. He hardly ever used the pool himself, and always remained in the shallow end—where he was mentally most of the time as well.

I felt as though we had hit the lottery with that 16' by 30' kidney shaped pool dominating the back-yard area. (Remember these were small South Florida backyards, which an infant could throw a stone across.) But like lottery winners, we were inundated by requests to share in some of the prize. "Can I come over and swim in your pool?" "It must be nice getting away from this heat in that pool" and "We'll just swim when you guys are away" were common requests and remarks we contended with. Living behind us was a family (army) of ten—eight of them children from the ages of thirteen to three. Many were the days that I'd get in my swim suit and be ready to dive in, only to see anywhere from four to eight bodies hanging on the chain-link fence like starving canines, licking their chops and whimpering—hoping that the evil fourteen-year-old would throw them a watery bone. But Nan made clear that this congregation (in any number) wasn't to cross the fence line, no matter what—not that I needed such instruction. She wasn't being snobbish but only wise. We needed neither a drowning nor a lawsuit to further complicate our lives.

But Nan also realized this merry band would do their best to ruin any relaxing afternoons and evenings out by the pool. (It's not easy to enjoy one's cigarette and cocktail while listening to murmured begging and seeing little urchin hands reaching through the chain links of the fence.) Accordingly, since she was against the idea of a concrete wall to block the steely and pleading gazes of the gang of eight (one should also recall that this was 1961, the year the Berlin Wall went up—and Nan was no communist), she decided instead to have the back landscaped with Firebush and Hibiscus shrubs and small palm trees closing in one side and the rear of the pool (the converted patio room and the back of the house took care of the other two sides). When the work was completed, the backyard pool area was pretty darned impressive—and better than that, private. Before long, the crowd behind us gave up the watery ghost and returned to their screaming at each other and their "scream-right-back-at-you" mother. (The father walked around lobotomized whenever he was home.) Needless to say, the landscaper was also taken with Nan and cut her a sweet deal on the excellent work he and his team did.

The pool was an escape for me, whenever I didn't care for the tense vibe inside the house whenever H2 was home. Oh, he'd come and join me in the water by turning his chubby body into a cannonball—a rather easy feat and leaping into the water, as close to me as he could get. Again, he wouldn't do this in the "deep end" (what was it, six feet?) where he felt less comfortable to helpless, and he never wandered too far into the ocean—up to his thigh would be good enough. H2 just wasn't at home in the H2O.

When H2 took his act elsewhere a few years later, Nan remained at the house (she wouldn't give it up or share with him any profits from a sale) and continued making her changes. A dishwasher—not necessary, according to H2 (who never washed dishes, of course)—now enhanced the kitchen, and several chairs received a new coat of different colored paint. Soon, Nan purchased an impressive oil painting of a Renaissance minstrel strumming a lute. The minstrel was a handsome devil, complete with a floppy Renaissance cap. That this figure bore a striking resemblance to Tom, who became H3 a year later, was simply a coincidence—surely. In every home or apartment

Nan owned afterward, the painting hung in a most prominent place—much to Tom's embarrassment after they married. And it was displayed at Nan's Golden Harbor apartment until the day she died. Now it hangs proudly in my living room.

Nan's decorating need was often re-stimulated by the number of places she and Tom lived for the eighteen years they were married. From the house with the pool, they moved to a second-floor apartment in Stuart, Florida, which necessitated my helping lug that elephantine sleeper sofa up a flight of stairs. The move was in conjunction with my mother and Tom's opening a patio furniture shop. Running the gamut in her previous employments— riveter, telephone operator, receptionist, waitress, secretary, and real estate agent—Nan now had her own business, which she ran while Tom was at work. Already an upscale patio furniture store before they took it over, Nan added to the height of that scale. That the store was right next to the most upscale restaurant in the area only inspired further her interest in home decorating. She purchased a number of her own store's items—at a discount, of course—and they ended up decorating her own apartment. After my wife and I married, she provided us a full living room's worth of furniture for our unfurnished dwellings. Many said we had the finest looking patio furniture they had ever seen in a living room.

Nan and Tom moved to two other apartment/condos in the area over the next few years, and in each Nan added new pieces while discarding others, giving them to charity or to me—such as a large ceramic owl for our floor and an oversized painting of a yellow moth (okay, it was a butterfly) for our wall. Finally, with their finances in good shape, Nan and Tom sold the business and moved into a new house, complete with a pool, a pool table, and an attractive stone fireplace (for show—this was lower Florida, after all). Most sadly, they weren't in the house much more than a year when Tom received his cancer diagnosis. Eight months later, the movers brought to Nan's next residence what Nan chose to keep with her, and the rest of the furniture was donated. She couldn't bear to bring with her Tom's favorite chair and their bed—nor the table where they shared meals. When she moved to the condo in Lake Park, she found newly decorating the residence a much needed activity in the first months of her widowhood. Now she decorated only for herself and her living room was much remarked on—with its faux fireplace façade, luxurious cushions, all-white sofa, glass dining room table, and impressive lighting fixtures.

Following the example of her mother, who decorated the living room of her house to her liking and then refused anyone the right to sit in it, except on Christmas and the occasional special day of celebration, Nan did most of her living in her TV room, where some of the furniture consisted of pieces she constructed or repainted. It was at this point—Nan was now in her mid-sixties—that she began leading a bipolar decorator's life. Choosing gorgeous furniture and display pieces on the one hand and fixing up bargain basement shelving, side tables, and the like on the other. But when company was over, she shut the door on the basement pieces and showed only the penthouse ones.

Over the next eighteen years, she remained in the condo and continued accumulating lovely pieces of furniture and a host of impressive knick-knacks from a glass unicorn collection to interior (though artificial) plants, which put another kind of spin on her living room—Mythic Tropical. The guest bathroom also had a royal flair to it—with gold fixtures, soap dishes, and soap dispensers. She bought new furniture for her bedroom—an Asian motif dominated by the colors black and gold. But she seemed always to be piddling with the furniture in the TV room—wall papering the shelves of the several-times-painted bookcase and creating storage pieces for her vinyl recordings, tapes, VHS collection, and later her CDs and DVDs.

The move to Georgia at age eighty, gave Nan a chance to further scratch her incessant decorator's itch. And she also demonstrated a peculiar reaction to the normal problems that come with a move to a new residence. My wife and I, with Nan's permission, picked out a modest-sized and recently built townhouse—downstairs a kitchen, dining area, living room, and bedroom; upstairs a master bedroom and a walk-in attic space. Nan converted the downstairs bedroom to her TV room, and had all of her bedroom furniture hauled upstairs—by the moving company, thank heaven. But upon setting the sofa in the living room, we found that it was too long for the wall she wanted to put it against. All right. Not an insurmountable problem . . . for almost anyone else, that is. "I can't take the house. I'll just store all the furniture [already moved in] and come live with you until we can get me another place."

"Now, wait!" was my involuntary reply. But my gears slammed shut and I couldn't come up with anything else, I was so stunned. Fortunately my wife's wheels were still turning. "Let's just have part of the sofa cut off so it will fit. I know an upholsterer who will do a great job cutting it." Catastrophe averted.

Nan purchased some new decorative items and continued with her make-shift pieces in the TV room. And now she had that attic space off her upstairs bedroom to play with, so she decided that some new shelving would fit nicely, along with a table for her sewing machine. Whereas she was in her element whenever she shopped for pieces at furniture stores and upscale home accessory shops, she was equally comfortable rummaging through the aisles at Goodwill for distressed pieces she could fix up with a few nails and two coats of paint. But there was still room in the attic for something else and before long the space was completed by a treadmill, on which Nan strolled almost daily. "You'll have pick it up at Walgreens, John. I don't want to be bothered with paying someone to bring it out here. It was fine though that I could be bothered with borrowing a truck and loading and unloading the damn thing. Anyway, when I got the truck and arrived at our brand new Walgreen's, I knew from Nan that I had to go to the back and ask to have the treadmill brought out for loading. When I did as she instructed, I was knocked back by the expression on the young pharmacist's face (the only person free to help me)."Gee, sir. We don't sell treadmills here," she said. I pulled out my cell phone and called Nan, who exploded with frustration. "Walgreens told me they'd have it ready for you to pick up." Did she know the name of the person who told her that? "Yes, it was Jason or Mason— something like that. He was a nice young man. He said that I reminded him of his favorite aunt." I then asked the pharmacist if either a Jason or a Mason worked at this Walgreens (the only one in town). "No, but we do have a Jamison who works on weekends and Wednesdays." That sounded hopeful until the helpful pharmacist volunteered, "I can leave her a message, but again we don't sell treadmills here." Jamison was a "her." Not a nice young man after all.

I finally asked Nan the right question. "Are you sure you bought it at the Walgreens here in town?" The silence was long and suggestive. "Didn't I say 'Walmart'?" No you didn't, mom. Well with the mystery solved, off I went to pick up the treadmill at the right location. But sadly, I never got to meet

Mason or Jason.

Nan's new residence also had a small deck attached to the rear door. But that word—"small"—made her less than satisfied with the area than she wanted to be. Enlarging it meant contracting with a builder or a business, and Nan wasn't willing to do that. "Do you know anyone who likes to work with wood, John?" She knew better than ask me, given my limited experience with wood. I was deft with a pencil and I've had my share of splinters over the years, but that was about it. In any event, I did know two fellow community theater actors who had the experience and talent with construction jobs—so I asked if they'd be interested in doing the deck project. Blank faces greeted my request until I added that Nan would actually pay them. I had done my job— as middle man, agent, or go-between—and I was spared the splinters. Evan and Arnold, whom we called "Swifty" because he was always the first actor in the production to memorize his lines, took to the deck enlarging like two old pros and did a great job, earning Nan's high praise and the insistence that they do other projects at the house. Her praise of Evan and Arnold was effusive—"They're like my second and third sons." Having made it so many years as the only child, I wasn't all that keen on having two siblings who both possessed talents I didn't have. Anytime my faux-brothers came to do work, Nan would have cocktails ready for them, which provided them more of an opportunity to charm my mother and encourage me to dwell on horrendous consequences—such as having to share my inheritance.

While she was living at this residence, she turned her attention to making her downstairs (the company) bathroom one never to be forgotten. She already had the gold soap dishes, ornate soap dispensers, and black and gold towels—so I couldn't figure out what she had done to warrant her "Wait until you see the bathroom. You'll be so impressed." Did she install a urinal for Evan and Arnold? Or a two-way bathroom mirror? No, I prayed it wouldn't be that. Well, my wife and I came over, and we found Nan standing before the closed bathroom door. "Ready? Close your eyes and step inside." These bathrooms weren't designed to accommodate three grown human beings, but my wife and I—and Nan—managed to squeeze in. "All right. Open your eyes!" Amazingly, she had done it again. There before us was a gold toilet seat and lid. "It matches the soap dish—see?" In shock, I was still able to nod. "Now, John—sit on the toilet seat." She had to be kidding. I hesitated, but my wife nudged me with a look on her face that said, "Don't you dare hurt your mother's feelings." I sat and immediately my rump sank what seemed like an inch or two. "See, John. It gives, and the fabric makes it so you don't have to sit on a cold surface, which I always hate—especially in the cold months." I fully expected her to say, "Pull your pants and underwear down so you get the full effect," but the gods were with me. I managed a "Wow"—a word that in this case held a world of meanings.

I was quite surprised when after several years in her new digs, Nan told us she wanted to move. "I've done all I can with this place. Try to get me closer to you." I had previously teased her about living near us with the caveat "You can move anywhere just as long as you're not within walking distance of our house." But in truth, the twenty-mile round trip between her place and ours was a little longer than I preferred, so I was all for her moving closer. We did some checking and secured a real-estate agent, who found a very nice single-level home only five miles from our house. Yet she was excited about the move mainly because of the decorating possibilities the new residence provided. It was a three bedroom and two bath unit, with a large kitchen and living room, complete with a gas lit fireplace and handsome hearth. There was also a spacious two-car garage for her car, washer, dryer, ironing board, and storage boxes. This house didn't have a deck but rather a concrete slab serving as a back patio—and whereas she regretted leaving the deck that Evan and Arnold expanded, she was happy to leave behind the stairs she had to mount to her bedroom. She was now in her mid-eighties and the nightly climb upward was becoming too much of a discomfort.

When we toured the new house, Nan informed us that her plans for the master bedroom and master bath would knock us out. The dining room would now include statuary to go along with the glass table, and the infamous treadmill would go into the guest room. Her TV room would again be the repository for her make-shift furniture and cumbersome sofa and chair. All the interior walls would be painted, she added, as well as the outside of the house—painted, that is, by her and her alone. She was disappointed, however, when I informed her that both Evan and Arnold had moved away—one to Florida, the other to Thailand. "Who am I going to get now for my special projects?" she moaned. I told her I had a candidate in mind, and with that assurance nothing remained but the move from the old house to the new one.

I asked if she'd employ the same moving company who brought her stuff up from Florida. "No, they were too expensive. Jeanette [one of her neighbors] said she used a local man for her move and was very happy with him. She called him for me and I hired him." "A local man"—as in the singular "man" and not the plural "men." I knew at that moment that I wasn't going to be freed from any moving duty—as I had expected or at least hoped. The man was on time with his truck—and he was more than willing to work—but some pieces of furniture have a way of being too large for a single person to move. What to do?

"Yes, mom?" My wife was called out of her elementary school classroom to take an "emergency" call from her mother-in-law.

"Where's John?"

"He's teaching at the university."

"Can I call him there?"

"No. Don't do that. I'll send him an email, and he'll read it right after he's done with his class."

"He needs to come over now. He has to help move the furniture."

I read the email as soon as I returned to my office, and within a half hour picked up my son, who was done with his university classes for the day. We made it to Nan's house about the same time my wife arrived and found my mother collapsed on a lawn chair in the kitchen, looking as though she had just been rescued from a hostage situation. Her face revealed exhaustion and fear. Fear? "I was so afraid you wouldn't come," she explained. "I tried to help the man, but I wasn't strong enough to lift the heavy pieces."

Other than the living room sofa and cumbersome TV room sofa-monstrosity downstairs, we had to bring down from above a chest of drawers (un-emptied, of course) and the box-spring and mattress, which were quite a joy to maneuver down the narrow staircase. And then there was the upstairs *étagère*—a word I had never heard of, I'm ashamed to admit, but one I never want to hear again. The piece wasn't all that heavy, but Nan had failed to empty the shelves, which housed valuable and easily-breakable knick-knacks and curios of various kinds. Once we carefully removed the items and gave them to my wife to wrap in newspaper, my son and I took the *étagère* out the front door but found that the truck had already left with its last load. No problem, because Nan then informed us that the piece was to be was walked across three lawns and delivered to the person Nan had just this morning given the *étagère* to. But we no sooner took the piece from the stoop than the rain began. My son and I slogged across the lawns and made the delivery and then ran back to Nan's in the now pelting rain. We stepped back in the house soaking wet and saw my wife's painful expression. Now what? In her fatigue, Nan had forgotten to empty the dishwasher—which was, you guessed it, completely full. Fine. Get us a couple of boxes and newspaper and we'll pack the dishes, pots, and silverware and put the boxes in our cars. Well . . . not a single box or strip of newspaper remained in the otherwise empty house. Since Necessity is the mother of invention and Aggravation the father of mental strain, we took each item and placed it as carefully as possible in the trunks of our cars. (The back seats were already jammed with lamps, towels, shower curtains, one small television, and sofa cushions.) After an hour of such careful and strategic placement, we were ready to head on off to the new place, where the mover had put all the furniture in the garage with the assistance of a friend who was then free to assist with the heavier pieces. Not so luckily, my son and I had to bring the heavy stuff into the house from the garage, where the men had left it—enduring the additional agony of crushed knuckles in the door jamb and Nan's "Wait, let's try it against the other wall" and "No, not in that bedroom. Put those [especially heavy] boxes in the other room."

Now that all the furniture was in the house, we reconstructed the beds and asked Nan where the sheets and pillowcases were so we could makeup her mattress. "No, you go home. I know where everything is. I'll do it." We protested but she insisted we leave. We should have protested more. The next day, my wife went over to see how she was and asked how well Nan had slept. "Not too good. I couldn't find the sheets, so I had to pull a shower curtain over myself, because it was so cold in here." My eighty-six-year-old mother sleeping while wrapped up in a shower curtain like the filling of a burrito. Next to the famous moment in Hitchcock's *Psycho*, I can't think of a more distressing shower-curtain scene—ever.

Nan was cold because she was too tired to locate the thermostat for the central air and heat. I was to blame for setting the air conditioner at 70 degrees because it was a hot day and the house hadn't yet been regulated to a comfortable temperature. I left without resetting the AC to the 79-80 degrees she preferred in the summer. In this significant way I wasn't her son at all. We liked our air and heat about ten degrees different from each other. She'd come to our place in the dead of summer, and I'd notice her wearing a coat or sweater as she sat down for dinner. And I had made the supreme sacrifice of pushing the thermostat up to 72. When we went over to her place for an August dinner, I wished to strip off my shirt so I could survive the heat—barely. Finally, my mother took pity on her sweaty and only child and said, "Okay, you can turn it down to 79."

I'd often moan, "Are we living at the equator, mom?"

Nan's aversion to cold weather wasn't helped by the colder (and occasionally icy and snowy) days we have in Northeastern Georgia. On one dark day during the holidays, the area lost power owing to an ice storm. We rescued Nan from her "frigid" house—the temperature had only dropped to 71 by the time we rescued her. We have a wood-burning fireplace in our home, and Nan sat inches away from the protective screen calling out in a pathetic voice, "More wood; more wood." I had to sit in the hallway because it was so hot in the living room. But that was nothing compared to the morning she awoke and found her house the temperature of a meat locker. Outside, it had fallen into the teens during the night, and it was too cold for her to get out of bed. Now past ninety, Nan pressed her panic button and immediately the service called and asked what was wrong. "I'm cold," she replied. "Can you make my house warmer?" Soon, we were awakened by a call from the service sharing with us what Nan had told them. Up we got, and off we went to Nan's. I failed to hear the heat blowing through the house, so I checked the thermostat, saw the low 50s reading and attempted to get the unit working again—but to no avail.

Bringing Nan back to our place, I called one of the A/C companies in town, and they came over to pronounce the existing unit dead on their arrival. A new unit was purchased, and the company got right on it and promised to install the new system by the following afternoon, meaning that Nan would spend the night with us. After a delightful supper and several glasses of sparkling wine, Nan announced she was tired and wished to go to bed. "Okay, Mom. We'll make up the couch and you can sleep there." With both our children grown, why didn't we suggest a bed in either of the children's rooms, one might ask? All our bedrooms are upstairs, and by this time Nan's endurance was very low for any kind of physical exertions such as stair-climbing, and her arthritic knee made any stepping up very painful. But before we retrieved the bed linen for the sofa, Nan got up—to go to the downstairs bathroom we assumed. But I heard some movement on the stairs, so I went around the corner and there she was—crawling up the stairs like a four-legged ninety-two-year-old spider.

"Mom, what are you doing?"

"I want to sleep in a bed. Bring up the oxygen machine, baby."

I leaped up the stairs as she was approaching the landing. "Mom!"

"Don't help me. I'm almost there. Go back down and get my bag after you get the tank. No, wait. I'll get it myself."

"How are you going to go down from here?" I could see her attempting a backward spider walk the way young Regan pulled it off in the director's cut of *The Exorcist.*

But she had another idea in mind. "I'll just sit on my butt and slide down step by step."

"No you won't." At least I had my way this time. But it shows, very well I think, to what lengths Nan would go to hold on to whatever shred of independence she could.

After she moved into her new house, Nan redecorated the living room, adding an aqua green rug, glass side tables, and a glass coffee table. On the side tables were new and ornate lamps and several glass figurines—mainly of unicorns, which had become her favorite collectable as she moved into her eighties. Her white sofa set the tables and figurines off nicely, as did the mirror-tiled opposite wall and faux tropical standing plants strategically placed. But one morning she dropped one of the heavy Moroccan pieces she had placed on the coffee table, shattering the glass table top. A search through her boxes of household stuff in the garage discovered two pieces of cut glass, exactly the same width of the shattered table top but not the same length. Nan felt it would do for now and set both pieces—one edge riding over the other—on the coffee table frame and *voila!* I assumed this was only a stop-gap measure, but the rest of the time she remained in the house, she never replaced the two pieces of uneven glass. I suppose the look just grew on her.

The prized new piece, however, was a glass futuristic grandfather's clock (which is what I called it, anyway), highlighted by gold trim and gold apparatus pieces. It surely was attractive, but it always seemed to me a tad vulnerable—as though one of the glass panels would work itself loose and bring the whole clock crashing down at midnight. Yes, it was beautiful, but it didn't keep time worth a damn. After a year or so of losing forty minutes a day, the hands just stopped moving. I told Nan that she should just set it at midnight and be done with it. It would likely be too expensive to fix, and who'd want to take the piece away to be fixed and then bring it back again—when it appeared that a good sneeze would collapse the whole thing. Nan agreed not to have it fixed, but she disagreed strongly with setting it at midnight—or noon, if one is an optimist. "I want both hands showing." Okay, that sounded reasonable enough to me, so I suggested 12:30. "No, I want the hands closer together."

Very well—11:45 then? "No, I want them even closer."

So for the rest of time she owned the clock it read 11:52.

At the end of the hallway, Nan set up an attractive curio, with four glass shelves, on which she set more of her unicorn collection, glass carriages, a statuette of Clark Gable, and other assorted and fragile bric-a-brac. As one might expect, a few of these pieces went the way of all glass during her time at the house—but nothing quite compared to the unexpected slippage of one of the heavy glass shelves in the curio (as Nan was attempting to dust it), which resulted in shattered glass, a shortening of several unicorn horns, and the cracking of two knock-off Fabergé eggs. Fortunately, Gable survived the glass collapse fully intact. Whether he gave a damn about the whole thing, he didn't say.

Nan set up a new *étagère* in her bedroom, which contained all of her religious pieces—effigies and small statues of Jesus, Mary, and St. Anthony, as well as several Pietas, a bottle of water from the River Jordan, and several rosary beads. Unfortunately, the unit wasn't secured, and one morning she bent down to plug the vacuum cleaner into the socket right near the bottom of the *étagère*. When she stood up, she lost her balance and grabbed for the first thing nearby to prevent her fall. She not only fell, but she brought the *étagère* right down on top of her, along with Jesus, Mary, and St. Anthony. Were she of good puritan stock, she might have pointed to the bump on her head and claimed that Christ had deliberately clubbed her for her sins. Instead, she was more concerned about the shape of the icons than she was of her noggin. Nan phoned my wife—"Can you bring some glue?"—and ten minutes later my wife was performing delicate reattachment surgery on holy arms and hands—and two holy heads. Naturally, I teased Nan about what she had done to the holy relics, which didn't go over very well. "God is going to remember this, John. Then you'll be sorry." I imagined myself spending eternity decapitated holding two empty tubes of glue in my hands.

Nan's bedroom also included a fully mirrored wall—from baseboard to crown molding—right behind the head board of her bed. Oh, yes. I teased about that as well—and Nan took it that teasing in much better spirits. "Have you thought of mirrors on the ceiling, mom?"

As "suggestive" as the mirrored walls were, they were only a mere hint when compared with the master bath. Again, Nan featured the gold-padded seat and gold accessories, but now she had an oval tub to decorate in the "Cleopatra Palace" style. With personal safety an issue, Nan had given up baths for showers, but she still didn't wish to tamper with the oval tub, since it looked so regally Egyptian. The tub was elevated with an altar-like step, on which Nan placed two urns. I wondered if was planning sacrifices to Osiris. Surrounding three sides of the tub were long strands of plastic vegetation, and on the rear corners stood two statues of two mythological-like female figures. I named them Minerva (the Roman temple goddess of the spas at Bath) and Artemis (the Greek goddess seen by the male Actaeon while she was bathing). The allusions didn't catch on with Nan, but her pride in the tub shrine was fully understood by all of us. Finally, as the decorating *pièce de résistance*, Nan had a fancy chandelier placed directly above the tub, providing the tub shrine even more celestial light. I wondered if in fact the historical Cleopatra ever did her business in such a majestic setting.

The guest room included a nice queen-size bed but no lamp stand or bedside table. Instead a guest would have the treadmill as a bedfellow, along with two makeshift book cases—the first storing the favorite movie books and biographies Nan collected over the years—but which, because of her weakened sight, she could no longer read. The other shelves stored her audio collection of old 45s and record albums, superannuated cassette tapes, and more recent CDs—most of which were versions of the old vinyl recordings. Scattered on the top shelf were Nan's defunct cassette players, miscellaneous batteries, and headphones either non-working or serving only one ear. On the other side of the bed were a series of see-through plastic drawers—the home of her old VHS and newer DVD collection. The room's closet shelf was jammed with the paperback novels she had collected in the fifties and sixties, many noir mysteries with alluring covers I used to sneak peeks at when I was a teen. And on the floor of the closet was a safe—the combination of which Nan had forgotten. Like Pavlov's Dog, I salivated at any mention or glimpse of the safe, wondering what treasure might be resting inside. Nan simply offered, "I don't know what's in there. It can't be very important, since I haven't missed anything." Of course this was the same woman who sold her car for cash and kept (and then forgot) the stack of $100 bills in her dresser drawer, under her unmentionables. After her death, I had the safe opened with visions of cash and bonds dancing in my head. But the opening was reminiscent of Geraldo Rivera bursting into Al Capone's vault in 1986. All that rested in Nan's vault was a folded piece of paper—on which were hand-written bank and life insurance account numbers with dated amounts listed. I'm surprised the paper didn't say, "Ha, ha. Sorry, sucker."

But no room was as peculiar as the third bedroom—the TV room, complete with the stereo she purchased in 1973. After all, she needed something to play her old albums and 45s on. More on all these entertainment gadgets later, but I'll note here that the room was dominated by the 55" flat screen television, complete with VHS and DVD combo player. Given the chosen location of the TV and shelving beneath it, Nan had to negotiate her way through a maze of wires—from the TV, the VHS/DVD unit, her telephone, and the extension cord. The complex wiring looked like it needed someone from *The Hurt Locker* to disarm it. The simple act of hanging up her phone could lead to unplugging her big screen and sending her lamp crashing into phone table, thereby knocking Nan's cup of coffee into her lap or onto the floor, sending its contents splashing across the TV screen.

Nan wanted an office area in the new house. The previous residence had the attic alcove, where she also had her dial-up computer, which the loss of her sight eventually made expendable. (Not long after she bought it, she heard someone on television talk about "computer viruses." She immediately covered her unit with a sheet until I could convince her that her health wasn't in any danger.) But in the new place, the only space available was in the kitchen, where a breakfast nook might have gone. But she wanted her papers, stamps, and envelopes where she could hear and watch *Days of Our Lives*. Shrewdly, she decided to remove the closet door in the third bedroom (TV room), thereby creating a small alcove in which to place her desk and small desk chair. On the closet shelving above, she stored papers and boxes of old checks. The shelf and the desk drawers were soon stuffed, and the overflow found its way onto the desk top and on the floor underneath the desk, with the result that finding anything from a stamp to the latest electric bill became quite a challenge. Like most other surviving children of an elderly parent, I was flabbergasted by the unnecessary documents stored in and around the desk. Old water bills with accompanying canceled checks from the late sixties forward; personal notes from Martha, Patty, Genie, and Joan from the seventies and eighties; rug shampooer rental receipts from three decades back; and dozens of other proofs of purchase or payment were all kept as if they would be needed half a century after the fact. Following Nan's death, I threw away some of the innocuous papers but the rest I burned in our kettle grill. It took me four days to finish the immolation, and somewhere the pagan gods were smiling.

The boxes of checks and other papers on the top shelf of the office/closet remained undisturbed except for Nan's reaching up and placing papers in a shoe box she earmarked as the receptacle for her monthly bank statements. Then she received that call from the mortgage company saying that she had missed a payment the previous month. Insisting that she hadn't, Nan reached up to grab the designated shoe box and pulled it down to check her statement. One problem, though. She pulled down a lot more than that shoe box. I imagined the moment looked like something from a "Three Stooges" short, as she was showered by papers and two shoe boxes. Panic setting in, she unceremoniously hung up on the mortgage company and called me. That was the day I took over paying her bills—a chore she was loath to give up, even at her advanced age. I had already been accompanying her to the bank to make her deposits and pay one of her credit card bills. Even with her wretched eyesight, she insisted on writing the amounts on the miniscule lines of the deposit forms, which I would often have to redo for the sake of the poor bank teller. And then I'd wait for the monthly reaction when the teller asked Nan for her I.D. "I've had my money in this bank ever since I moved to

Georgia. You don't know who I am by now?"

Most incongruous—given the impressive furnishings in Nan's living room, bedroom, and bathroom—were the sofa, chair, and stand-alone shelving in the TV room. The matching print and fabric on the chair and sofa was an olive green and grey combo, the kind one might pass for camouflage. Both pieces weighed a ton and defied sliding across the carpet to readjust their position. I finally had to put wheels on the chair so Nan could pull it closer to the television when she attempted to see things more clearly. In the last year at the house, she said "the hell with it" and kept the chair a mere three feet from the widescreen. I then took the wheels off. As for the sofa, whenever we sat in the room, my wife and I found ourselves constantly sliding forward. Unlike the matching chair, the cushions didn't sink along with the carcass sitting on them. I assumed the olive green and gray material was constructed out of an old slip-and-slide Nan picked up at a yard sale. When we asked Habitat for Humanity if they wanted the sofa after Nan moved to Golden Harbor, they took one look at it and politely declined.

The shelves in this room, on which Nan kept knick-knacks, photo books, and pictures of her grandchildren and one of me from thirty years earlier, had been repainted so many times and in so many colors over the years that the shelving was half an inch thicker than it was originally. I came to believe that Nan just had a thing for painting walls and furniture—even when they didn't need it. The TV room's walls received their last coat of paint after Nan's macular degeneration had robbed her of so much of her sight and depth perception. When she finished the project she proudly displayed her work with a wave of the hand. "I love this shade of blue." It was actually a shade of green. Not surprisingly, there were many bare and thin spots throughout the room—from ceiling to floor. When we volunteered to add another coat, she took umbrage. "I can do that. What else do I have to do around here all day?" Her second coat improved matters somewhat but bare and thin spots remained—this time without comment from us.

The upper part of the walls required Nan to be on ladder, and nothing we could say would deter her from climbing two or three steps up. Miraculously, she never fell off—or so we believed—but just knowing she was going to mount the ladder made those days uneasy ones for us. She also climbed to clean the mirrors over the fireplace and her bed—and to put away boxes on the shelving in her garage. In spite of the worry, I was quite proud of my mom for her stubbornness and her dexterity. This was the same woman, remember, who attempted to jump rope at age ninety.

The loss of Evan and Arnold left Nan frustrated over the projects she planned for the house that were beyond the talents and skills she (or I) could provide. But it just so happened that the husband of one of my former students was quite proficient with a host of difficult household and construction tasks. For us, Lee built a new deck and fence and installed a new bathroom sink and counter, as well as performing miscellaneous electrical work around our house. I asked if he'd be interested in doing a few projects for Nan whenever he had spare time. Lee cheerfully agreed and during the course of the next year and a half, he put in a new kitchen floor, painted very hard-to-get-to areas, put up another large mirror, and replaced all of Nan's kitchen cabinets. My mother paid him, of course, but she couldn't quite comprehend that Lee had a full-time job—and a family—and that he wasn't "on call" whenever she needed something done. "Lee hasn't come back to finish . . . ," she'd moan, to which we'd respond that it had only been four days and, once again, that he had a job and family. On one occasion, Nan called AT&T when she was unable to reach Lee by phone, asking the representative what she could do to find him. I felt guilty (and sometimes horrible) for bringing them together, but Lee was always kind and understanding and very cheerful and respectful dealing with my mother. When Lee's success in his job led to a new opportunity out of state, I didn't look forward to breaking the news to Nan, who had another major project in mind for him. "Why is he leaving?" she asked incredulously. My wife explained that he was going to a better job with more pay. Nan's response? "I don't get it with you younger people. Money isn't everything, you know."

As for cleaning and dusting her house, Nan's eyesight made the job highly difficult to impossible. We would discover spots of pasta sauce on the kitchen floor and trails of it dripping down the kitchen cabinets. Food scraps took up residence on the floor near her chair in the TV room, and spilled remains clotted the inside of her refrigerator. As much as she fought the idea—"The house doesn't get dirty. It's just me here"—we eventually convinced her that she needed someone to clean the house regularly. At first she agreed on once a month; therefore we asked the woman who does our place to work also for Nan. Nan was fine with the idea and determined that Betty should receive fifty dollars for her day's work—only twenty-five dollars below Betty's rate. Unwilling to risk Nan's dismissal of the whole idea, we decided to pay the rest of Betty's fee without telling my mother. But because we soon discovered that a once-a-month cleaning wouldn't be enough, we proposed to Nan that Betty should come every other week—the second visit doing just the bathrooms and the kitchen. "Fine, I'll pay her $25.00 for that day." Good enough for 1962 wages to be sure, but not for 2012. In addition, the bathroom and kitchen were substantial jobs in themselves, and Betty felt badly about letting other sections of the house go. The result was that we also sweetened the pot for the "short day"—which became a "regular day"—again unknown to Nan. It at least did my wife and me good to see the house free from spots, stains, and debris.

Nan's projects expanded to outside the house. One might imagine the reaction of her son when she stated she was going to paint the outside of her house. The bottom of my jaw was sore for a week after hitting the floor. "Mom, I don't think this is a good idea," was my opening and, as it turned out, closing attempt to dissuade her. "John, I'm going to do it myself. I'm not quite an old lady yet, you know." She was eighty-nine at the time. Out came the ladder, the paint, and the brush, and up went Nan to begin the process of transforming the stucco outside walls from a yellowish tan to a darker brown. Fortunately, gravity took over and convinced her she couldn't climb high enough to reach the top of the wall. As a result, she painted up to the eight-foot mark and turned the rest over to Lee, who was kind enough to finish the job.

Nan had enough sense to hire someone to cut her lawn—much to the relief of my son, who had been doing it. Yet she still weeded in the hot Georgia summer sun and raked leaves in the fall. The problem with the raking was that her muscles gave out after five minutes or so, leaving the rest of the task to her grandson and his father. For some reason she refused to hire her grass cutter to do this particular job. But sadly, she did listen to her grass cutter when he remarked about her roof and the possible need to have it replaced. "Someone he knew" just happened to be in the area, and before long she bought the ridiculous tale that a recent hail storm had damaged the roof. In a trice, she agreed to have her roof replaced. I had no knowledge of this agreement until I drove over and saw two men working on the top of the house. I shook my head as I listened to her assurance that the insurance company would pay for almost all of the work. "Wasn't it nice of my lawn man to tell me that my roof was damaged and contact his friend?" Sure, mom. Very nice indeed.

As she got older, Nan developed a soft spot for polite young or younger men to the point that she trusted them explicitly. Whether it was this roof business or her finances, she would always ask, "Now are you saying that you'd advise your own mother to do the same?" The answer was always yes, and Nan would always agree. I finally said, "Mom, I'm younger and I'm often very polite—and you're actually my mother—so I'm advising that you contact me from now on before agreeing to anything involving significant amounts of money." That's when I went through her papers and discovered that she had two home owner's insurance policies, the second of which was purchased at the time she had her roof done.

At the age of ninety-one, Nan finally gave over to me the task of walking down to get her mail and dragging the garbage and recycling roll carts down to the curb. (Nan's front yard sloped fairly steeply to the road below.) But she remained adamant about shaping up her rear "patio" area. As mentioned, it was merely a concrete slab, on which she had placed two lawn chairs. First she wanted to paint the slab herself with a roller. "I can do that much—even if you think I can't." I didn't protest—and she would have ignored me if I had. "I'll buy some new patio furniture and spend an hour or so sitting out there every afternoon." Two problems with that idea. She couldn't see to read or do crossword puzzles as she used to, and the afternoon sun would be in her face—and in the warm months would bake her to a crisp. I shared these facts, to which she nodded and said she would think more about it.

A week later she assured us that she had solved the problem of the sun. It just so happened that during a break in *Days of Our Lives* she saw a commercial for a patio awning, which would provide adequate shade and fold up when unneeded. It was one of those "Not available in stores" products. Just call this number and provide credit card information and within days the awning would be shipped. Nan went on to make clear that the product was guaranteed and that she would get the electric motor option so that she wouldn't have to fold up the awning by hand. We awaited the next announcement about who would be installing the awning with the electric motor. The announcement wasn't forthcoming, so I asked. "Well, you can call someone if you think you can't install it, John." I agreed. That is, I agreed to the fact that I knew I couldn't install it. But since Lee had moved away, I had no clue as to the identity of an installer. On the car ride home, my wife observed that the awning was likely cheaply constructed and the motor likely to fail within a month. "And you know, she's not going to feel comfortable sitting out there when it's hot. It's a waste of several hundred dollars just uninstalled. Surely over a thousand if it is." I couldn't argue with that prediction and assessment. Suffice it to say that for the next few months we didn't bring the matter up, and when Nan did, we promised to check the reviews to see how other customers liked the awning—with or without the motor option. It was at this time that Nan broke her hip and had to move to Golden Harbor.

At Christmas time, Nan had me string some clear lights over her front porch and place on the porch a plastic Santa—with garden pebbles inside to keep it from blowing over. Completing the display was a three-legged straw reindeer, of which Nan was particularly fond. "Let's get one with all four legs, mom," I suggested. "No. I've had this reindeer out every Christmas since 1977." Therefore it was left for me to prop up the poor creature against the corner of the patio walls. Inside, Nan decorated with evergreen garlands on her fireplace mantel, an artificial tree with minimal lights and ornaments, including a miniature John Elway—the former All-Pro quarterback of the Denver Broncos. I bought it for her one Christmas as a gag gift to tease her about the Broncos winning the Super Bowl more recently than her beloved Miami Dolphins. For some reason, she placed sentimental value on the gag gift and displayed the little Elway on her tree every Christmas afterward. But no other Christmas decoration meant more to the both of us than the manger scene she purchased way back in 1953. Over the years the shepherds and two of the wise men went the way of all flesh and the manger itself lost one of its sides and most of its straw—but Mary and Baby Jesus remained undamaged by clumsiness or by age. My only objection to this manger display was Nan's calling it a "crèche." I have a visceral negative reaction every time I hear the word—the same way others respond when they hear words like "probe" and "swab."

The topic of Nan's projects can only end with another moment from the immediate aftermath of moving to her new house—the night she slept wrapped up in the shower curtain. After we moved all the furniture inside from the garage, my wife drove home, and my son and I took one more survey of the house for any boxes or furniture pieces that might provide obstacles for Nan during the night. After she assured us she would be fine, I told her to lower the garage door—and we left through the garage and walked down toward the car. We sat inside the vehicle and waited until the garage door started to lower. I was about to turn the ignition key when I saw the door stop before it reached the floor. Seeing that the garage door was stuck, I realized that Nan's car wasn't pulled up quite far enough to allow the garage door to hit bottom. I got out of my vehicle and walked up to the garage, bent down, and said under the door, "Pull the car up a little." A childlike voice replied, "Oh." I returned to my vehicle and waited until I saw Nan's car pull up and the garage door finally close tight.

The following day, my wife went over to Nan's and found out about her burrito moment with the shower curtain. But Nan had a benign look on her face, according to my wife, who had the pleasure of telling me the rest of the story. Yet it took my wife several minutes to tell me, she was so overcome with laughter. As my wife recounted, "I wondered why she seemed so serene, and your mom told me she had never felt so safe and comfortable in a new home. 'Oh, that's so nice, mom,' I said, and then she added, 'An angel spoke to me yesterday.' I was so stunned that all I could say was 'Oh.' Then your mom said, 'Yes. The garage door wouldn't go down, and the angel told me to move the car forward.' I said, 'Oh mom, that was John'—to which she replied, 'No, John had already left. It was not John's voice.' I knew then I couldn't convince her otherwise and decided I didn't really want to because she was so happy that an angel spoke to her."

After my wife's giggling subsided and her tears dried, I got to thinking about Nan's celestial view of the event. What kind of angel gets that duty, I wondered? A rookie angel? An angel on probation? I could imagine Michael the Archangel saying, "Hey, Harry. Got a job right up your alley. Head on down to Georgia and . . ." I just imagined the angel's reaction: "I lived a clean and sin-free life for this?" To the end of her life Nan never believed she was mistaken about the identity of the voice that spoke to her under that slightly opened garage door. Still, I'm really happy she was never the wiser.

Chapter 4
"Finally, a Good Martini"

"Prepare for mirth, for mirth becomes a feast."
William Shakespeare

To borrow from Lord Byron, when it came to eating and drinking out, Nan came down on waiters and cooks "like the wolf on the fold." Having been raised by parents who started a bar and eatery in Long Island the very day Prohibition was formally repealed in late 1933, Nan, like her father, grew up having strong ideas about how drinks ought to be made. In addition, her mother was an exceptional cook, leading Nan to judge all food—particularly Italian food—by her mother's example. Accordingly, my mother found most establishments failing on either culinary or potable grounds. "How was your meal, mom?" was most often answered with an "Eh" or "The pasta stinks." "How's the drink, mom?" usually elicited "I can't even taste the vodka" or "Why don't they fill the damn glass to the rim?" Yet Nan's relationship with food and drink—those savory staples of life and pleasure—provided so many delightful memories, but none more hilarious than those during her last years of life.

After my grandfather's bar, which he named *La Taverna* (The Tavern), began to draw a loyal following in the months after its opening (when Nan was twelve and thirteen), he decided the clientele might pay for the pasta he so thoroughly enjoyed four or five nights a week. My grandmother agreed (not sure how willingly) and plates of linguine and rigatoni with her special marinara sauce began to fly across the bar counter. It wasn't long before she added meatballs and sausage to the plate—along with a large chunk of Italian bread. Assisting her in the pasta pushing was her daughter Nan, who was taught how much salt to add to the pasta water, how often to stir the pasta (very, very often), and how to test the pasta so that it would always be served *al dente*. Nan moreover learned the trials and tribulations that accompanied the clean-up phase of the operation. Her mother would finish with the last plate of pasta and then help her husband count the cash haul for the evening, while Nan and her older sister submerged dishes, knives, forks, and bar glasses and scrubbed pots to an inch of their lives. (Not to mention the dinner dishes for a family of five and later six.). She absorbed much during these years working in the bar, but she informed me that the best lesson she learned was that she *never* wanted a life which would demand or include soap, water, and scrub brushes.

Nan's first marriage ended her "career" as bottle washer to my grandmother's chief cook. From what I could gather, she applied the lessons taught by her mother and did her best to satisfy the food requirements of H1. But during the war, Nan was quite busy during the day as one of the many "Rosie the Riveters" at aircraft plants—this one in California, where my father was also working on planes. Although Nan didn't at all resemble the woman depicted in the now iconic "We Can Do It" image (1942) by J. Howard Miller or the one depicted by Norman Rockwell on the cover of the *Saturday Evening Post* (1943), she did bear a striking resemblance to the figure on the cover of the sheet music for "Rosie the Riveter" by Redd Evans and John Jacob Loeb (1942), except that Nan had black hair and not red.

But with the end of the war and the continuation of her miserable marriage, Nan cooked her own meals and very rarely went out to eat. When she left H1 for her and my safety, she moved back to one of the two apartments above her parents' bar. But they had by then moved to Florida, and Nan rarely saw the inside of a restaurant for the remaining three years she lived on Long Island. The exception would be her weekly forays to The Florence, an Italian bar and restaurant owned and operated by good friends of my grandparents. To me (I was five when I was first taken there), they were always Uncle Sally (Salvatore) and Aunt Giustina. When Nan came back to Long Island with H1 after the War, the returning soldiers who served in Italy sent out a clarion call for something they had tasted and enjoyed overseas—pizza. Although pizza already had a long tradition among Italian families—and my Grandmother was quite adept at making them—the general public had very little experience with the circular treat. My grandfather was approached to include pizza on his limited menu at the bar, and Nan and her siblings were all for it. But her father said no—arguing that it might bring in undesirables (teenagers) and give the place a bad reputation. However, Uncle Sally saw it as his way to jump start his business at The Florence. As the saying went, he cleaned up. From then on, Sally teased my grandfather about the lost opportunity and the popularity of his place among Nan and her sister and brothers, in addition to the paying undesirables. The Florence hired a skilled and gregarious staff and was a "go-to" place in Baldwin, right around the corner from *La Taverna*. Whereas Nan ate out very infrequently, her experience at The Florence established expectations about restaurant dining she would continue to hold the rest of her life— namely good food, attentive service, laughter, and plenty of face-time with the owner. Also at The Florence was what Nan learned to expect from drinking at *La Taverna*—a full glass of wine, and by full I mean up to the rim of the glass. This expectation would bedevil her later in life, as I would see first-hand.

Nan's restaurant experiences after we moved to Florida when she was thirty-four until she married Tom eleven years later were even more infrequent—and there was no place like Uncle Sally's Florence to find solace in. I was old enough to have memories of The Florence, but after we came to Florida I cannot recall a real restaurant meal from the ages of eight to sixteen. Nor do I recall Nan and H2 going out for dinner while I stayed home. I do recall H2 bringing back pizza or sandwiches when he was so inclined, but mainly Nan cooked and heard the complaints about her serving dishes that were too mundane on the one hand and too costly on the other. But with Tom, Nan began to enjoy eating out more often. After an initial rough period financially, in which they saved enough each week for just one night at a chain-steakhouse, they expanded their culinary horizons and ate at a number of first-class establishments in south Florida and on their trips to San Francisco (Alioto's was a favorite) and Las Vegas and during their travels abroad to Italy and Spain.

Tom's excellent restaurant standards influenced Nan and sharpened her expectations for service. But Tom could also make her cringe with his response to poor service or improperly cooked food. He would actually send food back if the eggs were too runny or if the steak was overcooked, whereas

Nan would accept what she received and mumble her complaints at the table. In Washington D.C., Tom sent the runny eggs back only to see and hear the chef chewing out the server for failing to note that the scrambled eggs should be "dry." Tom sent back coffee and soup if they were only lukewarm. He would get up and hunt down a server if no one came to the table in a set amount of time, and he'd do the same if the coffee or drink took too long in arriving. Whereas Nan tried to hide her face, Tom believed that "if you're paying for it, you ought to get what you want"—and that included polite and efficient service as well as the taste and temperature of the food.

Perhaps the three most memorable stories of my mother's embarrassment and even fear over Tom's restaurant disappointments occurred on the same road trip to New York, on which I joined them when I was twenty-four. We had just crossed the Florida border into Georgia when we decided to have a late breakfast. Nan suggested a Holiday Inn or something of that ilk, but Tom had it in his head that the best breakfast places were the smaller local ones—with a distinctive southern flair. Soon we saw a sign for "Merle's," and Tom made a quick left into a white-sand and rock parking area with two dismantled cars along the side of the small establishment. The place looked so unappetizing that Nan suggested Tom and I go in and see if it was indeed safe to enter. Tom's face was aglow with delight—I suppose because he believed he found a culinary jewel of the kind he had read about. And this was the same man with such impeccable standards who often told me, "John, if you can't go first-class, it's sometimes better just to stay home." There were half a dozen tables and five bar stools at the counter. Of course, Tom wanted the bar stools. He grabbed a menu, as I glanced back at one poor soul who had the table in the corner while he drank coffee and stabbed at a white clump of something that could have been oatmeal, grits, or mashed potatoes. Tom had just asked me to drag Nan in, when Merle himself came out from the kitchen. His hands and arms up to the elbow were smeared with grease. He gave us a cheery hello and said we had come between the breakfast and lunch "crowd." "What can I get you boys to drink? Coffee?" He was about to reach for the pot—grease-laden arms and all, when Tom spun around in his barstool and headed out the door. It was left to me to offer the "I'm sorry" look at Merle while he stood there, coffee pot in hand—likely wondering what the hell had gotten into these two boys. Needless to say, after several hours of ripe teasing from Nan, Tom agreed that evening to have dinner at the Holiday Inn where we were to spend the night. But Nan's playfulness turned to panic when "Old Sarge" stomped up to the table to take our order.

She was a large-boned woman, as they say, somewhere in her fifties, whose attitude could best be described as impolitely surly. After a cheerless "You want a drink?" she took our orders while snorting through one nostril. Of course, Tom's martini came on the rocks when he specifically asked for a "Martini straight up." Sarge offered a charming "You should have said you wanted it without ice," but did take it back to the bar for a trade-in. Nan could see Tom's radiator overheating; therefore, she begged him to "let it go." Tom did well enough until his steak came. I was eating my chicken when I caught sight of Tom out of the corner of my eye. He was working his knife against the meat and the meat was winning. Finally he blew, "Jesus Christ, I can't even cut this!" Nan's head dropped in capitulation, while I tried to suppress my delight over what was sure to come. Second round of the battle of Titans was about to start. Tom aggressively signaled to Sarge; she un-aggressively shuffled to the table."I can't cut this damn thing," Tom barked." You're probably not cutting it right" was Sarge's rebuttal.

When the nuclear dust cleared, Sarge left and came back to the table. "You want another steak?" Tom replied that he didn't. "The cook says you can have a fillet." Tom still replied in the negative. Sarge sighed as though she had to offer up her pet Rottweiler for adoption. "The chef says you can have the fillet for free—and the rest of your meal and drink." Now Tom thought the idea simply grand, and Nan and I—both of us having finished our meals, watched as Tom enjoyed his appropriately cooked fillet mignon, brought to Tom by the manager—likely after Sarge pushed him to the table, refusing to serve anything more to that whining and rude guy in the blue shirt.

One of Nan's favorite bits of Aristotelian logic was that good things always come in threes—and bad things as well. The following morning's attempt at breakfast proved her philosophy correct. Arguing that he suffered substantially last evening for agreeing to eat at the Holiday Inn, Tom insisted on discovering that magical breakfast joint that we failed to find the previous morning. We were driving along I-95 when he spotted a sign for "Dewey's," which lauded their breakfasts as being the best in the state. First Merle's and now Dewey's. Hmm. Again Nan pleaded in vain; Tom was going to show her that such places—a truck-stop no less—were the hidden gems of the culinary world. In we went and were pleasantly surprised—and Nan greatly relieved—that our server was polite, personable, and highly efficient. She had the coffee ready to go, and when the scrambled eggs came they were dry, just as Tom had ordered. But somewhere between the toast and the bacon, I heard a coin drop into a juke-box situated right behind Tom. In a moment, the cheerful atmosphere of Dewey's was hit by a musical tsunami in the form of an old-fashioned country song with a prominent pedal steel guitar lead-in set at max volume. Forget hearing each other; forget Nan's being relieved. First of all, Tom's musical taste lay in the more relaxed world of Frank Sinatra, Dean Martin, and Tony Bennett—not the more impassioned land of Waylon and Willie and the boys. But it was the volume of the song that primarily drove Tom to shout "Jesus Christ! Turn it down!" While Nan grabbed Tom's arm and insisted we leave, I cast a glance around Dewey's and saw the truckers and other patrons staring at Tom as though they were all regretting that public hangings were illegal. Perhaps realizing the same thing, Tom threw down a twenty and hurried to catch up with his wife, who was already waiting at the car.

But for all that, Nan's taste in food, drink, and restaurants was clearly influenced by Tom. Again, they enjoyed many fine meals at impressive restaurants, and Nan added with Tom's encouragement such faire as *escargot*, caviar (modestly priced, that is), blue crab, Lobster Newburg, and the like. And it was Tom who introduced Nan to the martini—the drink of such significance in her later years. My mother was almost exclusively a red wine and occasional beer drinker after she came of age. (Well okay, the wine had been imbibed for a number of years before she turned twenty-one—she grew up in an Italian household after all.) She didn't care for Scotch, bourbon, or rye—and she wasn't a tequila or rum or drinker either. She would sip anisette, the family's favorite cordial, and occasionally amaretto, but she didn't have a drink (other than wine) that she always ordered at restaurants. As for sparkling wines, she had for a period an infatuation with "Cold Duck," probably because the brand and its "champagne" sibling cost only $2.99 a bottle. But after that phase, she chose *Asti Spumante*—with its sweeter taste—as her go-to sparkling wine. In her last years, I tried to introduce her to the more delicious sparkling Bruts—at "$15.00 to $25.00 a bottle, but she insisted they tasted no better than the old $2.99 variety, which my son and his fraternity brothers doused each other with after football games. "Hey, it's cheap and tastes terrible, dad." But Nan did say that if I ever sprung for *Dom Perignon* she was sure she'd like that. So on New Year's Eve—less than four months before she went to Golden Harbor—I laid down a couple of hundred for a bottle. Much to our pleasure—and hers—Nan announced her approval and said, "Get this stuff every time, and I'll give up martinis."

But we didn't believe her, because the martini filled the void, one might say, but it also pushed her toward the edge on a number of occasions when she was married to Tom. She could get loopy to the point of snuggling Tom (or me) to the threshold of embarrassment, and she'd offer a litany of all the reasons why she loved Tom, me, or the great U.S. of A. After Tom died, Nan told me she was afraid of drinking too often during her grieving period and early widowhood. She began to ration her in-house drinks to two glasses of wine a day—one in the later afternoon and one with her dinner. The exceptions came when she went out to eat—with friends or whenever she came to visit us in Georgia or when we were down in Florida during the holidays. My wife and I were surprised when on one restaurant outing, she ordered a vodka martini rather than the usual gin. I teased her about trying to emulate James Bond—"Shaken, not stirred, right Mom?" No, she switched to vodka because it tasted smoother and she wouldn't get as buzzed with vodka. "Everyone knows that gin is more potent than vodka, John." I didn't know that, so I looked it up and informed Nan of the results. "According to one source, both drinks have an upward number of fifty percent alcohol content. The other source states that Gin has at least 35% alcohol, the same as Vodka. So the numbers show that Vodka does not have less alcohol content than gin and may have more." Nan's response to the science? "You don't know what you're talking about."

Whenever we visited each other, I would make the martinis using a two to one mix of vodka to vermouth, but in her seventies she began asking for a three to one ratio. And also at this time she always asked for two or three olives—one of which she would eat and the other one or two she'd give to me, like a parent gives candy to a toddler at a grocery store. It was hard for me to drink anything else whenever we ate together. "You're not going to make me drink alone?" she'd say in pathetic tones. "I'm having a beer, mom. I'm drinking with you." She'd get that disgusted look on her face as though she had inadvertently swallowed a fly. "Beer. That's not a drink." Of course I'd almost always capitulate—and end up with anywhere from three to six martini-soaked olives. But as they say, it's not the thing itself but rather the effect of that thing that was the issue. Somewhere near the end of the first martini, Nan would begin to praise me or my wife for our talents and loving nature (my wife) and for other less significant and more embarrassing matters (me). At this point, she would commence the "Something great is going to happen to you, John. I just know it." About the time the second martini arrived, she'd have pushed the rhetoric up to "You're going to be famous. I just know it." The problem with the second assertion—other than its ludicrous nature—was that it was delivered at louder volume than the first—a most distressful factor if we were in a restaurant. By the time Nan was through predicting my ascension to international fame, other diners probably expected a bolt of lightning to skewer me and lift me away (or they probably hoped that would be the case). Somewhere in that second martini floated the notion that I'd make a great president along the lines of Washington or Lincoln. My counter that I'd be closer to William Henry Harrison or Millard Fillmore elicited the familiar "Don't argue with me. You don't know what you're talking about."

Also when Nan reached her seventies, my wife and I noticed a number of quirky restaurant behaviors and preferences on her part. She got into an Olive Garden kick at this time. But it wasn't the chain itself, but rather a single restaurant some fifteen miles from her condo in Florida, not the one that was five minutes away. She had gone with some condo friends and liked their server Allison. (This was before she moaned whenever we had a female server.) When the group went back, they again had Allison, who found in my mother a kindred spirit—they were both widows from Long Island who adored Sinatra. Nan would afterwards drive herself down to this Olive Garden when Allison worked, and they would continue their server-customer interaction. My mother insisted we go for her birthday dinner when we were down for Christmas (Nan was born on December 23rd), and for her seventy-sixth and seventy-seventh birthday, Allison topped off Nan's meal with a large slice of cake complete with a glowing candle. But on her seventy-eighth-birthday celebration, Allison brought a small dish with a lit candle stuck in some candle wax.

"Happy Birthday, Nan!" Allison trumpeted. My immediate thought was that Olive Garden or the manager of this particular one stopped the practice of free cake, but that Allison wanted to do something to honor the occasion. Needless to say, Nan wasn't honored in the least. She said nothing, much to Allison's surprise, and after I paid the bill we walked to the car expecting Vesuvius to blow. Nan waited until we were pulling out of the parking lot before emitting her lava flow. "What the hell was that! A candle? That's it? What did she think I was? That was insulting! I'm never going back again!" And she didn't. What I saw then was that my mother could take serious umbrage at perceived slights, regardless of their nature.

We assumed the following birthday dinner (her seventy-ninth) would erase the taste of the bare candle in her mouth, especially because the event took place at a new Italian place she had discovered during the past year. *Un Momento* was as authentic as it gets. Italian owners, chef, and staff—with a double-veal chop entre *per morire per* (to die for). So we knew the food would be ideal for Nan, but I made sure there would be no repeat of the candle episode by calling ahead and ordering a piece of birthday cake to be delivered to the table after the meal. And sure enough, the meal and wine (no martinis) were outstanding, and the piece-of-cake delivery flawless, complete with an Italian birthday ditty sung by the strolling mandolin player Piero. When he finished, Piero asked if we'd like more cake. I jumped on the offer, considering that our children were with us and weren't satisfied with the small cannoli each had for dessert. We finished the sweets and I awaited the check. When it came my jaw dropped open. Our hosts had charged me for the extra cake that Piero seemed to suggest was gratis. I was about to put on my best "nothing to see here" face when Nan ripped the bill from my hand. "You look concerned, John." And then she saw what they had done. By the time we stepped out of the restaurant, Piero was safely wedged into a corner with his mandolin and the manager was sputtering a reluctant apology with an explanation that they never gave away free cake for the table—only for the birthday person. When he forced out "I'll take it off the bill, then," Nan told me to pay the whole tab because her anger and principle weren't going to be "bought off." Knowing Nan's belief that bad things come in threes, we never ordered cake at any of the subsequent birthday meals (we bought a cake and had it at home); nor did we even accept a free piece when it came. On her eighty-sixth birthday, Nan (now with martinis) refused the complimentary piece of cake with "I remember what they did to us." Somewhere I could hear the sound of a mournful mandolin.

Patterns held firm after Nan moved to Georgia, but now in her eighties, she began to find more and more restaurants unsatisfying for a host of reasons. Some places had a serious flaw in their otherwise acceptable offerings. "They have great appetizers here, but the entrées aren't much" was a common observation. Now she became much more of a critic of the surroundings than she had ever been. "I hate coming in here with that ugly green door we have to walk through"; "How can they let anyone serve food with an earring in her nose [or tattoo on his neck]?; "I don't understand why they have brick [or stone] walls in here. "I hate these paper tablecloths. The ends always curl up. Cheap, cheap, cheap." Or if there was nothing on the table, "I feel like I'm eating in a prison." If Nan chose an Italian dish, she would always tell the server "I'm Italian, so I know what's good." But then she'd take one bite and immediately lift her nose. "My mother never made it with thick sauce like this. It ruins the dish." Eventually, I would ask, "You want them to take it back, mom?" "No, no. It's fine." She'd then sigh and eat the pasta—thick sauce and all. On one occasion I took it upon myself to ask the server to replace the dish Nan said she could hardly get down, only to have her protest vigorously that it was perfectly all right.

"Why did you embarrass me like that, John?" Why indeed. Matters came to a point that after another restaurant trashing by Nan, I started asking her "Now where do *you* want to go eat, mom?" Invariably, she'd answer, "Oh, anywhere's fine with me, baby." But of course.

Once a week—and then once every two weeks—Nan had us over for dinner. She'd always serve a pasta dish—most often *cavatelli*, which her mother used to make from scratch. Finding *cavatelli* at Publix was often a challenge, since it seemed to move around the frozen food section as if it was never welcome among the Hot Pockets, Lean Cuisines, and frozen peas. When they were out of *cavatelli*, Nan would complain to the manager, who explained that they didn't sell too much of that pasta. "I think you may be the only person who buys it," he'd add. "Aren't there any Italians in Georgia besides me?" she'd muse. Following the *cavatelli*—if available—Nan placed the salad on the table. Her salads exclusively consisted of thickly sliced cucumber, tomato, and onion with bottled Italian dressing. Her son had long been a devotee of lettuce dominated salads—whether romaine, iceberg, leaf, or arugula—or any combination thereof. Nan's response when I ordered such a salad was "How can you eat that? It's like eating grass. I'm afraid people will think I mated with a cow and had you." In any event, Nan's main course was either a variation of chicken *cacciatore* or sweet Italian sausage in a tasty marinara sauce—just like her mother used to make (almost).

Remarkably, Nan continued her bi-weekly cooking for us until her final year of life. As mentioned earlier, with her sight issues, we worried about her safety in the kitchen. She would turn on the oven and ask my wife to set the temperature. She put the palm of her hand an inch over the burner to be sure it was on. After she passed ninety, we insisted that one of us would pull the meat out of the oven. She received her share of oven burns—especially when she was warming up her breakfast or lunch meal, but she took her wounds in stride and never complained. Except for when we came over, she'd take her meals in the TV room, and we'd often find food on the floor leading from the kitchen and dropped food particles around her chair a few inches in front of her large-screen. When she was on oxygen 24/7, the plastic hose would knock food off her plate, which she often did not see. And she continued her strict regimen of only two glasses a wine per day when she ate at home. The red wine she chose was one of the less expensive brands, not by choice but because this brand was the only one who made her preferred red rose, which she purchased by the jug. If I only had a dollar for every time she insisted we try the inexpensive red rose and accept her view that it tasted better than any brand of merlot, pinot noir, cabernet sauvignon, or Valpolicella on the market. But at least she didn't crave wine in a box.

Food shopping was yet another adventure the older she got. First there was her visual problem. Many were the times she tossed into her cart the wrong sauce, crackers, cut of meat, milk, and vegetables. She'd get home and discover the errors—once even believing that someone had switched shopping carts on her. My wife and I decided that we'd take her shopping so that we could avoid such mistakes, but at first she was inclined to grab and toss as she always had, so that we'd have to ask, "Are you sure this is what you want?" Reluctantly, she'd tell us what she wanted, and we'd do the grabbing and tossing—except for that heavy jug of red rose. I'd tease that we could blindfold her, spin her around three times in the store, and she'd still find the red rose. In her last year, her stamina wasn't up to the up-and-down-the-aisles activity of grocery shopping, owing to her breathing difficulties. Now she would write down what she needed, and my wife and I retrieved it from the store. Yet two further problems. First, her handwriting was often semi- or fully illegible owing to her failed sight. We'd have to call her and try to decipher what she wanted. At times, she couldn't remember. "Mom, it looks like a 'g' and an 'i' but I can't make out the rest of it." (It wasn't an "i"—it was an "r.") She wanted grapes.) Part of the word was cut off by the edge of the paper. Some requests were written on top of one another, leaving us befuddled. A strike-out line would fall between two items, so we didn't know which one she changed her mind about. Finally, she'd make us chase wild geese by misstating the item she was looking for. She wanted "Velveeta crackers," which seemed to me a product we could find. A cheesy cracker, right? Wrong. We couldn't find the item. Suddenly, my wife shouted "John—look!" I thought she saw a tarantula crawling among the Triscuits. Not Velveeta crackers but *Belvita* crackers. I couldn't help recalling the Walgreens-Wal-Mart snafu with the treadmill. There were other such confusions: not oranges but *orange juice*; not the detergent Cheer but the cereal *Cheerios*; not wild bread but *white* bread.

Steak seemed to cross Nan's wires on a number of occasions. When she was younger—up to her seventies—she preferred her steaks medium rare, as did Tom—although Nan wasn't inclined to send back a medium or medium well the way he was. When the chain steak houses became popular in the late sixties and seventies, Nan and Tom enjoyed going once a week to Bonanza Steak House for sirloins and martinis—for around ten dollars. As they became more financial stable, Bonanza was supplemented with more upscale steak houses and the sirloin was ditched for filet mignons, which Nan swore by for the next thirty years. But in her eighties she only occasionally ordered steak, eating about a third of it and taking the rest home to be enjoyed later. (The same generosity that prompted her to hand two-thirds of her olives to her son never applied when it came to her steak.)

When she was ninety, she saw a television ad for a two-for-one steak special at Longhorn's. Great, she exclaimed. She wanted to treat one of my wife's friends to a steak lunch as a thank-you for the gardening work she had done at Nan's house. After the lunch, I asked if they enjoyed their steaks. "Oh, I didn't feel like a steak, and Winona told me she was a vegetarian." Funny how advertising works. Longhorn's also featured in Nan's classic *faux pas* regarding my talents with the grill. I had knocked myself out for the 4th of July meal when Nan was ninety-one. Grilled fillets and lobster tails made up the main course, and the steaks were a perfect medium-rare. Nan actually finished over half of her steak (in addition to two lobster tails)—so I smugly thought I had made her the best steak had in quite some time. The following Monday, my wife and I picked her up for lunch, and we assumed she was looking forward to Olive Garden—her now go-to spot, for reasons I'll soon explain. But no, she said, "Let's go to Longhorn's today." Okay. I knew she had raved about their Wild West Shrimp appetizer, which she had chosen as her entrée when she and Winona had lunch months earlier. Wrong again. Nan ordered their small fillet "medium rare." My wife looked at me while I stared in disbelief at my mother—who had the same item a mere four days earlier, prepared lovingly and expertly by her devoted son. She ate three-fourths of the fillet this time, and when the server came around and asked how she enjoyed the food, Nan grabbed his arm and pulled him toward her. "I think this is the *best* steak I've *ever* had." Not the best steak since the one she had four days earlier—but the best steak EVER. Needless to say, that night in bed I muttered something to my wife about never again making her steak—no matter if she lived to be a hundred and fifty.

Nan's habit of taking home her uneaten food increased five-fold during her last years. It was only when she reached ninety that we got her stop saying to the server that she needed a "doggy-bag." "Ask for a *box*, mom—a *box*." It got to the point that she'd ask for a box as soon as the server placed the food on her table. He or she would always say, "Now?" Of course it was most often hit or miss whether she would ever eat what she asked to take home. Sometimes the box would be left on her seat if we were in a booth. Sometimes she left it on the table—or in the car—or ON the car. With her poor sight, she at times left the box on the kitchen counter until she discovered it three days later, forcing her to toss the contents in the garbage. And if the box made it inside her refrigerator, she would either forget about it or fail to see it, so that my wife and I would open the refrigerator door, see the box, and begin the process of dating it. "Let's see. This is from the Olive Garden lunch in early November last."

But of all the stuff she took from the restaurant, nothing ever topped the evening she purloined two cloth napkins from an on-campus restaurant. Our son and daughter had joined us for this meal, and since we seemed to have baker's blood coursing through our veins, we ate through the basket of bread like undernourished locusts, prompting a request for another basket and even a third. At the end of the meal, however, we noticed that we hadn't finished all the bread in basket no. 3. My grandmother had taught her children that "to waste is a sin"—so Nan volunteered to take the remaining bread back to her place. She felt too embarrassed to ask for a box, so she whispered, "I'll just take the bread and put it in my purse." Okay. After I paid the bill and as we were walking out to the car, my daughter latched on to me and insisted that I let my wife, son, and mother walk on ahead. "Dad, grandma stole two napkins." What? "She wrapped the bread in two cloth napkins and put them in her purse." Oh, great. "Tell her she can't do that, dad." Wait. I can't do that. "Get the napkins and take them back to the restaurant." Me? I think not. With my daughter's disapproval I kept my mouth shut as we drove the larcenist back home and tried to forget the incident. But two days later I received the call. "John, can you guys come over?" What could this be about, we wondered? When we arrived, Nan was sitting on the formal sofa—always a sign that serious matters had to be discussed. "I talked to the priest after mass yesterday. I didn't want to tell you until I thought about it for a day." One can imagine what scenarios stomped through our heads. Had she rented pornography or something? "I felt so guilty taking the napkins from the restaurant that I had to confess what I did." And what did the priest say? "He laughed and said that God would not hold it against me." I bet he did laugh—God too. "But I've decided to wash the napkins and have you take them back and apologize for our taking them." Our taking them? I visualized the headlines—"Professor confesses to theft at university restaurant."

When Nan reached her eighties, she began to demonstrate a satisfied and titillating side if the server was male and/or if the manager or owner was also of that sex. Although she hadn't caught up with the new tipping normal, she would always instruct me to reward the male servers generously: "John, make sure he gets the full fifteen percent" (I'd tip him twenty). A male server would receive the "Nan treatment"—her hand on one of his hands or on his arm; the "pull-down" to hear that she was Italian; the little joke about her expectations for the food; and the "thank you, baby" for taking the order, delivering the food, or presenting the check—to me of course. For those male servers she found particularly excellent in their duties (read: if they were handsome and appropriately attentive), she would "super-size" the treatment with a hug and/or kiss on cheek. Female servers would always receive the pleasant smile and sincere thank you—and a few would merit a "honey"—but I never received the order to award the "full fifteen percent." She let me make up my own mind on the tip—which was always at least twenty percent (though I never told her that). Nan's political filter had too many large holes in it, to the point that she'd sing out to one of her more familiar male servers, "How come I didn't get you today, baby?" when the female server stood by the table taking our order.

And how she adored it whenever a male manager would stop by the table and pay proper court. Many of them put a hand on her shoulder which she grabbed like a striped bass trying to wiggle off a hook. The overt flattery was never received modestly. It was expected, after all. These managers came in all sizes, shapes, ages, and ethnic backgrounds. All homage was accepted equally and exuberantly, but there was one manager who provided Nan with both her all-time flattering and all-time insulting moment. We decided to try a new restaurant called *Nord Italia,* which emphasized "Northern Italian dishes," which told me that this was no mere pizza and meatball-sub joint, run by two German guys from Kansas whose Greek and French restaurants hadn't made it. Giovanni Ricci was a thirty-eight-year-old, handsome devil with lush curly black hair that befitted the meaning of his last name, who hailed from the Ravenna region in the Emilia-Romagna province. He had been in the U.S. for only two years; therefore, his Italian accent was as thick as any flesh and blood woman would want it to be.

We hadn't seen him yet as we ordered our Bardolino, Prosecco, and Valpolicella wines and studied the authentic Northern Italian menu featuring *Cotoletta alla Valdostana* (veal chop covered in fontina cheese and ham), *Zuppa di datteri* (shellfish soup), *prosciutto di Parma, Risotto Alla Pescatora,* and *Fettuccine Alfredo*. And then magic happened. Giovanni came to our table, welcomed us, introduced himself, asked our names, and stared at Nan before saying—*"Sei italiana?"* She was barely able to squeak out her "Sì" she was so enamored of the Adonis standing before her. Giovanni checked on us twice during our meal, and when we stood to leave after paying the check, he came by, thanked us again, and brought a little more magic to the proceedings. He kissed Nan and said, *"Grazie, mia nuova bella amica"* ("Thank you, my beautiful new friend").

Surprise of all surprises. Nan asked to be taken back to *Nord Italia* the following week and every other week thereafter. (I told her she needed a two-week build-up of her longings.) Each time we went, Giovanni came over and greeted us, made dish recommendations, and kissed Nan goodbye, complete with a delightful parting Italian phrase. (Nan had expert understanding of Italian, although she found it hard to converse in it, not having had any practice for over thirty years). But then tragedy struck. We arrived at our usual table for an early dinner and noticed Giovanni in the middle of a staff meeting. I could see he wasn't happy, but Nan was oblivious to anything other than her expectations of warm greetings and goodbye kisses. When the meeting broke up, Giovanni seemed preoccupied and walked past our table without acknowledging us and went straight into his office at the rear of the restaurant. Nan was literally shocked by his silent passing, and she ordered her drink and food in Zombie style as my wife and I tried to explain that Giovanni was upset about something relating to the restaurant. It just so happened that he reemerged from his den of gloom at the time we were paying the bill. Nan stood up, as if to prompt his proper behavior, but he just walked to the window and conversed with the chef and then returned to his office. On the drive back we tried to convince my eighty-nine year old mother that it was merely a bad night at *Nord Italia*.

Two weeks later when we picked up Nan, she asked where we were going to eat. I said *Nord Italia* of course, but she balked. "I don't want to go there tonight." Well, all right, we went elsewhere—to a place that employed the server with the swarm of ladybugs tattooed on her neck. During the meal, my wife asked why she didn't wish to eat at *Nord Italia*, since it been two weeks. Nan ordered another martini when she was only half-way through her first— so we knew her reasons were serious. "I can't believe what that man did to me." Who, mom? "Giovanni Ricci." What did he do? "He completely ignored me. No hello. No how's the food. No glad you came. No kiss." She placed special emphasis on that last one. "I felt like a nobody. He wouldn't treat a dog the way he treated me." I wanted to offer that he probably didn't kiss any dogs—or at least not all breeds—but I diplomatically kept my mouth shut. "I never want to go there again. And I never want to hear the name Giovanni for as long as I live. I *hate* that name." Of course the Italian version of her son's name is, you guessed it, Giovanni.

My wife and I discussed at length my mother's reaction/delusion, and concluded that she had evidently placed a considerable value on Giovanni Ricci's charming manner and affectionate offerings. We also agreed she had a massive crush on the much younger man—and that men her age (or not quite that old) had and would probably always have the same reaction to young or younger women, whether they be co-workers, bartenders, or bank tellers. Yet not many men or women in Nan's position would think to do what she did next to prove the truth of the seventeenth-century playwright William Congreve's line that hell hath no fury like a woman scorned. Part of my mother's heritage included the old grandmother's tale that a curse (*una maledizione*) had incredible power if uttered by a woman who had been harmed (or her family harmed) by someone's cruelty or betrayal. When I was a boy of ten, I had been "blown off" by the Yankee great Mickey Mantle when I asked for his autograph during a spring training game in Florida. Five years later, we were listening to a Yankees-Orioles game on the radio, and I reminisced about the autograph snub years earlier. My mother was in one of those moods and thought she'd avenge her son's insult by casting the "evil eye" and "the horns" at the radio when Mantle came up to bat in the first inning. I was amused by her silly gesture, though I certainly loved her motherly loyalty. Mantle came up in the second inning and singled. So much for Nan's curse. But she warned, "It's coming. Have faith." Mantle back up in the fourth—a walk. Sorry mom. "It takes awhile for the curse to travel from South Florida to Baltimore." Mantle next up in the sixth. A double. Sorry again, mom. "The game's not over," she insisted. The curse had so far resulted in Mantle being two for two with a walk and a run scored. If that's the result of a curse, then sign me up. Bottom of the sixth—Orioles at bat. A fly ball over Mantle's head in center field. He chased it toward the fence. He leaped up to snag it. But the ball sailed over the fence for a home run. What's that? Mantle down. His cleats got hooked in the chain-link fence, which bent his foot in a way it wasn't designed to go. Verdict: broken bone in his foot. I turned toward Nan, who wore an expression of complete superiority. "Oh, my son. Ye of so little faith." It took Mantle two months to return to the field.

Remembering that, I knew better than to slough off Nan's curse on poor Giovanni Ricci. And it was therefore of no surprise when some six weeks later *Nord Italia* closed its doors to the paying public. Giovanni tried again the following year with another Italian restaurant, but it too failed after a brief ruin. Being the modest person she was, Nan took FULL credit for the closing of both establishments.

Like Don Quixote, Nan strove to reach her impossible dream: the perfect martini. Often I felt like her Sancho Panza, riding my donkey and trying to dispense shots of reality and earthly wisdom about being satisfied with a world that provided good vodka and vermouth—no matter how flawed the presentation was. "Why don't they fill it to the top?" was her mantra, as she looked at the martini glasses getting larger, while the amount contained seemed to shrink. She'd gaze with utter horror at the large "tubs" that made up the bowls of the wine glasses and remark that it was a good thing my grandmother wasn't alive to see "so little wine" in the glass. She seemed to forget that her mother served wine at home in old-school small glasses, which were filled to the rim and over—the spilling of red wine being an indication of health and good fortune. When she poured her wine at home, Nan filled the glass up—but then she didn't own any of the modern "tub" glasses used by restaurants.

But it was the "insult" of paying full price for a martini and getting only a "partial glass's worth." She would also point out (not quite accurately) that the inclusion of two or three olives pushed the vodka and vermouth up the glass—so that when the olives were removed, one would "lose half the damn drink." Of course, she made up for the skimpy portion by having another— and at times a third. Very few of us can have two or three and not alter the tone and pace of our speech (let alone the coherence of it), but Nan also added volume to hers with every additional sip. Again not surprisingly, her sentimental side came forward as she made clear how much she loved us and how "no one" could love a son the way she loved me. Once again she'd predict great things for my immediate future and proclaim what a great president I would make. Speaking of politics, she would shake her head and wonder how she had been taken in by Richard Nixon. "I felt sorry for him— the way they made fun of his looks." She admitted that she never told her family that she voted for Nixon over Kennedy in 1960. "I didn't want to vote for him just because he was Catholic—but I should have."

Another go-to topic when she was in her cups was her family and the kinds of loving friends her parents had—and the integrity, personalities, and loyalty they possessed. We'd hear over and over my grandfather's discovering change or bills left on the bar counter at *La Taverna* and then putting the money in an envelope, which he would return to the patron, never once assuming that the money was left as a tip. But the down side to this nostalgia was whenever Nan ate (and drank) in the company of her teenage grandchildren. She would launch into a story about Uncle Sally and Aunt Giustina and then say to my daughter and son, "*You'll* never understand. You don't know what I'm talking about. You'll never know what it was like to be with these people—nuh-uh. Not you." My daughter especially bristled at what she felt to be a patronizing remark by her grandmother. On the other hand, Nan under the influence would inquire of my daughter or son which artists were "hot" in the music world at any given time. "I never heard of them," she'd remark as my children patiently explained the who and why. If we were at our place, Nan would insist that they play something by NSYNC or Widespread Panic. She'd listen and then make her judgment. "Eh, my boy Frankie [Sinatra] has nothing to worry about."

And how she praised my wife when she was sufficiently martinied. "You're not my daughter-in-law," she'd repeat more times than I can remember. "You're my daughter-in-love." A sweet and gratifying comment if there ever was one—but some of the shine was taken off by Nan's sharing her observation with other restaurant patrons—either deliberately or inadvertently. And while any son would cherish the appreciation his mother has for his accomplishments—real or imagined—Nan's insistence on telling every passing server or patron that her son was *this* and had done *that* put permanent wince lines on my face. Imagine being a server—or worse, a stranger in the next booth—and hearing a tipsy eighty-eight-year-old at full volume say something like "Did you know my son was the talking hamburger in a fast-food radio ad?"

But all ended happily because Nan finally realized her impossible dream. She discovered the perfect martini. She and I had been lunching at the local Olive Garden for a number of months when one June day she groused, as she always did, about the distance between her vodka and vermouth and the top of the martini glass. I don't know why, but I got up and walked to the bar and asked the bartender to add some more of the proper ingredients so that the glass would be close to full. The additional cost was no object. The young man was cordial and interested to know about Nan and her preferences. We exchanged first names—his was Eph (short for Ephram)—and he suggested that the next time we should sit at one of the tables in the bar area so he could make Nan the "best martini she ever had." I had heard that one before in other contexts, but I thought she'd like Eph (he was a young man, after all), and it would be a nice change to sit in the bar area rather than in one of the larger dining rooms. It just so happened that my wife joined us because she was not only finished with the school year but with her teaching career as well. Nan was eighty-nine and finished forever with inferior martinis— although we didn't know it yet.

When we sat down, Eph waited on us. "Nan, I'm going to fix you a martini I know you'll love." She lit up not only because of the personal attention Eph gave her but also because of the wild prospect that her quest would end there—in the bar area of the local Olive Garden. Before we sat down, I had maneuvered my way to the other side of the bar and instructed Eph again to fill up her martini glass with a first-rate vodka and vermouth but not to tell her it was a double. Nan wiggled in anticipation as Eph set about his work. I watched him pour a slight amount of vermouth into the chilled martini glass and then throw it out. Hmm. Then he selected from the top of the liquor pyramid a bottle of Grey Goose and poured it into a shaker along with ice. In true Bond fashion he shook and not stirred it—then poured it into the chilled glass with only a reside of vermouth, dropped in three olives (Nan's request), and brought it immediately to the table. Nan stared at the glass—filled to the rim and still cloudy from the shaken ice—as though she had been presented with the Lost Treasure of the Knights Templar. It took her several moments before she lifted the glass to her lips, being careful not to spill one precious drop. Her fact glowed with exaltation as the vodka slid its way down her throat and spread through her torso in that wonderful manner known only to martini drinkers.

On that day my mother pronounced that Eph's was "the best martini she had ever had," and I wondered if she would draft a letter to the Vatican asking that they canonize the young bartender. From then on, it was once (or twice) a week for lunch at Olive Garden—but only if Eph was tending bar. Thrice we walked out when he wasn't in, and Nan ignored the hostess who assured her that the other bartender could make a good martini. "Nah," Nan replied, and we headed off to another restaurant. The two years with Eph were among her happiest. He always came from behind the bar and waited on us. But more than that, he made a fuss over Nan and allowed her to hug him and kiss his cheek. On those occasions when Nan had two (that's two large), she would attempt to pull him down in the booth with her, but he would always diplomatically untangle himself and remind her that management expected him to stand behind the bar and make drinks for other paying customers. Nan insisted that I join her in martini heaven, and I had to agree that Eph's were the best I ever had. And on Nan's last birthday before she entered Golden Harbor Assisted Living, Eph came to our house as a surprise to my mother and made her two of his Grey Goose specials. She was in bliss that he had made the effort to make her birthday memorable. After Eph left and my daughter and granddaughter arrived to have some cake, Nan was blissfully knocked out on the couch, dreaming of olives and grey geese. "Wow," my four-year-old granddaughter said. "G-G [great-grandmother] must really be tired. I can't even wake her up."

Chapter Five
Planes, Boats, and Automobiles

"There is nothing in the world so irresistibly contagious
as laughter and good humor."
Charles Dickens

As much as Nan enjoyed renovating and redecorating her homes, she often seconded St. Augustine's view that "The world is a book, and those who don't travel only read one page."

Yet on a number of her travels she also felt the burning truth of Tom Sawyer's observation, "I have found out there ain't no surer way to find out whether you like people or hate them than to travel with them."

Whether her traveling consisted of driving, cruising, or flying, Nan found her way into hilarious situations both of and not of her own making.

She certainly didn't wait long to begin life as a traveler. When she was three, she accompanied her parents and elder siblings on an ocean crossing to visit the Abruzzo region in east-central Italy from where my grandparents hailed. She met her relatives and was immersed in the local culture for the next three months, and when she made it back to New York she had to relearn English. She wouldn't return to the land of her ancestors until forty-six years later, although she collected many photograph books about Italy and relished the visits of those from the region—uncles, aunts, a grandmother, and cousins—including her dashingly handsome cousin Abramo, whose arrival on Long Island for a short visit resulted in a deluge of visits by Nan's female friends and a fit pitched by the jealous H2, who thought his cousin-in-law was getting a bit too chummy with my mother. H2 just couldn't accept that the affection the cousins shared (hugs, cheek kisses, and some lap sitting) was just an Italian thing.

After her childhood journey to Italy, Nan's travels were limited to areas within ninety miles of her Long Island home. But after she was married, she traveled first to Lawrence, Kansas and then to Southern California, owing to my father's mechanical expertise, which was needed during the war. When she returned to New York in 1945, her traveling days went into abeyance until she left my father and drove with me to South Florida, where her parents were living part of the year. She took three further trips to Florida after she married H2, the third when we moved to West Palm Beach—and five years later we returned to Long Island to visit her two brothers. Nan had always liked to drive—she told me it gave her a sense of freedom when she was behind the wheel—and she had no problem having her hands on the steering wheel for two-thirds of the 2,400 mile round trip. Unfortunately, each of these trips had complications. During the first one she was mentally battered by her first marriage and had to answer difficult questions regarding her desire for a Florida divorce. On the second trip, her stupid son was riding on the back of a bicycle and got his foot caught in the spokes, tearing away enough flesh to require an excruciatingly painful iodine bath and a limp for several weeks. In addition, in his wisdom H2 thought he'd lie out in the Florida sun and take a nap—with the result being a serious sunburn requiring my mother's constant attention and application of medicinal cream. With me limping and whining and H2 hunched over and bellyaching, she drove the entire way back to New York wishing, I'm sure, she had entered a nunnery at eighteen. Finally, when we visited New York five years after moving to Florida, H2 had a heart attack at age forty, forcing a hospital stay while my cousin Trudy and I returned to Florida in high style—on a Greyhound bus—while Nan remained with H2. Later, she drove back to Florida by herself and a few days later the recuperating H2 arrived by train. We had been hoping he would take the wrong train and end up in Montana or Wyoming, but alas.

Later car trips would be joyous ones for Nan—the one taking her and Tom to Valdosta, Georgia to get married the best one of all. There were also treks to California with Tom, and two other New York visits, with stops in Washington D.C. After Tom's death, she came to Georgia to visit us once or twice a year, rejecting our advice that she fly to Atlanta, since she now (in her later sixties and seventies) could afford to take a plane. She still had the exhilarating feeling of freedom on the open road, to which she added a sense of style. When she was seventy-four, she purchased a brand new silver Mustang with which to make her journeys. I called her "Mustang Nanny"—a name she embraced, even though she had never heard the Wilson Pickett classic "Mustang Sally." But driving lost much of its luster when she moved to Georgia in her early eighties.

Nan had driven up to see us the year prior and insisted that we go up toward the foothills of the Appalachians to see a piece of property she was interested in. My wife and I thought it interesting that she wanted to invest in property, seeing that in the 1960s she had sold real estate located on the Gulf Coast of Florida and worked for a company that sold property in the Bahamas. On the drive up, I had to negotiate a number of elevated and winding roads—not my favorite thing to do by any means. We arrived at the location, which had homes in various states of completion. I had just made the statement that "It's beautiful up here, mom," when Nan replied, "I know. I will love living here." Come again? When my wife's and my jaws finally lifted from our laps, I sputtered and hemmed out a "You're not really thinking of moving up here, are you?" Nan explained that the old gang at her Florida condo was thinning out and that she was for the past year feeling bored and isolated. Isolated? "Mom don't you think you might feel isolated up here?"

We saw no shopping centers or restaurants other than the kind of places Tom would have dragged us into. "Don't you see, John? I figured that I'm equal distance between you and Trudy [my cousin from the 1960 bus trip, now living in Marietta, near Atlanta]. I won't feel isolated or alone." What she didn't seem to understand was that the "equal distance" was close to eighty miles between her and us and between her and Trudy. "I promised you a long time ago that I wouldn't intrude, so this way I won't be down the street." It was lucky we'd be in the same state. All I could think about was my mother trying to negotiate those winding and elevated roads at eighty years old—silver Mustang or not. Of course, we also thought of the distance we'd have to travel to visit her and the inevitable health issues that would call on us to assist her at a moment's notice ."Mom, I have a better idea. Why don't you move to Athens so we can be closer?" Her face exploded like popcorn. "Really? Do you mean that, John?" My wife and I assured her that we did.

We found her a nice two-story condo and then drove to Gainesville,

Florida to visit my wife's mother. I then headed back to Athens, leaving my wife, who would wait for my mother and drive to Athens with her. I awaited their arrival, but received a phone call from my wife instead. "Your mother got run off the road by a truck on I-75 near Gainesville." Apparently it was raining fairly hard, and when the semi behind her tried to change lanes, it clipped the rear of the Mustang and sent it off the road. The rig kept driving, but another truck driver stopped and saw to my mother's safety. (Thank you, kind sir.) Nan was quite shaken and concerned about her silver Mustang, which had to be left in Gainesville for repairs. My wife rented a car and brought Nan to Athens. (We later returned to Gainesville to retrieve the Mustang.) Nan vowed then that she wouldn't drive any long distances again, which we were glad to hear, but soon we realized that we had the shorter distances to worry about as well.

Nan generally limited her driving to the store, church, and our place—except when she decided to visit her niece Trudy in Marietta for a couple of days. She dismissed our warnings about Atlanta traffic and assured us that with the proper directions, she would have no trouble on the road. I warned her about I-285, which circles Atlanta and reminded her again of the right exit to take to get on I-75 North, which would then lead her up to Marietta. Trudy's directions to her house would get her there by the appointed time. Now, we grown children always worry about our elderly parents when they get on the road—and so we did about Nan. Since she was severely technologically challenged, she had no cell phone on which to call us if she ran into trouble. Fortunately for me, this visit to Trudy's occurred on a Saturday afternoon in the fall; therefore my thoughts left Nan and landed along with my carcass in the front of the television for some good college football viewing.

Some three hours after Nan was supposed to leave in her silver Mustang, I turned to my wife. "Well, she should have gotten there by now. She'll have a good time this weekend." And then back to football. A little over two hours later the phone rang. "John, this is Trudy." Uh, oh. Is Nan sick? Not quite. "She hasn't shown up yet. When did she leave?" That was my personal "Houston, we've got a problem" moment. I couldn't do anything about it until the game was over—no, not really—I immediately began to panic and envisaged my mother as the victim of a serious accident on I-285. I told

Trudy that Nan was supposed to have left around noon and that I would call her house and see if she had simply forgotten about going to Marietta. "I'll get back to you as soon as I know anything," I told my cousin.

My next call went to a policeman friend, who told me he'd contact the Atlanta area for any word on an accident involving a silver Mustang. I couldn't think of what else to do but wait for a call regarding my mother's fate. An hour later, the phone rang. It was Trudy. "John, we've got her!" I wanted to ask in what form she and the Mustang were in, but my relief was too great to get the words out. What happened was that Nan made it fine to I-285 and turned the car properly north. I had emphasized that she needed to be in the right lane so she could exit when she reached I-75. I could see her whipping the Mustang over from one of the left lanes and causing an eighteen-car pile-up. But Nan took me too literally and ended up in the next "exit only" lane. She'd get off I-285 and then have to get back on. She'd end up in the exit lane again and then get off again. I'm sure she was thinking, "That idiot son of mine told me to stay in the right lane." After doing it again, she pulled over one lane to avoid being sucked off the Atlanta by-pass. That was when she passes the I-75 exit lanes and headed west and then south on I-285—getting off and then getting again at several more exits until she finally—after several hours—made a complete circle of Atlanta on the by-pass—all sixty-four miles of it. Somehow she managed to exit at I-75 and somehow she managed to get off that road and call Trudy from a convenience store. My cousin ascertained roughly where she was and said, "Do you see the Big Chicken across the road?" Nan didn't hear her properly, so in her exasperation at Trudy's apparent desire to tell a juvenile joke, she replied "No, why?" Trudy said she ought to be able to see it. "See what?" Finally, Trudy got Nan to understand that the Big Chicken was a famous landmark in the area—a KFC restaurant with a fifty-six-foot sign in the shape of a chicken. "Just go there, and we'll pick you up." Nan crossed the road to the Big Chicken and awaited her rescue. After that fiasco, Nan permanently retired the silver Mustang from all trips of more than five or six miles. At least we had a new joke to add to the repertoire: "Why did the Mustang cross the road? To meet the Big Chicken, of course." Uh, I guess you had to be there.

In her last years, Nan's driving was severely hampered by her failing eyesight, and when we took her to renew her license—in spite of our tactful suggestions to do otherwise—we at least had the comfort of knowing that there was no way she could pass the eye-test and be allowed to drive for another five years. I stood with her as she strained to read the letters on the screen. "Do they have to make the damn things so small," she muttered. I was formulating the right words to sooth her disappointment when I heard the woman say to Nan, "This is good for the next five years." How in the world . . . Anyway, the real traumatic moment came when she had to pose for her driver's license photo. How she hated formal or posed shots. The muscles in her face would reconfigure themselves in a way that gave her the look of a woman who was suddenly awakened at three in the morning by a spider walking across her face. She'd invariably ask for a do-over on her license and passport photos—without success. She'd pull out one of her expired passports and ask why she couldn't use that far more attractive picture. "Because that was taken thirty-eight years ago, ma'am."

The end of her driving came when she was pulled over by the police on her way home from church. She'd been straddling two lanes because, as she said, "There was no one else ahead of me I could follow."

When the officer saw from her license that she was over ninety years old, he asked if she was under medication and volunteered to lead her home—letting the matter slide without issuing a ticket. Although she let us drive her for the next week, Nan wanted to give it one more try and decided to drive to Publix, since it was much closer to her place than was the church. She made it about two-tenths of a mile before she turned the car around and made it back home. She just couldn't see the white lane dividers. Still, she kept the Mustang in the garage for another four months, arguing that she would need it if her sight suddenly improved. With the most passionate reluctance she sold her silver baby and wore the same broken expression as if she was forced to sell her own baby. Or so I'd like to think.

Although she boarded her share of flights during her life, it was very difficult getting her airborne the first time. She was in her mid-forties and had never flown, frequently remarking that she'd be too scared ever to leave the safety of terra firma. But when she was working for the company that sold property in the Bahamas, she was informed she would be taking the short flight over as part of her job—and there was no getting out of it. "Why can't we take a boat?" she moaned. Right before she was to board the half-hour flight from West Palm Beach on a six-seater prop job, Nan loaded up on spirits to dull her fear—and I suppose the pain from when the plane plunged into the Atlantic. But as she said, "I didn't feel even a buzz," and she flew over and back fully aware of the dire possibilities. Subsequent small plane flights were easier—but not much; it wasn't until she flew on large commercial jets in her fifties that she began to tolerate the journey better. Because my grandmother had a habit of saying her rosary beads whenever she was in the midst of traveling—by plane, boat, or automobile (always comforting when I drove her to New York one summer)—Nan gave that a try but was just too nervous to concentrate on her prayers. "I'll have another martini" served her much better than "Hail, Mary, full of grace, / The Lord is with thee."

But without question, her favorite mode of travel was by ship. Perhaps it was a memory of the trip she took to Italy as a young girl that instilled in her a love of cruises, but she had to wait some forty years to have the experience again. Myrna, her boss at the time, wanted to reward Nan for her excellent work by taking her on a two-day cruise to Nassau in the Bahamas. Nan found that it wasn't the so-called destination that thrilled, but rather the ambiance, food, drink, and gambling on board the ship that provided the excitement. She was staked by Myrna and gambled for free, winning a modest amount but loving every die tumbled and card overturned. Still, cruising didn't really begin in earnest until she was in her mid-sixties and a widow. She took several voyages in the Caribbean, two along the New England Coast, and one each off the coasts of Mexico and Alaska. In each instance she raved about the food—"You can eat as much steak and lobster as you can handle, John"—and the ambiance, which included the glamour of the Captain's Table and the attention provided her by the personable male stewards and by the Captain himself when he came over to introduce himself. "We had a real handsome Captain this time, and I told him he was lucky I wasn't ten years younger." She'd top off her report with a strong suggestion that my wife and I needed to take a cruise: "You'll love every minute of it." When she moved to Georgia at age eighty-one, she took several cruises with my cousin Trudy and her husband Lewis, where she met many of their friends and always had a great time. She'd praise the "Broadway" and "Vegas" style shows on board the ship and note any celebrities who were on board—the most famous being William

Christopher, who played Father Mulcahy on M*A*S*H. And always she concluded with two or three doses of "So when are you two going on a cruise?"—which began as a series of cheery suggestions and ended up twenty-five years later as plain old-fashioned badgering.

I was always very grateful for Trudy and Lewis's invitations to Nan to accompany them, because I never found that method of travel or vacationing at all desirable. I know—I know. To quote Nan, "You're crazy. You don't know what you're missing." I accept that judgment without argument. However, I'd rather be on solid ground for the bulk of my trips—free to go where I want and eat where I want, rather than being sea-locked until arriving at a port, where I'd end up seeing sights in some kind of group tour, walking along with men wearing sandals with black socks. Again, I know. I'm crazy. And I was crazy to try to explain my view to Nan, who in her late eighties opened her bag of tricks and pulled out the old stand-by guilt in order to convince me. "I've always wanted to take a cruise with you two, John. It would make me so happy." Okay, so now I'd be responsible for denying my elderly mother her shot at happiness. I told her I'd think more about it while she was on her latest cruise with Trudy and Lewis. When the cruise was over and Nan flew back to Atlanta from the west coast, we picked her up and had dinner on the road. Nan had her two "lousy" martinis and deep into the second one shocked us with "Remind me never to take a cruise again." What was this? Nan assured us she had a good time with her niece and nephew in-law, but that she wasn't thrilled about the food the way she normally was. The Captain apparently was of the reserved and hand-shaking ilk, as opposed to the effervescent and cheek-kissing variety. But what bothered her most was the attention she received from a member of the male species. Really? "He followed me wherever I went. I'd go out on the deck and he'd be there wanting to talk. At first I spoke to him, you know, and asked about his family and what he did. He claimed he was a rich businessman and that he'd been married three times but wasn't married now—that in itself made me not like him." I didn't bother to remind her that she too had been married three times. She added that he made her feel uncomfortable by always flattering her and being where she was. "He didn't knock on your cabin door, did he, mom?" She said no, but that if he did she would have "punched him in the face." At least Nan's vanity still had its principles. When the cruise was coming to its end, the man asked for her address—and not willing to be rude she gave it to him. But it wasn't hers—it was mine. Fortunately, he never darkened my doorstep.

Over the years she had complained about various matters after returning from a cruise, such as watered-down drinks, too many superannuated gents winking at her as they strolled by with their canes and walkers, and one of her travel partners, who yapped and yawed non-stop on deck and in the claustrophobic cabin they shared—not to mention the hours spent jammed tightly together on buses and tours. Yet, she had never said that she was through with cruises as she did on this occasion.

As expected, Nan couldn't do without her sea-salt for long, and once more she started in on me to take her on a cruise, playing what she imagined was her final card: "I'll pay for it." But I countered with "*If* we go, we'll split the tab. Let's talk hypothetically," I continued. "Where would you like to go?" I had said several times earlier that since I grew up after the age of eight in South Florida and was a miniature beach bum, I had no interest in cruising to the tropics, to the Caribbean, to anywhere where the big attraction was sand and palm trees. (Feel free to call me crazy again.) "How about Italy?" Nan replied. Okay. I'd listen. She got up and retrieved a brochure featuring a Mediterranean tour—ten cities in eleven days. Did I say that my wife and I also don't care to be on the constant move when we travel? "Mom, consider the amount of walking you'd have to do"—she was about to turn ninety at the time and had been showing limited mobility with her arthritic knee. I noted as well that the ten cities in eleven days itinerary called for considerable getting off and back on ship with only a few hours in each city. "Mom, not all these places are right on the water, you know." It was as sure as death and taxes: "John, you're crazy. You don't know what you're talking about. I just want to show you Italy, that's all." What was this? An opening? I said that my wife and I would love to go to Italy with her. "We can fly. What city would you like to stay in, mom? Rome, Florence, Venice?" All those, she answered, "but we also have to go to Milan, Naples, and the Almalfi Coast." *Madonna mia*, I silently screamed. I could see us on a tour bus with older men in those sandals and black socks or my renting a car and driving into the Adriatic because I didn't know where I was going. Needless to say, the travel summit broke up without a signed agreement.

Fortunately for us, Trudy and Lewis asked Nan on another cruise. Unfortunately for Nan, she wasn't able to go. All was reserved and paid for, when a week before departure we took Nan to the hospital, owing to her inability to breath freely. It was at this time that she had to be hospitalized and was ordered to be on oxygen 24-7. After she returned home, she once more opened discussion about our taking her on a cruise. This time, we had the sad duty of reminding her she would have to make arrangements for the oxygen on the plane and then on the ship. "I can't be seen wearing this stupid hose in my nose on a ship. We'll forget it until I get better and can get rid of this damn thing." So we never did go on a cruise together. Do I regret not doing so with her? Of course I do. No one's fault but my own. But I regret even more not being with her in Italy. That would have been so much fun and so very special.

The great British Prime Minister, statesman, and author Benjamin Disraeli titled a chapter in one of his books "Travel Teaches Toleration."

Well, all I know is that he never travelled with Nan. Among the most memorable trips with her was to Disney World when she was sixty-five and our children were eight and three. We discussed getting a room at one of the nicer hotels off property (the Disney medium-priced resorts did not open until four years later), but Nan rebelled, arguing that all we were paying for was a bed to sleep in—so why spend $85.00 for each room when we can rack out in one that costs only $39.99. When she kindly offered to stay at a cheaper place while we "wasted our money," we knew we had lost the battle. The two rooms were secured, and our daughter was commandeered to sleep in my mother's room so my daughter wouldn't have to get in bed with her three-year old brother. As it turned out, she would have preferred getting in bed with a three-year old orangutan. "Grandma snored and kept mumbling something in Italian I couldn't understand. She got up three times in the night and walked into my bed all three times!" The accommodations inside and out at this "reasonably priced" establishment were, to use an agricultural term, "seedy." All that was missing was a chalk outline of a murder victim or two. The roaches were well behaved, at least.

But we had come to enjoy Disney World and to see for the first time the World Showcase at EPCOT, with its international areas featuring Mexico, Norway, China, Germany, Italy, Japan, Morocco, France, England, and

Canada. Nan was anxious to see how Disney incorporated Italy and was quite pleased, except that I had made dinner reservations elsewhere because the Italian restaurant was booked at the time we were there. (We—or rather I—had failed to make reservations in a timely manner.) As luck would have it, Japan's Pavilion had an opening at their restaurant—so in we went for some excellent teppanyaki food with the classic table-side preparation. Of course, instead of an Asian beverage, Nan ordered her martini—and then another—and then another. During her metamorphosis from a reasonable, though tired, tourist, she began thinking—and TALKING—about WWII. (Can't understand why that topic entered her mind, since we were eating at a Japanese restaurant.) As the seconds and the sips went by, she reminisced about the day she heard that Pearl Harbor was attacked. Even my eight-year old daughter knew that wasn't a proper topic in the Japanese Pavilion—and she joined her parents in shhh-ing and attempting to change the subject. I should pause here to say that Nan was always very proud of herself for her tolerance and lack of prejudice. She busted at the seams whenever she'd remind someone that her son didn't know what a Jew was until he was nine and that her son was later an honorary godfather of an African-American child. She frequently made the point that she was made fun of as a girl because she was Italian—and she knew how damaging that had been.

But we all have dents in our principles—and hers was the bitterness she maintained for December 7, 1941 and such atrocities as the Bataan Death March. That in its history America had committed its share of horrendous deeds made no difference—nor did the fact that those responsible for the two events she lamented were either all dead or about to be. In any event, with each successive sip of gin (her choice then) and vermouth, she added fuel to her indignation and raised the level of her commentary. My three-year-old son thought the whole thing a hoot, whereas his sister, mother, and father attempted to silence Nan and convince her that the fourth martini wouldn't be a good idea—especially in the restaurant where she was unloading her historical grievances. I felt sorry for the poor young staff—all Japanese—who did their best to display their politeness as they were forced to listen to Nan's "I'll never forgive thems" as we finally managed to get her out the door.

As a not-so-cheery postscript to the dinner, we headed to an outdoor pavilion to enjoy a performance by an All-American musical youth group.

Just our luck--they launched into Neil Diamond's "America," which got Nan back on the WWII battlefield. The following day she asked sheepishly if she had said anything that embarrassed us at the Japanese restaurant. I said, "No, but there are now photographs of you with 'Do not feed this woman' all throughout the Japanese pavilion. The Japanese ambassador has also filed a formal complaint in Washington about you, mom."

As Nan neared her eightieth birthday, we decided to realize one of her wishes—to have us all go to Manhattan at Christmas time. We flew to LaGuardia, took a shuttle van to the city, and checked into the Sheraton on 7th between 52nd and 53rd—all without a hitch. A splendid meal at Rosie O'Grady's across the street provided a nice cherry on top of the day. But the following morning brought its share of problems—as we should have expected. The long walk to Times Square and back again—with the assortment of diversions from pigeon droppings on Nan's new winter coat to having her arm grabbed by one of the doomsday prognosticators outside of Macy's. We returned in time to rest a bit, before our dinner reservation at Tavern on the Green. The room where we had our meal was decorated in gorgeous holiday style, so we thought the photo would be perfect. But Nan balked. "I walked a long way today. I don't look good when I'm tired. Just have her take it of the four of you. I'll move out of the way." The poor server wasn't sure what to do, as Nan tried to climb past my daughter and son to escape the all-seeing eye of the camera's lens. As expected, fellow diners found the ballet both amusing and annoying, as Nan nearly stepped backward into one of the lavishly decorated Christmas trees in the dining room.

After dinner, we returned to the Sheraton so that Nan could change her clothes (again) before we went to Radio City to see their famous Christmas show. Nan had been talking of the Rockettes for days and how much we'd all enjoy seeing them in person. But as we came outside to begin our walk to Radio City, a cold but very light rain began to fall. Now remember: Radio City is a short distance from the Sheraton—one block to the east and a couple of blocks south. I said we could walk to it without getting too wet. Wife, daughter and son were all for it—but there was one dissenter. "I'll stay at the hotel." Why, mom? "I don't want to get my shoes wet." The silence following that statement might have gone on for a week had not my wife jumped in with "We can take a cab." Good. Crisis averted. Until.

My son and I walked the short distance to Radio City and ended up waiting several minutes for the cab to arrive. When it did, we noticed Nan having trouble getting out of the back seat. When she finally managed to extricate herself, she walked into Radio City and headed immediately for the ladies room. I asked my wife what happened. "When we first got in the cab, she told the driver to take us to Radio City and the driver said, 'Lady, you're kidding. It's just over a block or so.' So we got in the cab and we made one turn, went a short distance, then made another turn, and we arrived." I asked about the trouble Nan had getting out of the cab. "One if her shoes came off and fell deep in the well and then under the front seat. It took forever for me to find it." So much for the sanctity of her shoes. God only knows what was on the floor of that cab. Needless to say, my daughter was utterly mortified by the entire episode.

The following night we went to Broadway to see *Kiss Me Kate*. Resting most of the day while the four of us toured more of the city, Nan was bedecked in all her glory for her return to the Great White Way after a forty-five-year absence. But once again luck was not on our side. BOTH leads were "indisposed" that night and the replacement female lead began with verse two rather than verse one in her big number "I Hate Men." Coming to a jamming halt, she even broke the fourth wall and talked to the audience before attempting to get the song back on track. Still, Nan was enjoying the production (and it was quite good), while I happened to notice sitting in front of us the superb author, journalist, and historian David Halberstam—whose books I had read with pleasure and appreciation. During the intermission, I begged his pardon for violating his privacy and told him how much I admired his work. He was the perfect gentleman and thanked me for my praise and asked if we were visiting Manhattan. I said yes we were and did a quick introduction of everyone. I then thanked him and allowed him to turn back to his program—not intending to say another word.

"Excuse me. But do you know my son has written books too? What's the name of that author you wrote about, John?" At that moment, I channeled my daughter's mortification and desired to be in one of the cages at the Central Park Zoo rather than at the Martin Beck Theatre on Broadway. But any hope that the length of the second act would erase the memory of that embarrassing moment was dashed when, after the final bows, everyone stood and made their way out of their rows and into the aisle. As it so happened, Mr. Halberstam reached the point where our row joined the aisle at the exact moment that Nan stepped out from her seat. Sure enough, her high heel drove into the top of the noted author's right foot, causing him to leap back, articulating something between a cough and a howl. I believe I pushed past several patrons in front of me to avoid hearing them beg me to control my mother.

Other vacation highlights would include a later Disney trip with my wife, Nan, and my mother-in-law. I know; I know. The proverbial male nightmare scenario. But I adored my mother-in-law, so I felt I could handle the challenge well enough. Nan and my mother-in-law—now both in their late eighties—succumbed to fatigue early in the day, but they thoroughly enjoyed what they saw and the rides they took in the Magic Kingdom and Hollywood Studios. This time we stayed away from the World Showcase and the Japanese pavilion. I vowed to do all I could not to damage further East-West relations. Instead, we had a lovely meal at the California Grill at the top of Disney's Contemporary Hotel. Of course, those vodka martinis (three of them) were the expected accompaniment to Nan's meal, and somewhere deep into the second one, she trained her eyes on the window overlooking Disney property. We thought her staring so intently somewhat unusual, so we asked what she was looking at (a fair question, I believed).

"Do you see it, John? Do all of you see it?" I think initially we all assumed she thought it was some kind of UFO. Is it an airplane? "No. Don't you see it?" she repeated as martini number three made its way to the table. Tell us what you think you see. "Isn't it obvious." No, it actually wasn't. We waited a few seconds for her to begin her new cocktail and then inform us what she was looking at. "It's the Washington Monument." My mother-in-law was too sweet to say anything—and she was probably frightened by Nan's identification of the floating object. But the rest of us—including our dear friends (both Disney employees) who joined us for dinner--did the requisite open-mouthed "What?!" We saw nothing out the large window until I walked behind my mother and bent down to her eye level. And there it was. No, not the Washington Monument, but rather the reflection of a large bottle shaped like an obelisk that rested on the counter of the bar area. At least Nan didn't spot Elvira Gulch on her bicycle floating by out there.

But she did see the real Washington Monument when my wife and I took her to the Nation's Capitol when she was eighty-five. During our visit, all went well. Nan made the long walks to the Capitol and then back through the Mall—with several stops at the Smithsonian Museums—to the Washington Monument and the World War II, Korean, and Lincoln Memorials—and finally to the fence at the end the south lawn of the White House. She only complained about the visitor-unfriendly post-9/11 security changes in the city. She enjoyed the good food and drink as well as the sights—and delighted in reflecting on previous visits to D.C. No, there were no problems or unusual moments while we were there. They all came before we boarded the flight from Atlanta to Reagan International.

When we picked her up for the ninety-minute drive to Hartsfield-Jackson, she wasn't quite ready to roll. "I forgot to pack my overnight bag." So while she packed it, I picked up her suitcase to place in the car. She had chosen not to go with the luggage we recently bought her, but rather her old bag because it was "pretty" with its rose-colored highlights—unlike the "blah" black set we purchased. Nan was at last ready with her carry-on and off we went. But something bothered me about her suitcase. It wasn't that she chose her old one rather than the new one we purchased. No, it was something else, and I just couldn't put my finger on it. When we parked at the airport I finally realized what it was when I actually put my finger on it—or rather my hand through the handle. Her old bag didn't have wheels. I was therefore left to lug her heavy (overweight as we discovered) suitcase rather than easily roll it from far out in the long term parking to the bag check inside the terminal.

When we entered the security area for the carry-on bag check, I was just getting the feeling back in my right arm from the bag-lugging when Nan's carry-on disappeared on the conveyer belt for its x-ray. One would have thought she'd won the sweepstakes the way the bells and lights exploded. As she explained, in her rush to get her carry-on packed—"I didn't want to keep you waiting, John. I know how you get"—she simply swept into her bag such verboten items as hair and nail scissors, two large can of aerosol hairspray, and three large containers of skin products. Nan grumbled when these items were confiscated, punctuating her grumbles with "If I didn't have to be so rushed."

Yet the most memorable trip was the one we took to Long Island for "one last visit" to where Nan was born and basically lived until her mid-thirties. She was eighty three at the time of our visit and most excited about going. While there we checked out the locations of my grandparents' bar and restaurant, the homes of my two uncles and aunt, and the restaurant owned by Uncle Sally, who gave pizza a try after the war. There we saw one of the waiters who worked at The Florence when Nan ate her pies in the late forties and early fifties. He now owned the place. Nan also ran into one of her brothers' childhood friends, still working at the same place for all those years. As expected, there was much that had changed or disappeared over time, but delight and warm memories didn't leave much room for the more philosophical and gloomier aspects of nostalgia. As a bonus, this was the trip on which Nan first experienced the joys of a Grey Goose vodka martini, even if the glass was only half-full.

But the old house-brand martinis the night before we left for Long Island fashioned Nan's most memorable travel moment. We had a very early flight to JFK, so we decided to get to Atlanta the night before and sleep at one of the airport hotels. We set up shop in our rooms and then headed to the hotel restaurant for a nice meal and a couple of drinks. Because Nan's earlier dread of flying had not been entirely eradicated, she still liked to shore up her courage with a drink or two before boarding. This time she had some twelve hours to kill, so she did a little too much shoring up. She wasn't on steady feet when she and my wife walked toward the elevator as I stayed behind to pay the bill. As I reached the hallway, I saw my wife looking around as if she had lost something. Well, she had—she had lost Nan. "I told her I needed to go to the ladies room and to wait by the elevator for me. When I came out, she was gone." My wife headed up to our floor while I went down the hallway where the ballroom and meeting rooms were located. I immediately heard exuberant singing coming from one of the rooms. I saw on the sign by the door that this was a gathering of one of the African-American churches in the Atlanta area. I paused for a moment, thinking "No, no. She couldn't have." A well dressed black man greeting fellow church members at the door looked at me and pointed inside the room. Not only could she have—but she did. Nan was in the first row rocking back and forth with all of her brothers and sisters, holding a woman's hand with her right and waving above her head with her left hand—fully in sway with the music. When I reached her row, I saw her eyes were closed tight as though she were feeling every ounce of the spirit in the midst of the celebrants. I whispered under the singing, "Mom, mom. Come on, mom. Let's get up to our rooms." She opened her eyes and put her arms around my waist, pulling me into the row and the rhythm she was enjoying at the moment. After the singing stopped, the minister began his welcomes.

"I want to say welcome to all our guests tonight."

I imagine he thought "Especially the obviously inebriated white lady here in the first row." He looked up and said, "Come on in—and welcome." Down the aisle came my wife who in her search for her husband and his mother was informed by the gentleman at the door, "They're in here."

After an opening prayer and another song, we finally managed to maneuver Nan out of the row, back down the aisle, and out the door. The gentlemen wished us a pleasant evening and then, I'm sure, looked forward to sharing the tale of the drunken white Italian, Roman Catholic woman who added a little amusement to their joyous Baptist gathering.

Chapter 6
"Baby, You're the Greatest!"

"With the fearful strain that is on me night and day,
if I did not laugh I should die."
Abraham Lincoln

Fully appreciating Nan meant fully appreciating her sense of humor. In spite of a hands-off and often dour father, Nan's mother, sister, and two brothers all loved to laugh—even though her mother and siblings came about their laughs in various and often contrary ways. Nan's own sense of humor frequently and inadvertently confused and insulted those who didn't know her or those whose senses of humor couldn't even approach the same county where this ironic and sophisticated wit resided. I was strongly influenced by her sense of humor, and the laughter and private jokes we shared are among my most cherished memories.

Through all of our challenges, we laughed. Nan taught me see laughter as a dependable hand that pulled one out of the mire—and that its strength to pull never waned. Laughter was our way of defying the enemy, of maintaining control of the battlefield, of finally securing victory. It therefore seemed to me that the hilarious situations, reactions, and responses involving my mother as she passed eighty were a joyous extension of the laughter that was such a major part of our lives. These stories delighted all who heard them, but no one who laughed at them ever lost the respect each held for my mother and the example she set.

Certainly, Nan was influenced by her mother, who not only brightened any company she was in but also served as the best audience any comic could ever have desired. Even when she didn't understand the joke or story situation, my grandmother would join everyone in laughing at the punch line. Even if we knew she couldn't have understood all of what she heard, her laughter was so natural—so sincere that we always felt highly pleased we had made her laugh. She loved jokes and stories about herself as well as those about others she knew and didn't know. Tears would be pushed out by her laughter as she grabbed her stomach and the person sitting nearest to her. In her wonderful way with English she would comment as soon as the laughter began to die down, "Have you ever seen a bigger bunch of nitwits in all your life?" Nan's sister also had a boisterous laugh and shared the family gift of humorous story telling. But my two uncles were utter craftsmen in their comic abilities—yet they were so far apart in the tone and subject matter of their humor.

Nan's younger brother was someone in whose company everyone desired to be. Charming, complimentary, warm, and desirous of entertaining and making everyone laugh comfortably. He told hilarious stories on himself and about such topics as work-related incidents, golf outings, New York traffic, and a series of odd-ball characters he met during his daily activities. He encouraged his wife and children to share their humorous stories and his nephew John to show off his latest impressions of celebrities and politicians. His older brother, however, had a more intimidating sense of humor—replete with insults, outlandish tales (though I never doubted the truth of them), exaggerated confrontations, and shocking predictions. "When John graduates from high school, he'll move back to New York and I'll get him into the numbers racket—and he can go from there." And boy would he get personal. "Nan, it looks like Tom is about to fall asleep. You keeping him up late at nights? Do it when he first gets home from work and he won't be as tired." He'd say that in front of all of us—making my aunt scold him, my grandmother try to show her disapproval before bursting forth in one of her patented laughs, and me ignoring the Freudian aspects of his advice to my mother so that I could laugh without hesitation. This uncle usually took the floor and kept it to himself, entertaining all of us with his comic insults directed at his wife, as well as the rest of us. On one occasion, while he was visiting my grandmother by himself and in front of all of us, he decided to call his dear wife to let her know he had arrived safely (two days after he arrived, of course). He told the operator he wanted to place a person-to-person call—but to someone other than his wife. Rather he asked to speak only with "Blackie," without informing her that Blackie was a dog. While we were breaking up at the dinner table, my uncle kept insisting he would speak only to Blackie while his wife was trying to explain to the operator that she was the one my uncle wanted to talk to. "No, no," he said—"I will only talk to Blackie. Well, I guess he's not home, so I'll call again later, operator"—and hung up the phone. Finally, when my wife and I were first married, we had him over for dinner and as soon as he walked into our apartment, he said to my new bride, "Johnny tells me you're a real icebox in bed." From then on, he tagged her with the nickname "Icebox." We could laugh heartily at this teasing assessment because my wife is anything but.

Nan loved both brothers' senses of humor, although she often had to get over the embarrassment of her older brother's jokes at her expense—as did we all. With these influences on the both of us, we developed a real appreciation for insult comedy. We so enjoyed the televised Friars Roasts and the "insult" stylings of Jackie Gleason, Rodney Dangerfield, Henny Youngman, Bob Hope, Joan Rivers, Dean Martin, and of course Groucho Marx. Whether it was the *Duck Soup* and *A Night at the Opera* Groucho—the *You Bet Your Life* Groucho—or the Talk-Show Guest Groucho, we laughed and laughed at his incomparable wit. But no one delighted us more in this vein than "Mr. Warmth" himself, Don Rickles. From the 1960s on, we looked forward to every appearance Rickles made on television—whether on a variety show, on a special event (such as Reagan's Second Inaugural) on Friar's Roasts, or on the "Tonight Show." For many of these, we watched individually (since I had moved away), but we always compared notes about the latest Rickles spot. A number of his lines crept into our lexicons, and we'd often blurt them out at the same time or I would comment on something we saw in a restaurant, for example, and tag it with a Rickles line. We finally got to see Rickles live, opening for Sinatra, when Nan was seventy. Nan saw much of her older brother in Rickles—and even her younger brother, because Rickles always ended his routines with kindness and compliments.

But Nan didn't approve of the younger generation of insult comics—for example, Andrew Dice Clay, Sam Kinison, Lisa Lampanelli, and Louis C.K.—and even some of the older generation—Redd Foxx and Lenny Bruce, because they were either too rough ("without charm" she noted) or they tended to freely use the "F" word—which she loathed. And then there was

George Carlin, whom she loved when he was doing his milder stuff (such as Al Sleet, the Hippy-Dippy Weatherman), but turned against when he shifted to social and political commentary and spiced up his sets with liberal sprinklings of profanity—including ample helpings of the "F" word. Nothing I could say could make her appreciate Carlin—and I often tried. Yet there was no one performer or show that delighted her more than the thirty-nine filmed episodes of Jackie Gleason's *The Honeymooners*, which ran originally in 1955-56 and have been rebroadcast ever since. The wonderful ensemble cast and the plots for the classic thirty-minute episodes made the show a success for over sixty years, and here too lines from the show entered our lexicons and were employed whenever the occasion called for it, whether it was a reaction to someone we saw, someone who displayed rudeness, or someone who behaved foolishly in public. We began this practice when I was around ten and ended it only a day before Nan passed away, when I quoted Ralph Kramden and told her "Baby. You're the greatest!" Part of my tribute to my mother after her death was to watch the entire thirty-nine episodes of *The Honeymooners* and recall how many of the lines we both quoted to each other in more contexts than I could possibly count.

I should point out that, in addition to Carlin, Nan and I didn't always agree on what was funny. For all we shared in this area, she couldn't abide slapstick or any kind of physical comedy—unless it was subtle. My childhood love of the Three Stooges was always met by the shaking of her head and refusal to sit down and watch one of the shorts with me. (She did concede and let me name our dog Moe, however.) Nor could she abide clowns—and not because they were Stephen-King creepy according to her sensibilities. She never wished to see anyone, for any reason, humiliate or otherwise make a fool of him- or herself. When I first discovered the joys of professional wrestling, she tried to dissuade me from watching because the matches were scripted. She'd tease me about believing the matches were legitimate, and wouldn't listen when I said I was drawn to the characters more than the action. I had always loved the bigger-than-life figures, whether they were from history (Davy Crockett), comic book (Superman, Batman, Flash, et al), film (James Bond), sports (Mickey Mantle and Sam Huff), and even wrestling (Killer Kowalski, Haystacks Calhoun, and Dick the Bruiser). Nan was especially drawn to "cerebral humor" or thinking-person's comedy—for example, Johnny Carson, Shelley Berman, Jack Benny, Billy Crystal, and Jerry Seinfeld. She wasn't a big fan of sketch comedy (never cared for *SNL*) but found plenty of laughs in the two great improvisational comedians Jonathan Winters and Robin Williams. Again, Nan leaned toward the witty rather than the overt in comedy—believing in general that the form should be marked by class rather than crass.

Nan was a teaser, especially gifted at "pulling one's leg"—or rather, pulling one's brain off its hinges. She was quite adept at the deadpan delivery and the "sincere" expression of something either facetious or just plain ludicrous. For example, she would hit servers with the "I'm Italian, and this isn't the way to make what I ordered." The poor server would explain that the chef wasn't from Italy but rather from Arkansas or North Dakota and wasn't quite up on the correct way Italian chefs or Italian grandmothers would make the dish. She would shake her head at the server's mispronunciation of *gnocci and pasta e fagioli* or if they didn't know the difference between *prosciutto crudo and prosciutto di Parma*. If we ordered *calamari*, Nan would look at the fried squid as it was placed on the table and sigh. "I didn't ask for *calamaretti fritti*. I like my squid fresh, not fried. On other occasions, Nan inquired if the restaurant had dishes like *tortelli di zucca* or *bistecca Fiorentina* and watch the server sputter out an "I'll have to check."

Now in each instance, Nan quickly put the server out of his or her misery by stating, "I'm only teasing you, honey." But at other times, she'd let the moment go uncorrected, expecting one of us to make the point that she was just goofing around. Late in her life, when a physician discussed the benefits of a Coumadin regimen, Nan was in one of her playful moods. The physician asked her a series of questions about her basic health and then came to "Do you smoke?" Nan shook her head. "I haven't in thirty years." "Good," the physician replied and then went to the next question on the sheet. "Do you chew tobacco?" Nan's answer: "Yes." "How often," he inquired with his forehead jumping into his hairline. "Every day" was Nan's answer. Nan then clamed up as the physician jotted down some notes. He was half through his lecture on the dangers of smokeless tobacco before my stunned wife found her voice: "Mom, tell him you don't chew tobacco." Nan smiled and responded, "He knows that. How could anyone think I would chew tobacco? I'm not a hillbilly." The physician, who apparently had no sense of humor, flipped his pencil around and grumbled as erased his notes.

The most unappreciated teasing moment of this kind (as far as my wife was concerned) was on another doctor visit, this time to Nan's pulmonologist, a young woman Nan had immediately taken a liking to. When the doctor came in, she offered the cursory "And how have you been doing, Nan?"—to which my mother replied, after pointing to my wife, "I'd do a lot better if she [my wife] stopped hitting me." My wife's mouth took the shape of a beach ball while the pulmonologist, being young and hip, looked at my wife for corroboration that Nan was pulling a fast one. My wife's look of horror was enough to convince her that Nan was joking—although Nan never admitted she was only having fun. On the way back home, my wife said, "Mom, you can't tease about something like that. They're looking for cases where the elderly parent is abused by her children or caretakers."

Apparently the word "elderly" didn't register with Nan, so she just laughed and observed, "Who would think that *you* would abuse me?" We weren't sure whether Nan meant she could kick my wife's fanny if she tried to get physical or that her daughter-in-law was too kind and sweet to ever do such a thing. I'd like to think it was the latter.

Of course being a chip off the old block, I did my share of leg pulling, with Nan as the owner of the leg. My mother had the proverbial "big heart" and was receptive to charity pitches. She designated a certain amount of her monthly budget to go to charitable causes, but since she had signed up with so many, the amounts were often in the $5.00 to $10.00 variety each month. In her last years, we researched each of these charities or so-called charities and found to our shock that many of them took anywhere from fifty to ninety percent of each donation for things other than direct aid, which they couched in such euphemisms as "outreach," "fund raising," and "hands-on costs." Nan refused to believe us at first and wondered how charities directed at children's hunger and disease could in any way be fraudulent. But after showing her several articles and lists on the subject, she came around and allowed us to recommend the charities she should be giving to. Still, the many others (and there were many) who were suddenly cut off continued their appeals by mail and phone.

During one holiday visit when she lived in Florida, I was informed that I was no longer her only child. It seemed that she had "adopted" a Korean boy via mail. I thought I'd throw out an innocent-enough question: "Why, mom?" She informed me the poor kid was having a rough go of it—orphaned at age three and living hand to mouth in a mountain village in South Korea. "You served in Korea when you were in the Army," she reminded me." And I couldn't help thinking of the village you said was near your Army post in the mountains." A nice sentiment, surely, but the "village" outside our post was dominated by prostitutes and black-marketeers, not by needy orphans. "I couldn't help thinking he was born in your village." She then shot me a devilish glance.

"Sorry, mom. I was long gone before his mother conceived him." She told me his name was Huey and showed me his picture. He looked rather well-fed for someone living hand to mouth. But I suppose he had big hands.

It didn't take me long to commence my teasing her about falling for a scam.

"Yeah, I can poor see little Huey now. Just celebrating his forty-second birthday, sitting at a poker table with your latest donation, ordering expensive Cuban cigars, Beluga caviar, *Dom Perignon*, and American hookers—saying every night before he went to sleep with a blonde and red-head on either side, "Thanks for the dough, Nan." And so this routine went year after year for the rest of her life—much to the enjoyment of both of us.

I was one of the lucky ones. I had a parent who had an inexhaustible supply of superlatives when it came to what I had done and was able to accomplish—or what she thought I was accomplishing. Nan's pride meant the world to me and sustained me during many rough times during childhood and adolescence. It was also welcome during my adulthood, except on those occasions when her bragging caused me a bit of embarrassment—even though the memories were amusing if not hilarious. Some of these moments I have noted, but there were many others. For instance, in the late 1960s (and every year afterward), she pulled me aside and lovingly pinched my jaw the way she did when I was three. "I want you to listen to me. I am so proud of you for volunteering to fight for your country." Forget that when I was in the Army I went to South Korea, not Vietnam, and spent my time there fighting boredom, the windy and frigid weather, and the occasional village prostitute I had inadvertently insulted. For years afterward, she was proud of me for a number of achievements—starting and staying in college after my Army days were over, for one. "I was the *only* one in the family and in my circle of friends who believed you wouldn't quit or flunk out." Thanks, mom. Of course, she'd always pick the absolute worst place to do her bragging when I was with her. To a check-out person at the food store, she'd announce loudly enough to be heard back at the meat counter, "This is my son, John. He's just written a book on . . . on . . . what was that again, baby?" It was an academic book on a relatively unknown eighteenth-century writer, but by that time I was already fleeing to the vegetable section so I could hide under the cauliflower. And then there were examples of such bragging at auto-repair shops, paint stores, doctors' offices, and discount stores—where no one could possibly give a damn about my academic successes. Whatever happened to *discreet* expressions of maternal pride, I used to ask her?

I fondly remember one of her last "I want you to listen to me, baby" talks. She was eighty-nine at the time and dealing with yet another medical scare. I assumed she was going to share her thoughts on how we should handle her passing—that is, burial or cremation, the guest list, the music, the readings, and anything else relating to the memorial service. But then she threw me a wicked curve.

"God has a plan for you, John. He surely does. You are going to leave a mark on this world. You're going to contribute something great. I just know it. It's going to be something really, really great." She gave me a "puppy-dog" look seeking corroboration for her belief. Unfortunately, I had to remind her that I had just retired from the university where I taught, and that my mark-leaving days were over, not to mention that what I accomplished during my career was just a "tad" short of being great.

"You know that, don't you, mom?"

Undeterred, she just smiled. "I just know it will be something great because God has plans for you." Pity poor logic; it had no chance when it came to my mother's faith in my destiny, especially when overseen by the Almighty.

There were many incidents that were, shall we say, inadvertently funny—causing her to laugh when these moments were revisited. On the first Election Day after she moved from her townhouse, she decided to drive herself to her new voting place, which she had never seen. As she recounted the story, she couldn't find the place where a friend told her it would be and was about to drive back home when she saw an American flag flying from a fairly tall pole. This had to be it, she thought. She parked her car, grateful there seemed to be only two other cars there (and thus a small line), and walked to the front door and rang the bell. A kindly old gentleman opened the door and was completely shocked when Nan just walked in without even a hello. He got in her way and demanded to know what she wanted. "I'm here to vote" was her now agitated reply. After he responded, she begged his pardon and headed back to her car with tail tucked between her legs. She had tried to force her way into a private residence. She'd been looking for an official building in which to cast her ballot rather the elementary school where the voting actually took place. That flag misled her, she explained.

Sometimes the humor had to wait a number of years before it could be appreciated. When I was between the ages of eleven to seventeen, Nan would ask me to run down to the convenience store for a pack of smokes and a box of tampons (Tampax). The manager of the store knew my mother and blinked at any regulations against selling cigarettes to those under eighteen, which at least saved me from feeling like a criminal—but those tampons. Even attempting to buy my first *Playboy* at sixteen couldn't compare with the dread of being caught purchasing a feminine hygiene product. I pushed the box to the clerk with my eyes lowered to the counter, and never raised them higher than the bottom of the bag into which he paced the cigarettes and tampon box. I thrust my open hand out to accept the change and then turned with the bag in one hand and the change in the other, walking Frankenstein-like out of the store. When I got outside, I looked back through the window to see if any of my friends had been inside and therefore might have seen what I bought. I was lucky the clerk never commented—seriously or humorously—on what my mother had sent me to buy. Had the clerk been female—of whatever age—I know I couldn't have gone through with it. All the way home, I clutched the bag tightly to my chest, preventing a gust of wind from blowing the bag out of my grip and exposing the contents just as a pretty teenage girl or young woman passed me by. Had that happened I would have expired on the sidewalk. Surely, Freud would have loved having me as a patient.

One of my all-time most embarrassing moments—although now I find it hilarious, as did many others at the time—occurred when I was up before a judge owing to my failure to have a driver's license while operating a Vespa motor scooter. I was fifteen at the time and neither I nor Nan realized that a license was required to drive one. My tail light was out one evening as I headed to a friend's house, and I was pulled over. When the license was asked for, I hemmed and hawed about not having one yet. "Leave your motor scooter here and get in," said that police officer. I ended up at the police station, where I had to call Nan to come get me. My court appearance time was set and the next day I secured my permit to drive my Vespa—legally, that is. Nan drove me to my court appearance, and I thought she was going to wait outside the small courtroom while I took my medicine from the judge. But no—she felt compelled to stand up with me and throw me and herself on the mercy of the court. As soon as she launched into "He's a good boy, your honor," I felt the mortification known only to a few, and by the time she was finished with "He attends the teenage dances here in this building" and "He goes to the Catholic church every Sunday," I honestly felt I would have preferred a five-year sentence at a work farm than endure one more special pleading from my mother. Finally, the judge laughed. "He's not going to jail, ma'am." One should have seen Nan when this mercy was bestowed by His Honor. Tears came to her eyes as her body almost sagged, "Thank you, Judge. Thank you, thank you." I almost made it out of there without anything further embarrassing, but as we hit the door, she called back one more "He really is a good boy, Your Honor."

Nan had true wit. By that I mean the mental dexterity to come up immediately with something amusing. Too often, we are confronted with a rude salesperson or fast-food worker and get back to the car, only then to slam the palm of our hands against our foreheads and say, "Damn, I should have said . . ." That's not wit. Wit is quick, sudden, unsaddled. My favorite Nan-as-wit story goes back to the time she served on a jury in Florida when she was in her sixties. The case involved the theft of some dozen bottles of spirits—gin, vodka, rum, bourbon, and Scotch. After both sides gave testimony, the jury was sent back to begin its deliberations. As soon as all of the members arrived in the jury room, the bailiff brought in the evidence—all dozen bottles of the booze. The bailiff set down the bottles on the jury table and then asked if there was anything else he could bring the jury at this time. Nan immediately responded, "How about some ice?"

Finally, my teasing of her (which she always appreciated) could at times be on the devilish side. After I began teaching at the university, I received a plastic parking card, which would raise a gate and allow me to park behind my building on campus. The first time I took Nan to show her my office it was early evening, after almost all classes were over. I drove up to the gate and rolled down the widow. "Mom, I need to get the gate up so we can park." As I slyly slipped my card into the slot without her noticing, I said with a hint of authority, "Hey Bill, this is John. Let me in." The gate immediately rose and Nan sputtered, so impressed by my importance, even though I had only been teaching there less than two weeks when she came up from Florida. I waited until the next day to inform her she'd been had.

Another good one on my part came when Nan was crowing about the "greatest generation" and the many sacrifices and contributions it made to the country (remember that riveting she did during the war). She couldn't help punctuating her remarks with a wicked smile, "That's a lot more than one can say about your generation, John. You baby boomers with your feelings of entitlement, your deafening music, your drug abuse, venereal disease, and general irresponsibility are a far cry from the legacy my generation left behind." Utterly elated that she had stumbled into my trap, I replied smugly, "That's all true, mom, but tell me—which generation raised us?" Regardless, I felt then and certainly now that she was truly one of the greatest of that greatest generation.

But my favorite rapscallion moment occurred when Nan had finally come to Athens to live at age eighty-one. The moving truck would arrive the next day, but she was most anxious to see her new digs, which my wife and I had secured for her—with her permission, remember. Just before the turn onto the road where Nan's townhouse was located there was another residential area and then a rather run-down trailer park. As we passed the first residential area, my perverse and impish spirit took over and I said, "Just wait until you see your new place. It's just the kind of home you can redecorate and make a showpiece." That's when I tuned into the trailer park. At first, Nan was silent, perhaps wondering if I was taking a shortcut to her new place. I added, "Let's see. I think it's right around this curve. Look for the one with the blue siding." That's when I heard a pathetic "John?" I drove on until I stopped in front of the one with the blue siding, which I had earlier seen from the road on the way to Nan's townhouse. "Here it is. Wait until you see it. You'll really love the kitchen. Come on." There was neither sound nor movement from the back seat. My wife could take no more. "He's only teasing you, mom. It's not in here. It's in the next area." It wasn't until I pulled back onto the main road and then into the complex in which her townhouse was located that Nan finally spoke. "John, you little ___." There's really no need to quote the last word (a scatological one consisting of four letters) of her comment. My defense of this diabolical act? As I told her then, "Mom, you taught me everything I know."

Chapter 7
The Battered Lamb
Returns to the Fold

"I know not all that may be coming,
but be it what it will, I'll go to it laughing."
Herman Melville

Oscar Wilde once observed that "Religion is like a blind man looking in a black room for a black cat that isn't there, and finding it." Just as one has to pause to capture the full meaning of Wilde's assessment, so too did I pause—many times—when I considered my mother's relationship with the Roman Catholic Church and with God, Jesus, the Virgin Mary, the angels, and her two favorite Saints—Jude and Anthony. She was a woman of unshakeable faith in God and a religion that did much to shake her loose from its numbers. In addition, there was the matter of "Am I worthy enough" in the eyes of mother church. Being a two-time divorcee (regardless of the treatment she endured from both men), Nan was from ages thirty to fifty-six ineligible for holy communion, and a vivid and painful memory is of my mother remaining seated while everyone else in the pew left to receive the sacrament. But the sadness of this weekly occurrence never stopped us from sharing grins and suppressing chuckles at some of the church's more colorful parishioners, nuns, and even priests. Through the years, Nan offered many amusing to hilarious estimations regarding the rules and changes in the church service and its philosophy.

Coming from an Italian immigrant family, Nan was exposed to the Roman Catholic religion and its many symbols, rules, icons, medals, and holy days. She was baptized as an infant, received her first holy communion at seven, and her confirmation around age twelve. Nan grew up with the mass's liturgy only in Latin (English came in the 1960s), the smell of incense on special days, the separation of parishioner from the altar, the dispensing of communion only by the priest, the covering on all female heads—whether with hat, handkerchief, or doily—and the presence of black and white clad nuns. Like all Catholic children, she was amused by the series of juvenile Catholic jokes and humorous narratives, such as "What did Jesus say when he was on the cross? He said, 'Hey Peter. I can see your house from here'—or the tale of a new usher named Dominic, who sent his "basket on a stick" down the rows to collect money, not just twice during the mass, but each time the priest said *"Dominus vobiscum"* ("the Lord be with you"). Asked to explain, Dominick said that he took collections every time he heard the priest say "Dominic, go frisk 'em." Not funny as all that? Well, perhaps you had to be there.

Going to mass in Nan's old-school Catholic church in the 1920s an early 1930s could be an intimidating experience, as she told me often enough. First, if she or her sister and brothers talked during mass, they would immediately hear their mother shushing them before the nuns descended upon them with looks that suggested the end was near. But that was child's play compared to the stare their father would give them—a look, she said, that could drain blood. I've always believed that the fear her father conveyed made it easier to frighten Nan with the horrors awaiting the sinful in hell. Catholic school did its best to keep its students on the straight and narrow with nuns who never feared parental interference, law suits, political correctness, or union restrictions on how they handled classroom discipline. There were no Ingrid Bergman Sally Field, or Whoopi Goldberg types in Nan's school. Rather the nuns were more of the Louise Fletcher (Nurse Ratched), Margaret Hamilton (Wicked Witch of the West/Elvira Gultch), and Kathy Bates (Annie Wilkes in *Misery*) variety. Whether it was chalk, erasers, canes, or open palms, the nuns had a free hand (sorry) in dispensing any discipline they felt warranted.

When I attended Catholic school from grades 6-8, I knew enough not to report to my mother my transgressions or punishments—whether it was being lashed on the back by Sister Helen's cane for cutting in line or being slapped full across the face by Sister Regina for tripping a fourth grader. Nan always said, "I don't care how bad your grades are, but you better get at least a B in deportment." I'll admit I had no idea what "deportment" meant—until Sister Regina called Nan in for a conference after the tripping episode. It wasn't even close: Nan was far more frightened than I was at meeting the intimidating Sister Regina (all four feet ten of her) and hearing her express disappointment in my behavior. But I did learn the definition of deportment that night—and I cleaned up my act and was a model citizen the rest of my time in Catholic school. Yes, I was blasted full in the face by a chalk-laden eraser hurled by Sister Regina—but she was aiming for the boy sitting behind me. True to her manner and reputation, Sister neither apologized nor gave me permission to leave class and wash my chalky face. When I mentioned to Nan what had happened, she offered sweet solace. "Next time, don't get in the way. A little chalk's not going to hurt you."

Nan was of the generation that held all priests, bishops, arch-bishops, and cardinals in the highest esteem—no exceptions. The local priests she heard mass from over her lifetime varied in personality of course—from the young and vibrant Irish Father Brian Donnan to the old and cantankerous Bulgarian Father Mihail Lacrima. Father Donnan was the type who made going to confession a looked-forward-to event. No matter what you confessed, you'd leave the confessional feeling like a million bucks, as Nan said. (And Nan occasionally went to confession, even though she was told that she shouldn't, since he was ineligible for communion.) She believed that if I went in and admitted to Father Donnan that I slew my mother, he'd say in that wonderful Irish brogue, "Well, that's a good boy, then. You showed initiative. Say three Hail Marys and put your mind at ease." The problem was that Father Donnan's confessional lines—one for each of the two "kneeler-boxes" as we called them—reminded Nan of the queues for Sinatra tickets and me for Santana tickets. But on the other side of the church was Father Lacrima's confessional. Normally his lines would consist only of the most elderly parishioners—those too deaf to hear him scream at them—and the unlucky visitor who was vacationing in South Florida and hadn't been to one of Father Lacrima's masses, which usually took a full twenty minutes longer than Father Donnan's. But owing to the disparity of line-lengths, Sister Helen would take it upon herself to herd half of Father Donnan's line over to Father Lacrima's. She was of course well equipped to do the job, employing not a shepherd's crook but rather that damned cane of hers, which she would apply to the backs, shoulders, and buttocks of those of us in Catholic school. Nan received no such corporal punishment, but if she had, she was the kind of religious woman who would apologize for possibly damaging Sister Helen's cane.

Both Nan and I agreed that going into Father Lacrima's confessional booth was as frightening an experience as we had in those days—and not just middle-school age boys and girls, but those much older as well, including Nan. First, Father Lacrima had no humor, no temperance, and no forgiveness—at least in his manner. It was quite easy to have an idea what sins others had committed just by listening in line. He blasted his reactions to one's stealing, cursing, missing mass, and failure to obey parents. There was no, "Well, that's a good boy, then. Just say three Hail Marys." Father Lacrima offered no encouraging words and his sentences were far rougher and lengthier. A dozen of these prayers, twenty of another, and twenty-five of a third. Nan would laugh when I'd tell her that I was late for my fourth period class because I was down at the altar rail doing my penance. And we didn't skimp on the number assigned. We just believed father Lacrima had a way of knowing if we had said all twelve, twenty, and twenty-five. And Nan would always say, "Tell me the truth. Did you say every prayer?" I didn't have to ask if she did. She probably said an extra five or ten just to be sure. The memory haunted both Nan and me. Entering the confessional box; closing the door behind; kneeling while facing the sliding panel which would soon reveal the frightening outline of Father Lacrima's head; and looking up at the crucifix above the sliding panel wondering which would be worse—having nails driven through our hands and feet or having Father Lacrima reacting to our modest sins? When I was in college, I ran into the word *lachrymose*, which means "tearful or given to weeping; inducing tears; sad." I shared that information with Nan, who replied that she'd never forget the definition since it sounded so much like *Lacrima*, which also meant "tearful" and "inducing tears."

When the English mass began in the 1960s, Nan and I weren't fans of the change. First, she had been hearing the mass in Latin for over forty years and had come to love the language, with its rhythm and majesty. No one interfered with the priest's voice, but after English came in, others took it upon themselves to speak parts of the mass along with the priest—parts they weren't previously supposed to interrupt. Admittedly, we loved hearing Father Donnan's Irish-English, but when Father Lacrima began in with his lumbering and often unintelligible Bulgarian-English it became quite a chore for the rest of us to endure. In the last fifty years of her life, Nan heard the mass in English with Irish, Spanish, French, German, Korean, Italian, African, and Polish accents—some she enjoyed, others not so much. At times she couldn't understand anything the priest said—or so she claimed—and she frequently lamented the unnecessary changes wrought by the Second Vatican Council in the 1960s.

In an attempt to square the church with the modern world, one "brilliant" idea was to deemphasize the more "high" church aspects, including statuary, high mass, stations of the cross, the distance of the parishioner from the altar, and the dispensing of holy communion. Some of these changes evolved over time, but they all seemed to stick in Nan's craw. St. Leo's—the church we attended—decided that the stations of the cross be removed and the statuary be pushed more to the side to make room for a French artist's mural taking up the wall space over the altar all the way to the ceiling. The artist painted Christ on the cross looking up at his heavenly father. In other words, the perspective was from God's place in the sky. Christ's body was therefore elongated—the cross barely seen—and the two colors limited to shades of brown and yellow. Without question, the mural was far more gar-ish than God-ish. Then the powers-that-be decided to get the parishioners in step with the times by transferring to the church a musically inclined nun, who saw to it that the resident organist, who played only for the school choir and occasional guest choir, was canned--leading to the hiring of a young musician right out of college. I was just discharged from the Army in 1970 when I accompanied Nan to our old church. As we and the other parishioners walked in, the new organist launched into "Entry of the Gladiators," the later nineteenth-century military march by Julius Fucik, which was eventually appropriated as the familiar circus entry anthem—or the entrance of the clown song. Hardly *Handel's Messiah*—more a complete mess. After most of the pews were full, the new nun, "Sister Shrill," berated everyone for failing to sing loud enough at last week's mass. It seemed that most in the church had come for religious reasons, not to increase the odds of impressing the panel on an early version of *The Voice*. Sister then asked (ordered) us to take from the pew rack a copy of the song we'd be singing at the start of mass. I almost choked up my breakfast bagel when I saw that we'd be singing the Beatles's "Let It Be"—then a fairly new release. The rehearsal went poorly and we were chastised for our efforts, but before we could try again, the mass began and Sister Shrill grimaced in embarrassment as only one-tenth of the parishioners took a stab at "Let It Be." The rest of us decided just . . . to let it be.

The revelation of child sexual abuse committed by Catholic clergy hurt Nan deeply. She was stunned and at first dismissed the accusations as overblown. Surely, a few (very few) priests had on rare (very rare) occasions violated their vow of celibacy with attractive women who threw themselves at them, but she was hardly prepared to learn that the chastity vows were violated with young boys. She finally accepted the truth of the devastating findings, but she could never talk about it. She remained to her death completely in awe of the priests she met and heard mass from. This was a topic I could never tease her about, criticize, or ridicule in any fashion.

Over the years, Nan initially growled at such changes in church law and the mass, such as no longer requiring a woman's head to be covered, the loosening of rules regarding meat eating on most Fridays, and wearing of "casual" to "shameful" clothing by mass-goers. She eventually came around on all of these changes—although she deplored women in shorts at church and she lived her life without ever attending a guitar mass. But of all the changes made to the Roman Catholic service, the one that bothered her the most was the practice of having "temporary" lay persons—deemed "Extraordinary Ministers of the Eucharist"—to dispense wine and communion wafers. She had grown up, as had I, with no one but a priest placing a host on the parishioner's tongue. And only the priest took the wine during the Consecration. Arguments about the need to save time, especially in large churches, did not fully satisfy Nan as the years went on. She always made her way to whatever line had a priest at the end of it. The wine she would take from a lay person but never the host. Calling these communion assistants "Extraordinary Ministers of Holy Communion" didn't fly with Nan. They were just ordinary Joes and Janes to her way of thinking.

There were times when Nan's observations and teachings regarding God, sin, communion, morality and the rite of confirmation left me sympathetic, laughing, confused, unprepared, or stunned. Ever since I could remember she informed me how lucky I was to be born male and free from the limitations and expectations of young females. She'd tell me of the lectures her mother gave her. "Nan, don't do anything that's a sin. When your father finds out, he'll kill you and then he'll kill me" was one I hope my grandmother was exaggerating—but then again . . . Another example would be my grandmother telling her, "As a girl, you must walk the razor's edge in all you do. If a man falls in the gutter, he'll get up, brush the dirt from his coat, and he'll still be *Mr.* Smith. If you fall in the gutter they will call you a whore." When I was preparing for my First Communion at age seven, Nan said I had to come completely clean with the priest. "Don't leave anything out. To make a good confession, you have to tell him everything." I was so wired when I went in the confessional that as soon as I finished saying "Bless me, Father, for I have sinned. This is my first confession," I began singing like a canary. But among my list of heinous sins, I included such atrocities as jumping on the sofa, pulling my Chinese neighbor Ling's hair, and eating bubble gum I picked up from the sidewalk. It may have been the only case in our church's history when a priest refused to allow the confessor to finish his litany of sins.

As expected, the list of sins as defined by my mother (and taught to her by my grandmother) was long indeed. These three were mentioned daily: leaving food on a plate, leaving at least a quarter of a glass of milk un-swallowed, and refusing to eat whatever was put before me. Each of these three was followed by a reminder of the starving children in Europe. Other sins included walking anywhere near the railroad tracks, coveting my neighbor's Roy Rodgers bicycle with handlebar fringe and saddle bags, and of course my particular favorite—touching myself. (Nan even bought me a yellow book on the subject—endorsed by none other than the Catholic Church.) And then there was Nan's preparing me for my confirmation—a sacrament and the fourth of the initiation rites in the Catholic Church, which in my case was at age eleven. Nan made sure I understood that I would be receiving the Holy Spirit and that a bishop would be performing the ceremony. She explained that he would give me a "light tap" on the cheek and say *"Pax tecum"* (Peace be with you) and then send me off as a defender of the faith. She had witnessed the ceremony only three months earlier; therefore she assured me she was up on how it went.

Oh, but there was one more thing. Nan said I needed to have a sponsor to stand with me during the procedure. Before I could make a suggestion she announced that she had asked my grandfather to do the honors. My grandfather? The man I was completely frightened of? The man who never spent any quality time with his eldest grandson? Instead of hugs and ice cream, I received only grunts and frozen glares from this lion of a man, whose roar was just as bad as his bite. Of course, I realized that my mother was anxious to do something to please him, especially now that he was in his mid-sixties. But how could she sacrifice her only child? Wouldn't a goat have done as well? The day came and grandpa met me at the church and barked, "Are you ready?" After another minute's silence, he muttered with a slight smile, "The new bishop is going to confirm you." New bishop? Not the one "light tap on the cheek" bishop my mother saw in action three months earlier? We started down the line—since it was in alphabetical order I was near the end of it—and the closer we got to the altar I detected a certain sound coming from that location. At first I thought it was a metallic click, but soon realized that it was actually the sound of bone and flesh against bone and flesh. Now about tenth in line I could easily see the other kids coming off the altar area—pressing their cheeks with wild looks in their eyes. By the time I reached number four in line I was panicking. The new bishop must have gone to a seminary fight club because he was hauling off and whacking the confirmation seekers with a full open hand. I cast a look at my grandfather walking at my side. He was now smiling—of course he was. When it was my turn I did what probably every other kid did—except Billy Aaron, who was first in line and didn't know what was coming. I closed my eyes and awaited the blow. When it landed, my grandfather dragged my arm so I'd keep moving. Otherwise I might have dropped down on the spot. When I reached the pew where my mother and grandmother sat, Nan asked if I was all right—although she was laughing too. Only my grandmother saw the assault for what it was. "My poor Johnny. Why did he have to hit you so hard?" I wanted to reply, "Because grandpa paid him," but I received the same blow everyone else did—girls as well as boys.

Nan supplemented her attendance at mass and firm devotion to the church with a wide assortment of religious paraphernalia. Statues ranging in height from two to fifteen inches were collected over many years and displayed in several rooms and on her dressers, but primarily on a series of shelves she had in her bedroom. A good number of effigies of Christ and the Virgin Mary were joined by those of St. Anthony, St. Joseph, and St. Jude, as well as two popes, five *Pietàs* (the Virgin Mary cradling the dead body of Jesus), the twelve apostles, several rosary beads, a host of crucifixes, one Mother Teresa, and assorted medals featuring the Blessed Mother, St. Benedict, and St. Christopher. Her desk drawer was stuffed with religious and Mass cards she had accumulated since girlhood. If she received a request for a donation (and she received *many*), she cut out and kept whatever religious depiction was on the letter and saved that. If the organization sent a dime or quarter asking that ten to fifty times that amount be donated, Nan kept the money and gave it to the church on Sunday. She felt it sinful to throw anything out that depicted—in photo or even illustration—the image of God, Jesus, Mary, the Saints, or the Pope.

As noted, accidents did happen. She stumbled several times into her shelving unit and knocked several of the items to the ground, causing some of them to break. An armless Christ or a headless St. Anthony would not be tossed. God had given us glue for a reason. Of course, a number of the reattachments were less than perfect. Sometimes a piece of shoulder or leg crumbled into unglueable pieces; therefore one Jesus would have a hole where his left knee once was and another blessed the multitudes with severed hands. When my wife took over the gluing duties, she did her best to put a chin back on St. Joseph and a head back on Pope John Paul II. As I also mentioned, nothing tickled Nan and me more than the manger scene she displayed every Christmas. She bought it when I was six, and then it included the manger, the infant Jesus, Mary, Joseph, a shepherd, the Three Kings, two sheep, a donkey, and an angel. But figures somehow disappeared over the years, until all that was left were the baby Jesus, Mary, Joseph, one sheep, and only one of the Magi, the one with the frankincense, Caspar—"the friendly Wise Man" as I used to call him. But poor, poor Joseph. The top right-hand side of his head was missing—parts of the temporal and parietal sections of the skull, to be clinical about it. I would entertain Nan by coming up with blasphemous reasons for the head wound—from an agitated donkey kick to a high-powered rifle shot from one of Mary's jilted old boyfriends to a deadly and explosive reaction to Frankincense.

When she was ninety-one, I took Nan to church and assured her I'd be back to pick her up when mass was over. But before I headed back, I received a call from my wife's cell telling me that she had a blow out and was parked in someone's driveway. I assumed I'd have enough time to meet her, change the tire, and then get to the church to pick up Nan. Unfortunately, the driveway on which my wife's car rested was all sand and dirt. The car jack kept slipping as I raised the car's frame, causing me to call my son-in-law to come with his larger jack. Since Nan didn't believe in cell phones, I called the church office and told them to look for her and tell her I'd be on my way as soon as possible. With the tire finally changed and my wife back on the road, I headed to the church, assuming that Nan would be sitting on one of the outside benches or in the church office. She was at neither location. And so the search began. No one in the office had seen her. No one standing outside had seen her. I thought at first she might be sitting in the church itself, even though there was a mass currently in progress. It was a Spanish mass, but the church secretary managed to slip a note to Father Moreno while the scripture lesson was being read by one of the parishioners. As he stood to give the homily, he addressed the attendees in Spanish. I could make out the words *El esta buscando a su madre* ("He is looking for his mother) as Father Moreno pointed at me standing in the rear entrance. Naturally, everyone turned and smiled at me, followed by Father Moreno asking if Nan was presently sitting among the parishioners attending the mass. I retreated from the doorway as no one came forward to claim she was my mother, and I saw a teenage girl heading for the bathroom. "Excuse me, but I can't find my mother. Would you mind looking in the bathroom and seeing if there's an elderly woman sitting on the. . . I mean, if she's in there." The girl nodded as though she had run into one of those men her mother warned her to run away from. After a few moments, she came back out, shook her head no, and high-tailed it to the parking lot.

My next assumption wasn't a pleasant one. Perhaps Nan had suffered some kind of health event and was presently wandering around the outside of the church not knowing where or who she was. I went on a hunt, looking all around the church and then down the sidewalk going both east and west from the church. I saw nothing. Thank goodness there was no ambulance in the busy street, but she might have crossed the road and headed down any one of the side streets going in several directions. I checked one more time with the church office, a janitor, another priest, and one of the women who knew my mother, but none had seen her. I was about to brave the traffic to see if she was somewhere on the other side when my cell phone rang. It was my wife, whom I had called and kept up to date on my searches. "I don't know why, but I called her house," my wife announced. "She's home and wants you to come by to get her CD player to work. "Did you tell her I was looking all over for her at the church?" I softly inquired.

"She said that when you didn't show up she asked one of the women she knows to drive her home."

"Without telling anyone at the church to call me?"

"Right."

"Without telling the church secretary to tell me when I got there?"

"Right. She said she just figured you'd know she was home."

Of course. What was wrong with me?

Less humorous, however, was the fact that her status as a Roman Catholic was ruptured following her re-marriage after divorcing my father at age thirty. That made her ineligible to receive Holy Communion, according to church law. I'll quote from one source explaining the rule: "It can happen that one of the spouses is the innocent victim of a divorce decreed by civil law; this spouse has not contravened the moral law. There is a considerable difference between a spouse who has sincerely tried to be faithful to the sacrament marriage and is unjustly abandoned, and one who by his own grave fault destroys a canonically valid marriage." Nan was therefore still eligible to receive communion after her divorce from my father. But when she married H2 she learned that she had violated church law, which in part quotes Luke 16:18: Jesus said, "Whoever divorces his wife and marries another commits adultery against her; and if she divorces her husband and marries another, she commits adultery." The new union cannot be valid if the first marriage was lawful. If the divorced are "remarried civilly, they find themselves in a situation that objectively contravenes God's law. Consequently, they cannot receive Eucharistic Communion as long as this situation persists." In short, Nan was out of luck. (See https://www.catholic.com/qa/may-a-person-who-is-divorced-but-not-remarried-receive-communion.)

I remember so may Sundays when my mother was the only one in the pew who did not go to the altar for communion. She would pray—usually with her rosary—the entire time communion was given. It was so distressing for me to see the expression on her face—-one of want and deep disappointment——that I stopped looking at her during that part of the mass. I could only guess at the intensity of the hurt she experienced. I felt guilty going myself, although she always insisted I do so. Therefore, as a boy I began to build resentment for such canonical law, knowing that many others very likely took communion with un-confessed sins on their souls. Nan's marriage to her third husband Tom (a non-Catholic) brought her no closer to receiving communion, of course, and her "banished" status continued until she reached age fifty-six.

Twelve years after marrying Mr. Right, she read an article about the church's decision to become more "liberal" in dispensing annulments—which would then wipe the slate clean enough to allow the marriage-annulled to receive communion. She would have initially to make the case that her first marriage to my father wasn't lawful or appropriate in the eyes of the church in order to be "cleansed" enough to receive the Eucharist. Wishing to act on this possibility, however slim, she made arrangements to speak with a young priest about the chance of being accepted back to the church with full rights restored. He got the ball rolling and, after a series of embarrassing, sometimes humiliating, and time-consuming interviews with other priests at the Diocese offices seventy miles away, Nan and Tom had their first marriages expunged—meaning the vows never happened in the eyes of the church. Somehow her second marriage (the civil ceremony) was washed away as well, and Nan and Tom re-married in a Catholic church. On that day she received her first communion in twenty-six years. I vividly recall sitting next to her after she received the host and watching the glow on her face. Few events in her life meant as much as this one did, and I could only lament that she was denied the sacrament in the first place. But I decided not to allow any bitterness to spoil the moment for me and I relished in the happiness exuding from Nan. Yet as the mass came to an end I sat in the pew thinking about the annulment—smiling over the fact that my mother had something in common with Henry VIII, who of course annulled his own marriage to Catherine of Aragon so he could marry Anne Boleyn. Then another thought kicked me in the head. The annulment of my mother's marriage to my father (it never happened) meant that I was now—at the age of thirty—a bastard in the eyes of the church. I mean to say I was illegitimate. Good thing I wasn't of the Royal Family, because I wouldn't be able to become king or inherit title. This new status delighted me to no end. When I shared my new title with Nan, I expected her to react with horror. Instead she grinned and said that I shouldn't worry, because she'd always "own up" to her "bastard child."

Chapter 8
"You Call This Music?"

"Smiling novices, I can hear the music of your laughter of joy."
Mother Teresa

When Nan was a teenager and listening to her treasured recordings of Benny Goodman and Glenn Miller, her gruff and opera-loving father opened the door to her room and grumbled, "You call this music?" Nan's relationship with music, television, film, and stage productions sustained her (and me) during many rough years and continued to please and comfort her during the final period of her life. Showing that she was her daddy's girl at least in one sense, she liked to open my bedroom door and snarl, "You call this music?" which she had to shout because John, Paul, George, and Ringo were dialed up to seven and eight on the volume meter. She'd playfully harass me until her death about there being nothing in Ringo's repertoire that could come anywhere close to Gene Krupa's iconic drumming in the 1930s and 40s. Together we watched and listened to much relating to the musical and visual arts, and I learned a great deal from her about old music and old films that has remained with me to this day—and, I might add, has come in handy whenever I've played trivia.

Nan's birth coincided with the beginning of radio broadcasting to the home market, and by the time she was six both NBC and CBS were disseminating musical, dramatic, comedic, and sports-related programming. As a young girl (pre-Depression), Nan's family listened to an Atwater Kent wooden-cabinet model costing around $80.00, which would roughly equal one thousand dollars in today's money. Ten years later, the family, now much better off financially, had an RCA console model in the living room costing around three hundred dollars (close to five thousand dollars of buying power now). On this radio Nan's family listened to Roosevelt's Fireside Chats; comedies such *Fibber McGee and Molly, The Goldbergs, Burns and Allen, Amos and Andy;* and comedians, particularly Jack Benny, Bob Hope, Groucho Marx, Red Skelton, and Abbot and Costello. Having first priority, however, were *The Voice of Firestone*, the brand-new NBC *Symphony Orchestra*, and the live Metropolitan Opera broadcasts. Nan's father's soft spot was classical music, especially opera. For him, this was the only legitimate form of music, even though he also enjoyed Italian and Neapolitan songs such as "*'Avucchella*," "*Funiculì, Funiculà*," "*O sole mio*," and "*Torna a Surriento*."

But for Nan (when she was able to commandeer it), the radio was most significant when it broadcast the popular singers of the time—Bing Crosby, The Andrews Sisters, and Fred Astaire (yes, he also sang)—but primarily the Big Bands, most notably those of Glenn Miller, Benny Goodman, and Artie Shaw. It was during Nan's listening to Goodman's "Sing, Sing, Sing" when she was fifteen that my grandfather made his famous statement "You call this music?" The 1940s continued broadcasting these and newer artists on radio broadcasts Nan listened to—including her favorites Tommy and Jimmy Dorsey, Dick Haymes, Peggy Lee, Harry James, Perry Como, and some guy named Sinatra.

Yet she couldn't command the radio (again, whenever she got use of it) to play what she wanted when she wanted. But the phonograph could. Nan's family, like many others who could afford them, had an RCA "Victrola" to play their 78 rpm shellac discs. Nan's small record collection began at this time, with discs selling between thirty five to fifty cents each. In the 1940s the phonograph became a piece of furniture for the family, and as the forties gave way to the fifties, the family phonograph was supplemented by the smaller compact models—all with automatic changers playing the new 33 1/3 and 45 rpm records. Nan purchased a small one for me when I was eight and I spent my allowance money on 45s and the occasional EP (4 songs). Nan would listen in on what I had and although she didn't think too much of Elvis, there were some records I bought that she appropriated, leaving me to hunt in her collection for the 45 I spent my allowance money on. "Blueberry Hill" by Fats Domino, "Who's Sorry Now" by Connie Francis, and "Mac the Knife" by Bobby Darin were three she purloined and kept with her collection up until her death.

As I got older and the music became more electric-guitar oriented, she stayed away from my room—to "protect" her hearing, she exclaimed. But on occasion she found something I played to her liking, such as George Harrison's "Something" and Judy Collins's "Both Sides Now," and gave me credit for having at least some musical taste. But when she was "bombarded" (her word) by The Kinks, The Who, Hendrix, and Cream, she'd stick her head in and shout over the wailing guitar and pounding drums, "You call this music?" I'd laugh and threaten to convert her to the dark side. She often referred to the Beatles appearances on the Ed Sullivan Show and mockingly praised Ringo for his congenial backbeat, flopping her head back and forth as Ringo often did, and then demand that I listen to Gene Krupa playing his guts out on the famous 1937 recording of "Sing, Sing, Sing." She wouldn't relent until I admitted that Krupa was the better drummer.

When I was fifteen and had a paper route, I managed to save $150.00, with which I bought our first stereo record player. We had up to that point a console model so she could listen to our records in high fidelity. I surprised her with the new set up by insisting that she kept her eyes closed until I started playing the demo record that came with the purchase. Both our eyes expanded and then shifted left and right as we "watched" the sound go from speaker to speaker. We were both like two seven-year-olds, utterly amazed by a magician's bag of tricks. The only problem was that Nan had to re-purchase in stereo so many of the albums she already owned. Fortunately for me, my purchase of albums was limited (pre-Beatles), but Nan had bought nothing else for ten years. Still, there was no going back now; therefore, she put aside new clothes and house decorations in order to welcome the new stereo discs. As for anyone, stereo soon became the norm, but she and I never forgot our eyes dancing left and right when we first heard the new stereo record player, as though we were watching an audio ping-pong match.

For all our mutual teasing, Nan taught me much about the music of her period and of music in general. I was one of the few of my age who was up on his Glenn Miller, Benny Goodman, and Frank Sinatra. In addition, she purchased many Broadway show albums—usually with cover artists, not original Broadway casts—at discount rates, usually purchased at food stores. I soon became a fan of all Rodgers and Hammerstein musicals particularly, as well as those of Cole Porter, Lerner and Loewe, and Irving Berlin. Many of the songs from these shows of the forties, fifties, and sixties were covered by Nan's favorites, including Sinatra, Tony Bennett, and Dean Martin. She would point out particular orchestral and vocal moments, and we'd talk about them and why they were important to the success of the song. She also had a number of "sing along" albums by Mitch Miller and others, and from them I learned to appreciate the tunes pre-dating her teenage years, such as "Ol' Man River," "California, Here I Come," "Alexander's Ragtime Band," "By the Light of the Silvery Moon," and George Gershwin's classic "Rhapsody in Blue." We would sing them together and occasionally harmonize, providing our normally tense domestic life with H2 with much needed escape and delight.

Nan had her favorite singers throughout her formative years and into adulthood and old age. They ranged from the very popular Tony Bennett and Dean Martin to the lesser appreciated Sergio Franchi and Engelbert Humperdinck. But no one could tickle her fancy like Old Blue Eyes. Nan heard Sinatra on the radio (Lucky Strike's *Your Hit* Parade) and on record when he sang with Harry James and Tommy Dorsey. But it wasn't until she went with some friends to see him at the Paramount Theater at the end of 1942, when she was twenty-one, that she witnessed first-hand the full magic of Sinatra. Frank had been looking for singing gigs after he left Dorsey in the fall of 1942 and late in December he secured a spot at the Paramount right after Benny Goodman performed. The reaction to singer was electric—not again matched until Elvis and later the Beatles. The comedian Jack Benny couldn't believe all the screaming and carrying on for a crooner he had barely heard of, but that night five thousand youth would be served—and heard. Even Goodman admitted that he didn't know what the hell was going on.

Not surprisingly, the Paramount extended Sinatra's run initially for a month-and then two, with Frank doing anywhere from six to even eleven shows a day. Roses thrown at the stage were supplemented by panties and bras. Frank's teenage girl fans became "Bobbysoxers" with their rolled-to-the-ankle white sox. Swooning often followed on the heels of Sinatra's crooning. Times Square traffic became snarled with screaming, shrieking, and hysterical girls and young women, while others stayed in their seats so they could see the next show—and the next. Frank even had sandwiches brought to the sitters to show his appreciation for their enthusiasm and dedication. This was the atmosphere when Nan came into the City and became as addicted as those five and six years younger than she. I have studied as many photographs of that time as possible—hoping to see my mother in full-fledged frenzy. Regretfully, I made it only to the point of "Well, that *could* be her."

Throughout some very trying years, Nan took comfort and enjoyment from her music, Sinatra being supplemented by Dean Martin and other artists, from soloists to orchestras. I can never recall a time when the record player, hi-fi, or stereo were silent for a single day. When Nan finally found happiness with Tom, they shared a common interest in music and discovered together several artists they hadn't listened to previously. For example, they saw the clarinetist Pete Fountain during a trip to New Orleans, and Fountain became a favorite from then on. With the loss of Tom when she was sixty-two, Nan initially intended to keep the stereo quite during her mourning period, but she discovered that her music was an important source of comfort—and it remained so for the rest of her life.

When she bought her first car that contained a cassette player, Nan was overjoyed by the prospects of hearing her favorite music while she drove. But that would require repurchasing her albums on cassette—and as she did when she switched from mono to stereo discs, she bemoaned the cost of the new technology. At this time CDs were also beginning to make their mark, but she'd have none of that. Instead she kept her records and stereo and bought a cassette player for her house, so that any new albums she purchased could be played both in house and in the car. Yet she wouldn't listen to me when I suggested she purchase a new system with cassette player and decent speakers. "Why waste the money?" she countered. "The tape player [she always called the cassettes "tapes"] works well enough." But she'd often complain that they never sounded as good as her records. "Of course," I reminded her, "You have better speakers with the stereo than you have with that $19.95 cassette player. Years later my son made cassettes for her of her favorite individual songs, which she couldn't believe was possible. She never caught on to the dubbing and recording techniques that allowed her to listen just to her favorite selections on an album.

Much to my shock, Nan (now in her eighties) pointed to the CD players at the local Best Buy and asked if I thought she should get one. I managed to say yes, and we left the store with a nice system, with good quality speakers. I also bought her a Sinatra CD in appreciation of her willingness to upgrade musically. When she heard Old Blue Eyes on a good sound system, she beamed with happiness. Even though she asked if the CD discs could be played on her stereo through the stylus, she seemed this time to accept with little protest that she'd have once again to buy her favorite recordings in another form. She next had installed a CD player in her 1997 silver Mustang, so now she could really enjoy her drives about town. She bought the CDs and only complained about how she could once buy record albums for $3.99 to $5.99 a piece. I reminded her that while more expensive CDs were more durable and one couldn't accidentally drag the phonograph needle across a vinyl disc causing permanent scratch marks and altered sound. Besides, my son could now make "mixes" of her favorite songs on CDs, cutting down on Nan's costs and her complaints.

When Nan's sight began to go in her late eighties, playing her music became much more of a challenge. The CDs played fine—that is, once Nan could find the "play" button. Locating a particular track on a CD was now almost impossible because she couldn't see the right button to click or the number of the track on the device. Working the tape player, which had now been relegated to the kitchen area, was even more difficult. The play, fast-forward, rewind, and volume buttons had to be guessed at, with the result that Nan kept turning the player on and off when she wanted the sound louder and rewinding when her intention was for the tape to go in the opposite direction. My wife tried her best to make things easier for Nan by putting bright tape below each button—different colors for the differing commands. Yet even that didn't always work. "I forgot whether red meant stop or rewind" and "Is that blue or green—I can't tell" being common replies.

But our most memorable music event would have to be surprising Nan with tickets to a Sinatra concert almost fifty years after she saw him at the Paramount. While visiting us in Georgia, Frank appeared at Chastain Park—a popular amphitheater and outdoor venue in Atlanta. Our seats weren't half bad, although we couldn't afford to sit up close to the elevated stage and have our meal catered in with champagne chasers. Nan's excitement was impossible to suppress, of course, and it was all she could do to tolerate the opening act. She muttered such comments as "How long is she going to keep singing," "I don't want Frank to be half asleep by the time he gets out on stage," and "Get off the stage, honey. We didn't come to see you." There was a second opening act, but this one Nan—now age sixty-nine—anticipated with considerable pleasure. Our favorite insult comedian—Don Rickles— took the stage and was as good as we hoped he'd be. As expected, he shredded the opening act and the conductor of the orchestra—none other than Frank Sinatra, Jr. When Sinatra came out and "kicked" Rickles off the stage, the moment was right and ripe for a wonderful evening. And although he was seventy-five, Old Blue Eyes sounded great. Great, that is, until several near the front pushed aside their catered lobster and bottles of *Moet* and lit sparklers to add "magic" to the concert. That is, if "magic" meant "voodoo." The sparklers set off considerable amount of smoke which the wind blew right into Sinatra's face. He started his set with "You Make Me Feel So Young" and was cruising by the time he began "The Summer Wind," which in this case helped bring the smoke into his lungs, causing him to add coughing and throat clearing to the wonderfully melodic lines of "My Way." Nan's way—if she could have had it—would have been to dismantle finger- by-finger the idiots who lit the sparklers, and then feed those digits to the wildlife that inhabited the area around Chastain Park.

Nan was in her twenties and married when television took up residence in the home. At the end of the war, most Americans didn't even know what a television was—but within five years everyone wanted one. The family's first set was a mere ten inches wide on the diagonal, although her parents could soon afford one of the sixteen-inch models and within a few years upgraded to a twenty inch console model—all of them black and white. Some of Nan's favorite shows of the late forties and early fifties were the *Texaco Star Theater* (with Milton Berle), the *Jackie Gleason Show*, a number of the game shows, including the infamously-rigged *Twenty One* and *The $64,000 Question*, and several of the live drama series. When she wasn't at work, she would sweetly tolerate my addition of *The Lone Ranger* and *Howdy Doody*—and in the later fifties *The Three Stooges*. We had a seventeen-inch and later a nineteen-inch television, which was a fairly big screen back then. Only one television, however, until the mid 1960s, when we had a seventeen-inch black and white in the "TV Room" and a color television in the main living room--a twenty-one-inch RCA console model costing around five hundred dollars. What a wonder that was. I can still recall our mouths hanging open when the NBC Peacock spread its colorful feathers at the beginning of each color show.

Nan's television size made it to twenty-seven inches by the time she moved to Georgia at age seventy-nine, but we easily convinced her to double that size, noting that the new wide-screens were affordable and they would help if her eyesight became less "sharp" as she got older. As for her favorite shows at this time, she complained that there were no real variety shows on anymore—such as *The Ed Sullivan Show, The Dean Martin Show*, and *This Is Tom Jones*, all of which ended their runs between 1971 and 1974. As Nan reached her eighties and to the end of her life, there would be the occasional show she wouldn't miss—such as *Dancing with the Stars*—but she was most devoted to the five-times-a-week episodes of *Days of Our Lives*. She began watching the soaps in her later twenties, and when she wasn't working during the day she would park herself in front of the set and view such favorites as *Search for Tomorrow, The Guiding Light, The Edge of Night, As the World Turns, The Young and the Restless*, and *All My Children*. But *Days of Our Lives* was her baby, which she started watching when it debuted in 1965, expanding from thirty minutes to an hour ten years later. The characters became like my siblings, even though I never saw a full episode. Over the years, the Blacks, the Bradys, the Johnsons, the DiMeras, the Hortons, the Donovans, the Kirakises, Chloe Lane, Kate Roberts, Maxine Landis, Doug Williams, Melanie Jonas, and Calliope Jones all vied with me for Nan's love and attention. Hell, these characters came and went, but I stayed loyal. And yet . . . "John, I'd love to see that movie, but I don't want to miss tomorrow's *Days of Our Lives*. Something big is going to happen." I'd reply, "Mom, something big happens every day. Whatever that's big tomorrow will be big again the next day—and it will be joined with something else that's big. Doesn't anything unimportant ever happen on that show?" None of these characters came to Nan's memorial service, but I'm sure that when I see her again and mention that fact she'll say, "No but something big was happening that day in Salem and they didn't want to miss it."

Nan also was a big fan of the *Turner Classic Movie* channel. Her favorite films from the thirties, forties, and fifties made their appearances on the channel—mercifully free of commercials. But as she aged and could no longer read the small print in TV listings, watching a full movie was mainly hit and miss. She'd moan about coming in halfway through *Casablanca* or at the end of *Pal Joey*. And boy would she howl when she learned that her favorite musicals of the thirties—such as *42ⁿᵈ Street, The Gay Divorcee,* and *Gold Diggers of 1935*—were on *after* she went to bed at 10:00. But years earlier, she found the answer to all her scheduling problems with the advent of the VCR and VHS cassettes. She bought one of the units in the mid-1980s for five hundred dollars—a large expense back then. Cassettes of movies were almost unaffordable, although Nan sprung for the one movie she most dearly wanted to own—*Gone with the Wind*—for a staggering ninety bucks. At first she mainly dubbed favorite movies from the television broadcast—most with the commercials—but at times she dubbed as she watched, pausing the recording during the advertising. She quickly collected over forty dubbed tapes—some with two or three movies on a cassette, others with a combination of a movie and selected television shows. But in 1987 the cassette prices came down to below thirty dollars, so Nan bought a few more of the classic movies, but not many. As the 1990s progressed, the cost of these cassettes fell further, allowing Nan to build her collection to an impressive size. As for renting cassettes, when she first inquired, it cost an individual one hundred dollars just to "belong" to the rental club (never mind the cost of renting a cassette), which she refused to do then or at any time later when the membership costs were phased out.

Of course, technology marches on, much to our delight and expense, and the DVD player was pushing the VCRs off the shelves and into the refuse heap. But Nan resisted. "The tapes are good enough for me," she often remarked. When she moved to Georgia she eventually came around to the idea that the old dubbed tapes were of poor quality and that, now having watched a few movies on our DVD player, she would enjoy seeing her favorite old films on the best technology available for home use (let's just ignore Blue Ray for now). I told her she could get a combo VHS/DVD unit so that her VHS tapes wouldn't be wasted. At first all went well. She bought a good number of DVDs and alternated between watching her tapes and her new discs. But when her eyesight became affected by her macular degeneration, new problems began.

Simply playing a manufactured VHS cassette wasn't too difficult for Nan, seeing that the tape began to play as soon as it was loaded. She could turn her television set to Channel 3 and then enjoy the movie. But if she wanted to stop the tape, she would have trouble locating the stop button—and never mind the problem confronted whenever she needed to fast forward or rewind. Still, she could watch her movies—that is, until she upgraded her television unit and had to negotiate her remote to be able to play cassettes or DVDs. It was impossible for her to find the button that switched from television viewing to cassette/DVD viewing. Invariably, she'd hit the wrong button on her forty-six-button remote and she'd end up unable to watch anything. She'd try over and over again until only a floating icon remained on the screen. Then I'd get the phone call.

When I arrived to untangle the electronic knot, Nan would launch into her litany of complaints. "Why did they make it so difficult to watch a damned program? I used to put it in Channel 3 and that's all I needed to do. Now you have to be scientist just to change the channel. Show me what you're doing so I can fix the damn thing the next time." I'd show her, but she only became more confused and intimidated by the remote. On several occasions, we'd pick her up for lunch and I'd ask how things were going on *Days of Our Lives*. "I didn't see it yesterday." Why not? "I hit something on that damned remote and I couldn't watch a thing." Why didn't she call me? "I hate having you come over for something like that." I always assured her that I would come whenever the TV didn't work. And as much as it was inconvenient from time to time, I hated to think of her being unable to enjoy her programs—especially *Days of Our Lives*. My wife tried every way to make the remote easier for her. She taped up the entire remote like it was an Egyptian mummy from the days of Tutankhamun in fourteenth century B.C.—leaving uncovered only the buttons Nan needed for basic watching of the television. Still, the wrong buttons would be pressed and we'd be back at square one. By the time Nan hit ninety, she had given up on watching her movies, seeing that she couldn't jump through the multiple electronic hoops to get them to play.

As for *going* to the movies, Nan was like everyone else of her generation; she went often and allowed the films and their stars to inhabit many of her waking thoughts. Clark Gable, Cary Grant, Errol Flynn, and Fred Astaire were her male heartthrobs, and Rita Hayworth, Lana Turner, Ingrid Bergman, Merle Oberon, and Olivia de Havilland were the women she admired the most for their talent and beauty. When she was a girl of ten, she and her older brother took in a little picture called *Frankenstein*. When they came out, they had two and half blocks to walk before she was able to dive under the covers and hide from Boris Karloff, whom she was sure had been spotted terrorizing southern Long Island. With her brother's deliberate attempts to frighten her by pointing to imaginary monsters closing in on them, Nan revealed to me that it was the longest and most terrifying walk of her life.

But mainly, as it was for everyone else, the cinema was an escape from the harsher realities of life, and from the 1930s through the middle of the 1960s, Nan never missed a chance to hunker down with popcorn and a soft-drink at a local movie theater. After she married Tom, her movie-going was more occasional—one reason being that she so enjoyed being with the man in her life, but also because, as she told me, "Movies had changed too much" from the late 1960s onward. The new breed of Hollywood stars—Dustin Hoffman, Catherine Deneuve, Clint Eastwood, Julie Christie, Charles Bronson, Faye Dunaway, Jack Nicholson, Jacqueline Bisset, Gene Hackman, and Jane Fonda didn't quite measure up to her favorite stars of the past—and the grittier anti-hero films never appealed. She certainly enjoyed blockbusters like *The Godfather* films and *Patton*, yet she wouldn't even bother to see *Star Wars, Jaws,* or *The Exorcist*—the first because it was filled with "machine characters"; the second because it was "bloody and scary"; and the third because it was "too frightening to see." After Tom died, Nan went to the occasional movie by herself and later with us—the last being *Lincoln* when she was ninety—but television and videos made up the bulk of her film watching.

One of my most cherished memories was any occasion she took me to the movies when I was a boy—from the ages of six to seventeen. I therefore saw many movies I wouldn't have seen had I made the choice of films myself. True, some of the films she took me to would appeal to young or teen-age boy, such as the circus film *Trapeze, Ben Hur, Spartacus, Lawrence of Arabia, The Bridge on the River Kwai,* and Hitchcock's *The Birds*. Nan always took me to musicals—*Guys and Dolls, The King and I,* and *South Pacific*—and I received some bible/religious training through *The Ten Commandments* and *The Greatest Story Ever Told*. In addition, I saw many movies I might not have appreciated at the time but I have since found masterful, including *Marty, Elmer Gantry, Breakfast at Tiffany's, Giant,* and Hitchcock's *Vertigo*. Another category were the films no mother should ever take her young son to see: *The Seven Year Itch, Butterfield 8, A Streetcar Named Desire, Baby Doll, Peyton Place, Cat on a Hot Tin Roof,* and, yes, *Lolita.* For my seventeenth birthday, Nan gave me the choice of film we were to see—and it just so happened that it was the last film we saw together (just the two of us, that is) in a theater until she moved to Georgia almost forty years later. Reflecting the comfort we had with each other, as well as the precedent of the naughty films she took me to, I chose the then notorious shocker based on the Harold Robbins novel, *The Carpetbaggers*. And how could I ever forget that I first felt the pangs of love after Nan took me to the period drama (and forever since panned) *Raintree County* when I was only ten years old. No, it wasn't a girl sitting next to me or the young lady selling Jujyfruits and Junior Mints behind the concessions counter. It was rather the stunning beauty on the big screen—Elizabeth Taylor. For some time afterward, my stomach ached as my mind concentrated on the beautiful Elizabeth—then aged twenty-five. When Nan reminded me that Miss Taylor was twenty-five and fifteen years my senior, I said that I didn't care one hoot about the age difference.

Up until the time I graduated from high school, Nan was a devoted reader of several movie magazines—which included features on the new films and plenty of gossip about the stars. Our extra bedroom closet was piled high with copies of *Motion Picture, Photoplay, Silver Screen, Screen Life,* and *Modern Screen*. After she married Tom and her movie-going became more infrequent, she tossed out her collection as blithely as she did my baseball cards when I was in the Army—never considering, of course, that there might have been money in them thar magazines. As for her reading in general, Nan read more often pre-Tom—and I can recall some of the more racy covers of her sensational paperback novels—the kind she could finish in one afternoon or evening. She would also read the occasional best seller, but she would always look forward to the film version of these books. As for non-fiction, she'd peruse volumes on exercise and diet, interior decorating, and fashion, but only rarely something historical. She didn't actually say it, but I could her thinking, "I can get my history through my movies." Once we were discussing Queen Elizabeth I, and she disagreed with a point I made about the Renaissance monarch by noting, "Bette Davis never did that in *The Private Lives of Elizabeth and Essex* [1939] or in *The Virgin Queen* [1955]."

Every once in awhile she'd read something baseball related, that is if it had to do with her beloved Brooklyn Dodgers. Having been to Ebbets Field several times in her life, Nan had a special fondness for the boys in blue, particularly because they always managed to fall short of winning the big prize. And this is not to forget the 1951 team that blew a 13 ½ game lead in mid-August and ended up tied with the hated New York Giants at season's end—only to lose when Bobby Thompson hit the famous "Shot Heard 'Round the World." Nan had to go to work at my grandfather's bar and confront her devilish older brother, who just happened to be a rapid Giants fan. Big brother made the Dodgers' defeat even more painful, especially as he greeted her entrance with the first verse of the song, "Sound Off": "The heads are up, / The chests are out, / The arms are swinging / And cadence count. / Sound off (sound off)./ Sound off (sound off)." That the Giants lost to the Yankees in the World Series didn't help much, since Nan's father, mother, and younger brother were big Yankees fans.

In any event, Brooklyn fans embraced the motto "Wait 'til Next Year," and it finally came in 1955, when the Dodgers beat the Yankees in seven games. Reflective of Nan's luck at the time, we had just moved to Florida from Long Island a few weeks before the World Series, so she wasn't able to savor the win locally or get back at her brothers, who were still on the Island. "No one cares down here," she lamented. And the following year the Yankees righted the universe by again beating the Dodgers in the World Series. But that defeat had only a fraction of the pain than what occurred at the end of the following season (1957). The Dodger brass decided to move the team to Los Angeles—the loyal fans in Brooklyn be damned. No other national event was as traumatic to Nan, with the exceptions of Pearl Harbor and 9/11. She immediately cast an Italian curse on the Dodgers and rooted for them no more. It took awhile for the curse to be effective, for the Dodgers won the World Series three times between 1959 and 1965, but another sixteen years passed before they won another, which they followed with one seven years later in 1988. And for the next twenty-nine long years they failed to reach another World Series—mainly because of Nan's efforts. Or so she would tell you if she were still around. Believe me, I learned much from Nan about loyalty and the severe price of disloyalty.

Nan attended only a few sporting events in the last thirty years of her life: one pro football game, one college football game, and one major league baseball game, to be exact. But in the last forty years of her life, she became a fixture at the theatre—the live theatre. As a widow she began attending dinner theatres in Florida and a number of "Broadway" musicals in the area, as well as selected musical events. When she moved to Georgia, we took her to more "Broadway" musicals at the Fox Theater in Atlanta and here locally in Athens. We saw Sinatra (as noted) and Andy Williams's Christmas show, an opera (*La Bohème*), and a good number of musical revivals, such as *The King and I, 42nd Street, Mame,* and *Damn Yankees.* We took her to *Cats* after we had bragged how great it was. Verdict: she didn't at all care for it—except when Grizabella sang "Memory." It seems she wasn't a fan of both clowns and humans dressed as cats. Even "Memory" took some heat. "It would have been a better number if she wasn't dressed in that ridiculous cat fur." We later offered to take her to another Andrew Lloyd Webber smash, *The Phantom of the* Opera, but she said no. "I don't like being afraid when I watch musicals," she noted and then reminded us how absolutely horrifying it was when Lon Chaney was unmasked in the silent film version of 1925.

One of the last shows we took her to see was a night of Glenn Miller, performed by the official Glenn Miller Orchestra. Yes, Miller had been dead almost seventy years, but we assumed that the orchestra would more than make up for Glenn's absence. When it was over, Nan shook her head in disappointment. "What's wrong, mom? Didn't you like the show?" "Did you hear those songs?" Indeed we did—all of them, including such masterpieces as "In the Mood," "Chattanooga Choo-Choo," "Moonlight Serenade," "Kalamazoo," and "String of Pearls." What was the problem, then? Nan, who had listened to these songs for half a century, had a ready answer. They didn't play the songs "exactly the way Miller did them on record." Nan would cut little slack when it came to her favorite musical moments.

My own involvement with local theatre as an actor and director allowed Nan to experience stage drama and comedy as well the musical. After all, she came to all my shows—something that was very special to me. When she reached ninety there were a few times when even her son's best efforts couldn't keep her eyes open, but for the most part they were and she was a wonderful audience member. When I had my own theatre group, my wife sold tickets at the door, and Nan would sit with her occasionally handing out the programs. Until her last few years she would also attend the cast party following the final show of the short run. The actors thoroughly enjoyed her praise of their efforts and a few tales of her having seen the movie version of what we performed. That she couldn't always remember their names didn't bother anyone at all. Some of the shows we performed didn't quite reach her level of comprehension or leave her in all ways comfortable, owing to the situation depicted on stage or the language used to convey character and mood. And she'd always gently complain when we did something that conveyed horror. "John, why don't you do *Our Town*?" Yet she was in her own way the ultimate theatrical trooper, even at times lending furniture and props for the production. I always offered to put her in one of our shows— "Just a walk-on, mom. How about it? You don't even have to have any lines." She could have been a censorious town woman in Shakespeare's *The Taming of the Shrew*, for instance, but she was too frightened by the prospect of walking out in front of an audience. "I'll pass out in the wings," she predicted.

Perhaps my favorite theatrical memory of Nan was on a New Year's Eve, when she had just turned ninety. We had a nice dinner out and then headed to the Classic Center in Athens to see one of the "Rat Pack" touring shows. Needless to say, Nan thoroughly enjoyed the show featuring facsimiles of Sinatra, Dean Martin, and Sammy Davis Jr., complete with the shtick that made their joint Las Vegas appearances in the early 1960s so memorable. Following the show, Frank, Dino, and Sammy made their way to the exit doors to greet the audience as they left. Nan waited patiently, and when her turn came, she of course got hugs from all three men. "It was wonderful, she gushed to them, but then she grabbed the Sinatra by the arm and lowered her voice—but not low enough for me not to hear her. "I saw Frankie at the Paramount fifty years ago, and when he sang 'I'll Never Smile Again,' he didn't sing it that fast." The Sinatra looked at Nan as though he she had pricked a water balloon in his face.

Chapter Nine
Docking at Golden Harbor

"From there to here, from here to there, funny things are everywhere."
Dr. Seuss

With Nan's hip surgery scheduled for two days' time, we headed to Golden Harbor to make arrangements for her move. Only Nan didn't know it was going to be a move. We found that out when I brought up the subject of selling her house. "What?" she almost shouted. "What are you trying to do to me?" I reminded her of what her doctor said and her apparent willingness to make the transition to assisted living. "I didn't know he meant permanently. I just thought it was for a few weeks." My wife and I relied on all the lessons of patience and tact we had learned during our lifetimes and finally got Nan to see that moving into Golden Harbor would be the best—no, the only—course. I couldn't blame her for exclaiming "My life is changing so fast," and my wife and I had to control our emotions after hearing that one. But all of Nan's anxiety and despondency miraculously disappeared when they showed her the only two-bedroom apartment they had available. She had poo-pooed the efficiency-size room and wasn't crazy about the one-bedroom apartment either. "Where the hell am I going to put all my furniture?" she moaned. But when she saw the two-bedroom apartment, she lit up and started pointing to where this should go and that should go. "I can see living here." Great. We'll take it. Wrap it up.

As earlier mentioned, the surgery went well but the recovery did not. When she arrived at Golden Harbor, they assumed her stay would amount to hours, let alone weeks. The following morning she couldn't keep her eyes open for more than moments at a time. She didn't eat and could barely articulate a syllable. Later that day, my children came to see their grandma for the last time, and I had the priest come in to give her the last rites. Nan was in one of the vacant one-bedroom apartments, not in her palatial two-bedroom one—not that she needed any space more than the bed in which she lay. I had also steeled myself for telling her—if she asked—that she was leaving us and that she would soon be having a joyous reunion with Tom and her mother. I planned to tell her we would be fine and would know she'd be looking down on us. Yes, these are the expected things one says at such a moment, but until someone comes up with something better, why not offer happy prospects?

That night my wife and I feared we had seen her for the last time. I instructed Golden Harbor to call me right away if they sensed she was passing so I could be with her when she died. There were no calls during the night—so around nine in the morning we walked into Golden Harbor and made our way to Nan's bedroom. If I was shocked seeing her in the hospital bed with her dentures out, looking utterly dead, what we confronted when he stepped to the foot of her bed blew "shock" completely out of the water.

"Where have you two been? Can you have them bring me some food? I need to go to the bathroom." Somehow my wife and I groped our ways to the two chairs by Nan's bed without falling to the floor on our rear ends. "Mom?"

"I need a chair in here." My wife uttered something between a gargle and a spew.

Nan stared at us as if we had lost our minds. "What's wrong with you two? You don't want me to have a chair? By the way, I feel fine."

And so began her seven and a half months in residence at Golden Harbor. When she made the seemingly miraculous recovery, we assumed it was what the hospice handbook called a "rally"—a brief interlude (day or two) suggesting a recovery, only to be followed by a rapid decline. Accordingly, we were not convinced Nan would be with us the following week. She informed us she had seen a beautiful woman in a white dress standing at the foot of her bed, which I chalked up to a near-death hallucination rather than a nice dream vision. The hospice nurse walked in—the one that predicted Nan's not lasting the night—and dropped her jaw, as did the entire staff at Golden Harbor. It was as if Nan had walked into a battlefield and took a bullet in the chest, which went only 699 pages through the 700-page Dickens novel she had clutched to her heart.

To us and to anyone else, Nan complained about the room she was in. "Where is the two-bedroom apartment you said I could have?" We of course fudged the truth. "For right now, they want you to be near the nurse's station. Besides, you need to stay in bed for now." The next day, she repeated the request to move to the larger apartment, which was followed by her pushing off the covers and attempting to get out of bed. What was she doing? "I have to go to the bathroom." All right, we said, we just have to call the nurse to help you. "I don't need the nurse. I've already figured out how to do it myself." My wife and I almost choked. Nan had come straight from the hospital after her hip replacement and had absolutely no physical therapy. But she insisted, and so we watched her get out of the bed (with our hands outstretched ready to grab her) and make her way by holding on the bed railing and then a section of the wall and then the doorway to the bathroom, then to the sink, and finally down on the toilet—or so my wife said about the last step, since I didn't watch that part. And Nan made it back to bed retracing her route exactly. "If I have to stay in this room a little while longer, then bring in my television and get me a chair to sit in." I brought the television, hooked it up along with her portable CD/Tape player, and watched hospice bring her a Jerry Chair—or more technically a 3-Position Reclining Geriatric Chair. "Much better," Nan exclaimed after sitting in the chair instead of reclining in the bed.

Amazingly, her vital signs improved and her renal functions began working normally again. After some ten days in her room—and after Nan told me to "get on my knees and beg" Golden Harbor to let her have the desired two-bedroom apartment—we decided along with the staff that Nan could make the move. Nan was considerably delighted and relieved. "I was getting stir crazy in that room," she informed us. "Can I move to the new room tonight?" We had to inform her that, no, the two bedroom—which I will from here on refer to as "The Penthouse"—was devoid of any furniture. I promised to contract some movers and get the furniture still at her old house (which we had already sold) delivered and set up in the new apartment. The following afternoon, the truck pulled up at Golden Harbor and the unloading began. Because there were only two young men unloading the goods, I stepped in to make it a three-man job. But we had a problem of geography. The entrance doors to Golden Harbor were about as far away as possible from the Penthouse (which was tucked away in the very back corner of the building). Imagine the entrance doors as Miami and the Penthouse as Seattle, and you will get an idea of what I'm talking about. In between was negotiating the dining room and the early diners making their way to their tables. Down a narrow hallway with other residents—with walkers and in wheelchairs coming the other way—then a sharp turn—and then down a longer hallway and game room—crowded with other residents, of course. I heard one old gentleman mutter, "It's good to see furniture coming in instead of going out—the way it usually is around here." Given that I wasn't exactly twenty-three anymore made my afternoon an exhausting one. Getting the furniture in the Penthouse was one thing. Placing it in the right spots was quite another. The powers at Golden Harbor made sure that Nan's bed—now a small single delivered by hospice, rather than the grand queen-size she had at the house—was ready for her and that the Jerry Chair was set up as well. Somehow I had the strength to wheel Nan to the Penthouse, and she immediately went into full-bore decorating mode. "John, I want one of the TVs and all my records, tapes, and books in the second bedroom there—as well as my coats and shoes." I asked if we could postpone the setting up until the next morning. "I have waited patiently for over a week to get into this place. I don't want to wait another night before it's fixed up." Naturally, there was no counter argument I could come with, and with the help of my wife, I set the *very* heavy Asian-style bureau in one place, only to have Nan change her mind about the location—so we had to move it again. But that damned glass grandfather's clock was the real evil star of the show; we placed it in four locations before Nan was satisfied. The large flat screen was set and hooked up. The sofa was situated with her Jerry Chair behind it. "It doesn't matter because I'll be out of this chair soon enough and we can give it back to hospice. We never did.

We put boxes of her stuff in the proper rooms and talked Nan out of putting her glass dining room table in the main room. "I'll want to cook and have dinner here." She never did. Oddly—no, *most* oddly—Nan rejected our suggestion that we buy her a small/narrow chest of drawers to place in her bedroom, which was very small. The next day she asked for a cardboard box, out of which she constructed a make-shift two-shelf unit on which she placed her undergarments and small hand towels. We replenished the glass shelving-unit in the main room with her expensive looking knick-knacks, including her unicorn collection and the small statues of Clark Gable and Vivian Leigh as Rhett and Scarlet. We also set up her religious shelves in her bedroom, complete with all the icons she had in her house before she broke her hip. Needless to say, her main room looked pretty ritzy, especially in comparison with the other apartments which we looked into as we walked down the hallways. As for the second bedroom, Nan wanted it set up so she could have a TV room, the way she had previously. "I'll go in there to watch television and my movies and listen to my music." She never did.

For the first month, Nan tried to keep up with *Days of Our Lives* on the TV in the main room. She would get out of the Jerry Chair and sit on the sofa to watch and to "entertain" when we came over every day. But I began to notice that whenever the television was on when we arrived, it would be set to a particular network whose political perspective Nan didn't agree with. I knew she wasn't paying attention to what was being broadcast so I had to wonder if she just turned on the set to hear persons talking. She stopped trying to watch *Day of Our Lives*. "I either can't follow along or I fall asleep." The hospice nurses told us that it was all part of the "transition," which in Nan's case could take a month or more." They were a little off on the estimate, however.

As sad as the evidence of her decline was, Nan continued to amuse us in so many ways. When we assured her that the food was good at Golden Harbor and that she'd likely make some friends in the dining room, rather than taking her meals in her apartment, she proceeded to give us one of her famous incredulous looks and replied, "Why would I do that? I don't want to eat with all those old people." Believe me, there wasn't even the slightest hint of humor or insincerity in this ninety-two-year-old woman's assertion. Certainly, taking all of her meals in her apartment costs more, but we thought "what the heck."

As one would expect, some of the meals satisfied, while many others didn't. She liked best the scrambled eggs, the toast, coffee, and of all things, the pasta (or spaghetti as it was called at Golden Harbor). A woman raised on some of the most delicious pasta dishes ever prepared (by my grandmother) and a very good pasta cook herself—a woman who brutally judged restaurant pasta, even at one of Atlanta's premiere Italian restaurants—enjoyed the pasta fare at Golden Harbor. Go figure. Yet occasionally even her favorite bites didn't quite measure up, either because they weren't prepared well enough for her tastes that particular day or because she didn't quite recognize the dish for what it was. A hamburger could "taste like a rock," the eggs were so cold "you could skate on them," and a crab cake "had the softness sucked out of it." Regarding the last of these, we had to tell her that the item wasn't a crab cake but rather a cookie. Nan even echoed Uncle Junior on *The Sopranos* when she noted, "even the coffee's old in here."

As she began to lose more of her perspective on the time and events of her daily life, she would share a number of imaginary concerns. "I didn't care for breakfast this morning. They served me sour salad." It was lunch and it was coleslaw. "They haven't given me breakfast for three days." What happened was that she slept late for several mornings in a row and her first meal of the day was actually lunch. On one occasion she was quite out of sorts because she didn't have any money in her apartment. I assured her that she didn't need any cash. She shook her head. "What if I can't pay for my meals when they bring them by? Today, a nice lady came in with the food, and I told her I didn't have anything to pay for it. She was so nice and said that she'd give me the food anyway. But what if someone else brings it and demands the money?" We assured her that she had indeed paid for her food—every month at the beginning of the month and that she would never have to pay for it otherwise. That calmed her, thank goodness.

When her health initially improved after the scare following her surgery, we brought her to our house for dinner. But she could barely make it from the car to the dining room table, and she decided not to venture out of Golden Harbor again. At Thanksgiving, we convinced her to have the holiday dinner in the dining area—the only time she ever dined there during her seven-month stay. They brought her plate and a bottle of wine for the three of us. The turkey and dressing were fine, she said, but it was really the wine delivery that showed the place had "class."

Before her hip replacement surgery, Nan had her two glasses of wine a day—the first a Blush Chablis, the second an only slightly heartier Red Rosé. When she was moved to the Penthouse at Golden Harbor, she wished to continue her daily intake, but after several days she confessed that she had lost the taste for both wines and asked for an occasional variation from years back: *Asti Spumante*, the sparkling Italian white wine. We stocked her refrigerator with several bottles and shared a glass with her when we came to visit. Fortunately, her taste for the *Asti* remained for the rest of her time at Golden Harbor, but on one occasion the sparkling wine led to one of the most memorable and humorous moments of this period. For her ninety-third birthday, we had a little party for her in the Penthouse. Attending were my wife and I, our daughter, Nan's great-granddaughters, and our son. As our son kissed his grandmother, she asked "When are you two getting married? I have my dress all picked out." Our son wasn't yet formally engaged, but he had brought his then girlfriend (and now wife) Mary to Golden Harbor to see Nan when she first moved into her apartment. My son diplomatically handled the situation—made easier because Mary couldn't make the birthday gathering. But great-granddaughter Leah was there—and she was blonde like our son's fiancé, but was only twelve, though tall for her age. As the *Asti* was being poured, Nan told me to be sure that "Terry" got some too. We assumed she meant Leah, so we all laughed and sipped on our *Asti Spumante*. When it came time for refills, Nan again insisted that Leah be given some of the wine. "She can't," said my wife. "Why not? "She's only twelve, mom." Nan reared up and denied the truth of my wife's observation. "She's not twelve. My grandson would not be engaged to a twelve-year-old girl." It seems that with her very poor eyesight, Nan confused Leah with "Terry"—her incorrect name for *Mary*, my son's girlfriend. We all laughed heartily at that mistake—except poor Leah who later wondered aloud why Nan was trying to "get her drunk."

Nan was a big hit with the staff and young female volunteers at Golden Harbor. She encouraged and praised them, often offering advice to the volunteers on negotiating the occasional rough waters of dating and romance. Nan never complained to them about anything—not the standard behavior of so many residing at such places as Golden Harbor. They loved Nan's sense of humor—one staff member dubbing her the "Genius of Sarcasm." Nan liked to tell us, "You should have seen the nurse's eyes pop when she saw me getting from my Jerry Chair to the bathroom without the walker." As for that walker, she used it to hang her robe on—never for locomotion. In fact, one day she told us that she was not "getting any better" because she wasn't getting enough exercise. "Let's walk down the hall, John."

I dared not attempt to convince her she couldn't or shouldn't make that effort in her condition—I surely didn't want her to accuse me of making an old lady out of her. I helped her up and we made it to the door of the Penthouse. One step into the hallway and she said, "You better get me back to my chair." By this time she was spending all of her waking hours in the Jerry Chair; no longer did she sit on the sofa. The effort was simply too tasking, and she had to save her strength to get herself—without help—to the bathroom and at night to her bedroom.

Nan thoroughly enjoyed the visits by the head hospice nurse Josie, who had northern roots and spoke "New York," as Nan put it. Yet she believed that Josie was a full-fledged doctor—always calling her "Dr. Josie"—a misapplication we never bothered to correct. But there were days when Nan's frustration with her declining conditions led to such remarks as "Maybe I should get a new doctor. I'm not getting any better."As the months went on she'd ask me more frequently, "What is it that's wrong with me, exactly?"and "What am I here? A patient?" We'd always answer her last question by telling her she was a resident. She eventually lost all memory of the precarious situation she was in when she first came to Golden Harbor, which we felt was a good thing. She never asked me if she was terminally ill. No, not Nan. Her thoughts were always on getting better and making plans for future activities and events. "We need to go on a cruise soon. I'm getting stale sitting around here all day" and "I have my dress picked out for my grandson's wedding. I'm wearing lavender" were two familiar refrains. She was all about "next summer" and "next Christmas," so often beginning her conversations with us with an "I've been thinking . . ." I found her concentration on the future a wonderful thing—as well as an example of how to live out one's last months. Contemplating the future raised her spirits, not to mention ours.

Although Nan's attempt to walk the full length of the hallway outside her door went nowhere (literally), she remained cognizant of the need to exercise. Her walking from room to room in the Penthouse provided some of the desired work-out—even though it was precarious without the assistance of her walker. Early in her stay at Golden Harbor, a staff member encouraged her to attend an exercise session with other residents. They put Nan in a wheelchair and placed her among eight or nine others. When we next saw her, we asked how the session went. "I'm not going back." Okay. Why not?

"You just sit there and lift your foot and open and close your hands. What kind of exercise it that?" Did she expect to work out with barbells and bench press machines? In any event, her formal exercise regime began and ended the same day.

When Nan's ability to concentrate on television departed, we were hard-pressed to find activities for her, especially because her macular degeneration wouldn't allow her to read. One thing she asked for was bubble wrap. When we asked why, she informed us that she used to enjoy popping the bubbles. "It relaxes me." Very well, then. We brought in sheets of bubble wrap. But we discovered that the newest style of bubble wrap had smaller bubble pockets, which were much harder to pop. So much for the bubble wrap, although Nan wanted us to take it back because it was "defective." She also tried knitting, but was unable to sustain her stitches. The same with crocheting. So what now? My wife thought Nan might like the feel of winding yarn, so we gave her a couple of skeins to wind into balls. Success. Nan thoroughly enjoyed the activity and the feel of the soft yarn in her hands. She also felt she was contributing something, since my wife crocheted and would use the yarn after Nan wound it. Another problem, though. Nan would wind four or five balls of yarn a day. After a couple of weeks, we had enough wound yarn to open our own shop. Once more my brilliant wife came up with a solution. She bought a device that re-wound the balls Nan had already wound into a cylinder shape so we wouldn't have to add to our massive stock of yarn. Nan was never the wiser, but another problem reared its ugly head. Nan would start to wind one cylinder of yarn and then put it down when she ate or took one of her frequent naps. When she returned to her winding, she would often pick a different cylinder and so on—to the point that she had three or four cylinders in various states of being wound with the threads of all three or four tangled together. As I sat there with my wife trying to untangle three of these partially wound cylinders, I asked myself "What the hell am I doing?"

As Nan entered the last three months of her life, she would demonstrate many moments of disorientation. She'd awaken and ask where she was or how she got where she was. She'd wonder why we haven't been by to see her "in about a week," when it had only been a day. She'd ask which hospital she was in. She heard bells and a parrot's voice. When she insisted that a truck was driving past her window (there was nothing but grass and trees back there), we thought she was having periodic hallucinations—that is, until we were there when they started cutting the grass near her window with riding mowers. Mystery solved. Of course with her insistence on getting about on her own, she fell on more than one occasion, merely bruising her arm and knee rather than breaking them. After one of her falls, she realized that her lower denture plate had escaped her mouth during the fall—although she didn't tell us that initially when we arrived for our daily visit. "I lost my lower teeth" was all she said. So we began our hunt for the plate. She didn't see what we were doing; therefore, she didn't let us know that the denture couldn't be in the bed, in the pillowcase, in the drawers, in the sink, or in the toilet—all places in which we looked. My wife eventually opened wider Nan's bedroom door and heard the tell-tale sign that the dentures were on the floor behind it.

Finally, for some reason she always believed that the main area of Golden Harbor (the offices and dining room) were on a different (lower) level than her apartment, while in truth everything was on one floor. When she had just come out of her dire condition and was anxiously awaiting her move to the Penthouse, she mentioned to one of the student volunteers that soon she would be "going to her place upstairs." That evening the poor young woman called us at home to tell us that my mother was talking about going soon to heaven and that perhaps we needed to see Nan before that happened.

Spending seven months at an assisted living center usually means making a bucket-full of friends or at least acquaintances among the other residents. Not with Nan. As noted, she refused to eat in the communal dining room and only once joined others in the exercise class, and the Thanksgiving dinner she had was just with my wife and me. No, her friends were exclusively the staff, hospice nurses, and young volunteers. I came to call her the "Norma Desmond" of Golden Harbor. She only had two fellow-resident visitations—and they were completely unexpected. A woman rolled her wheelchair into the Penthouse, looked around while Nan was sitting here, and without a word rolled back out again. The second visitor was a woman who walked in (while we were also there) and proclaimed that another resident complained because this woman had used the word "piss" rather than "pee." I commiserated with her as best I could while escorting her out into the hallway. Nan's own colorful language did not alter during her final months. She asked my opinion on something by saying, "you're the sophisticate; I'm just a horse's ass." She also channeled her Yiddish side (not really) and pronounced herself a "schlemiel" for asking for a hassock and then finding it too uncomfortable to lift her legs on. "This blouse looks like crap on me" and "I look like shit" also came from her lips. But she never used the "F" word, reminding us to the end that she "loathed" it completely and found it to be the depth of crassness. On two or three occasions, she demonstrated her frustration with her condition by remarking, "I just sit here and rot"—a rather graphic image, to say the least. As for how she looked in the final weeks, she never lost her sense (or appreciation) of style and her own appearance. She had manicures and pedicures and had her hair colored and styled. But there was nothing she could do about that damned oxygen tube—except to take it out of her nose to eat and then forget to put it back in right before she fell asleep and awoke wondering why she was having difficulty breathing. Nan would occasionally play with the tubing, casting it as a fishing line and twirling like a lasso. Our five-year-old granddaughter, having seen Nan many times with the tubing in her nose, took some scotch tape and created the same look for herself—but fortunately not in front of her great-grandmother.

Nan didn't ask for much from my wife and me while she was at Golden Harbor, but when she did ask, she made clear she expected quick results. Early in her stay at the Penthouse, she mentioned that she wanted to hang some small pictures in the kitchen area but she didn't have a hammer or any nails. I told her I'd bring both items when we next visited. She let that go for a few minutes before she said, "I really want to hang those pictures over there." I repeated my assurance that I would take care of it the next day. "You would think that if a son loved his mother enough, he'd want her to have some pictures to look at." She was teasing of course, but not really—so off I went to get the hammer and nails. On another occasion she wanted us to cut our visit short so that we could get her a new pair of sunglasses and a scarf to cover her hair. Why? "I'll want you to take me [by wheelchair] outside so I can get some sun and fresh air." That sounded like a good plan, so we purchased both items and brought them to her the next day. "You want to try on the sunglasses and scarf, mom? We'll take you outside." No, not today, she answered. Nor the day after—nor the day, week, month after that. She never went outside. "I'm too comfortable here in my chair"—in the very same Jerry chair she wanted so much to ditch when she first moved into the Penthouse.

Other "accusations" against me weren't at all teasing ones—though they were quite hilarious. One morning when we visited, Nan was quite concerned that a man had come into her room, passed by her chair, and went into the second bedroom (the "TV room"). "He's in there now. Look, the light is on." A beam of light was indeed visible under the closed door. Being dubious, I walked to the door, opened it, and saw no one inside the room. The light source was actually the morning sun coming through the room's window. But what I did see was a large cardboard box. It was full of pads and personalized female items from hospice. But before I could explain its contents, Nan claimed it was proof that a man was moving in. I finally got her to understand that he was likely the delivery person, who put the large box in the other room. When she finally accepted my explanation, she breathed an audible sigh of relief—but for not the reason one might expect. "I was really mad at you, John, for renting out the other room. I couldn't believe you'd do that to make some extra money." I waited for the teasing smile but it never came. And there were more accusations to come.

Near the end, Nan decided she needed a phone. My wife and I immediately saw the problems with that request. "Why do you think you need one, mom?" First she wanted the ability to call "Dr." Josie when she felt too uncomfortable or anxious—and if not her then us for the same reason. We assured her that the staff at Golden Harbor would assist her and would call hospice, a doctor, or us if she was really in such need. We also reminded her that she would likely get annoying calls from telemarketers and salespersons of every stripe and that she would have to get out of bed to answer the call if she was asleep. We may have thrown in a couple of other reasons, but we never mentioned anything about the cost of putting a phone in. But Nan must have thought of that "rented" second bedroom, because she complained, "Why are you so cheap when it comes to my living here?"Again no teasing smile. At one point she had shown frustration at not having any cash in hand. We told her she didn't need any—that all her meals were paid for, as well as any necessities to be delivered. Again, "Why are you so cheap, John?" I made the mistake of saying, "Here I'll give you all the cash I have so you'll have some money." I thereby dug my own hole and I fell right into it. All I had on me were three one-dollar bills—which I dutifully handed over.

The look she gave me was one of those "Well, aren't you the generous one" expressions. When she passed away, and we were cleaning out her room I found two of the dollar bills, but never the third. We wondered what she spent it on. Of course my so wondering would only provide further evidence of Nan's claim that her son was cheap.

One of my favorite moments came when Nan was waiting impatiently for the birth of her latest great-granddaughter. Each day we saw her, she'd ask "Well, is she here yet?" Finally, the big day arrived and after spending time at the hospital with our daughter and family, my wife and I made it over to Golden Harbor to share the good news. Right on cue, Nan hit us with the now-familiar question, and I responded, "The baby's here, mom." After the expected and joyous reaction, Nan asked what her new great-granddaughter's name was. I replied, "Hailey Madison, but her sister wants to call her Maddie." Nan scrunched up her face as though she had just passed an open sewer line. "That's a terrible name! Harry Mason? And they're going to call her Eddie? For a little girl? What the hell were they thinking?" Once I articulated the correct name at increased volume, Nan beamed. "That's beautiful. Little Hailey Maddie. How darling."

The final three days of Nan's life began with further disorientation and another fall. The head hospice nurse came and informed us that Nan was going into transition and would likely be gone within the next several days. My mother asked me on the second day, "What's happening to me?" as she took to her bed for the last time. I couldn't bring myself to give her the correct answer to that question, and I said only that she needn't worry about anything and that we'd be bringing the new baby to see her tomorrow. It was at this point that the hospice nurse increased the drug level for Nan's comfort. Nan quickly fell asleep. We went to bed that night believing the end would come the next day. We arrived and Nan was conscious. She again asked what was happening to her and punctuated that with "I need to get out of here. Take me out of here." She tried to rise but was unable to lift her legs off the bed. We did our best to calm her as the nurse returned and decided that she would increase the drug level again because of Nan's continued discomfort and anxiety. And then our daughter arrived with the baby. "The baby," Nan muttered and raised her arms to feel the infant. That touch seemed to comfort her considerably, and even though the drug was doings its work, I like to think that Nan's seeing her new great-granddaughter gave her a kind of comfort no drug could provide. As Nan began to drift to sleep, my daughter and the baby left. I sat on the bed near my mother's head and expected her to fully close her eyes and sleep. The nurse advised that we leave and come back after dinner. Just as I kissed Nan, she somehow raised her arms and torso and hugged me—not once but twice. Then she fell asleep and later died before we came back. I looked at her in the state of death and knew it wasn't her. I imagined that she was now with Tom, smiling, laughing, and enjoying a little Sinatra. Perhaps she was even telling Tom about her cheap son.

Epilogue

"True humor springs more from the heart than from the head;
it is not contempt, its essence is love."
Thomas Carlyle

My mother was a one tough lady—not just because she riveted airplane wings during World War Two and actually hand-washed dishes, hung wet laundry on a clothes line, and got up from a sofa to change a channel. The challenges she faced and unfairness she experienced would have broken a lesser person. Put another way, life wasn't always kind to my mother; frequently it was downright cruel, but she never collapsed under the strain, although she came close on several occasions. She was always there for me, and when I grew big enough to defend her from physical harm, I happily repaid the favor. We therefore bonded in ways that most mothers and sons, thank God, never have to. I don't know what I would have done without her.

Talking about my wife's and my careers in education, Nan expressed regret that she didn't get a chance to affect anyone's life for the good. How she would have been stunned, then, to see all of those sitting at her memorial service and to read all the wonderful comments sent by email, card, or posted on Facebook. Beyond all the advice she gave, examples she set, and laughter she provided, she never fully appreciated how much she was loved. She once joked that no one would ever write about her because there wouldn't be anything of interest to fill the pages. I hope I have proved her wrong in this book—and she wasn't wrong all that often, if one discounts her prediction that Elvis and the Beatles were flashes in the pan and that Jackie would never marry Ari.

Since her passing, Nan has frequently visited me in a recurring dream. In that dream she's back—alive and apparently well. As happy as I am to see her, I am filled with dread at her appearance. Why? Because I've cancelled her

Medicare, sold her house, stopped her social security checks, and spent some of her money I received when she died. In every dream I'm faced with the same dilemma—how do I tell her what I've done and how the hell do I convince the government to start paying her again and reestablishing her health insurance? So far, none of my dreams have ended with my telling her—so I continue on, like some ancient mariner, reliving my mistake, while poor Nan has no idea what has happened to her income and retirement fund. That's what I get, I suppose, for being so cheap.

The End

View other Black Rose Writing titles at www.blackrosewriting.com/books and use promo code **PRINT** to receive a **20% discount** when purchasing.

BLACK⬤ROSE
writing™

www.ingramcontent.com/pod-product-compliance
Lightning Source LLC
Chambersburg PA
CBHW070957120726
47910CB00004B/1272